Currently Unchaperoned

by

Heidi Wessman Kneale

Currently Charmed Series, Book 1

Currently Unchaperoned

Cover Art by *The Wild Rose Press, Inc.*

The Wild Rose Press, Inc.
PO Box 708
Adams Basin, NY 14410-0708
Visit us at www.thewildrosepress.com

Publishing History
First Fantasy Rose Edition, 2021
Trade Paperback ISBN 978-1-5092-3297-0
Digital ISBN 978-1-5092-3298-7

Currently Charmed Series, Book 1
Published in the United States of America

Felicity exhaled sharply. What did it take to provoke him to some sort of reaction? Something she had once read in a novel came to her.

"There is one ultimate test that would prove beyond a shadow of a doubt, whether or not you belong in the church." She stood up.

"Is there?" Wariness tinged his voice. "I am not aware of such a test."

"Oh, yes you are. Everyone knows this one."

"Enlighten me."

She stood before him. "First, you need to put your hands before you."

He held his hands straight out. "Like this?"

She widened his arms. "Out more like this. Palms up."

He let her move his hands. "Now what?"

"Now close your eyes and listen to your heartbeat."

She did not know if he closed his eyes in the darkness. He did take a deep breath, then another.

"What's your heartbeat like?"

"Slow and steady."

"Good. Remember that. We'll need it later."

He let out a breath. "Now what?"

"Step two." Felicity hiked up her skirts in a most unladylike fashion and straddled Mr. Wyndell's lap.

So surprised was he, his hands went immediately to her arms. "Miss Abbot!"

"Sssh," she admonished before thoroughly kissing him.

Dedication

For Lady Sarah and Lady Amy.
Courage will serve you well.

Chapter 1
How Felicity Goes to the Party

Felicity Abbot of the Essex Colchesters detested the London Season. Her opinion might have been vastly different, had she been allowed to attend. But no, here she was, languishing away *again*, trapped in the mires of impending spinsterhood, awaiting Society's persnickety permission to be presented. For crying out loud, she was one-and-twenty this year.

She drew a calming breath. No, she was not a child. A temper tantrum was well beyond her. Grandmama said she had a plan, just before she left several weeks ago. Patience would serve her well…at least, that's what she had been telling herself ever since the Season started.

She flopped on her mother's bed while Mrs. Abbot prepared for a night on the town. Her mother had selected the loveliest red evening gown, all tucks and ruffles. She'd cut quite a stir among Society. All that remained were the finishing touches. Jones, the lady's maid, picked up the curling tongs from the spirit lamp and applied them to the next curl. The smell of hot hair wafted about the room.

Not that Felicity needed any help in that department. She'd been blessed with an exuberance of blonde curls. Jones had despaired over getting them into any semblance of order.

Her mother's hair, long and straight, submitted meekly to the curling iron.

Felicity sat up. "Any word on when Grandmama returns from Tunbridge Wells?"

At this, Mrs. Abbot narrowed her eyes. At least she didn't chide Felicity. "Your grandmother has not written since her last letter."

Felicity groaned. If her Grandmama kept this up, by the time she returned, Felicity would hate the Season so much she would refuse to go.

Lady Abbot was paying for her granddaughter's Season. She would be the one to present and escort Felicity. Said she'd had it all worked out, and Felicity would be a glowing success. Mrs. Abbot had bowed to her mother-in-law's wishes.

Her frustrations should really have been directed to her absent grandmother. Without her, Felicity had no official sponsor. But if she took her frustration out on Grandmama, then she was guaranteed never to have a Season at all. Ever. Not that she wasn't tempted. Many a time her pen sat poised over the letter, veritable poison dripping from its tip, alas, never to be applied to paper. That would have been ungrateful. It was only by Grandmama's generosity Felicity was in London at all. No Grandmama, no Season.

Grandmama's nerves were frayed enough as it was. That was why she was currently at Tunbridge Wells taking the waters, instead of here in London debuting her granddaughter.

"Couldn't you take me out to the Chesters' party? I wouldn't stay for long, and it is only next door."

"No."

Jones applied another lock of hair to the tongs

before they cooled too much.

Felicity stared wistfully at her mother's back. It was the best she could do. Not that her mother deserved her frustrations, not entirely. Well, maybe a little. After all, she was the one who agreed to Grandmama's scheme.

"I shall be an old maid before I am out."

Her mother, seated at her dressing table, ignored her daughter's protest. She poked at the new curl, still hot from the curling tongs. "Until you are properly debuted, I will not take you out in Society."

Jones set the curler back on the spirit lamp and brushed out another lock of Mrs. Abbot's hair.

Felicity sprawled facedown on her mother's bed. Though she had been putting her hair up for the past four years and her figure more than filled out her stylish frocks, until she was presented to the king, she would always be a child.

Her hand traced the stitching on the quilt. Who'd spent hours putting in all those tiny stitches? Must have taken them quite a while. Felicity called upon her magic and tugged at the thread. Stitch by stitch, it came loose. She pulled out the thread, unlocking the quilting that kept the spread together.

She should not be petulant, but how could one help it? She did not relish her powerlessness. Felicity let her magic glide across her skin, its cool, feathery touch lifting the hairs of her arm. It gathered in her fingers, this tiny force, subtle, yet present, awaiting her command. What if she pulled the whole quilt apart?

"Felicity..." Her mother's voice startled her.

In guilt, she looked away. "Found a loose thread." Of course, her mother sensed her magic. She pushed the thread back into its stitches, a more difficult task. Unravelling stuff was so much easier.

"Perhaps you would best put your talents to work to finish your charms."

"They're finished." And had been for at least a year. There was only so much magic one could force into a ring or a bracelet.

"Start a new piece."

At this, Felicity sat up. Personal magic in one's person wasn't terribly strong, unless one was fortunate. Instead, it was best to take the magic and store it in a suitable object, like a piece of jewelry or other personal item. It took a long time to imbue a charm with magic. Years even. One had to concentrate on the desired effect and push one's own personal magic into the object, little by little, storing it, until the object was strong enough to emit its own aura. *'Notice Me'* was a popular charm, as was *'Beauty'*. Felicity preferred charms such as *'Good Luck'* or *'Success'*

Felicity was fortunate. Alas, her talent wasn't anything special like singing or great beauty. She traced a finger across the restitched quilt. Undoing things was her gift. Not terribly useful if one was trying to build things up, like a debutante's charms.

Not that it looked like she'd ever be a debutante. "So I am to waste away another Season? I'll be on the shelf before I ever get a chance."

Mrs. Abbot froze. Her eyes narrowed. "Felicity Anne Abbot." Her voice was low with warning. "That is not fair."

In guilt, Felicity sat up properly. "I'm sorry." Truly she was.

Felicity should have debuted two years ago.

Instead, she spent what was to have been her first Season struck down with That Dreadful Illness. No sooner did she feel herself much improved than she was struck down again. An entire spring of never-ending illness.

What could have been her second Season was cut short before it even began. Three weeks before they were to have removed from Essex to London, her brother Timothy had died in a riding accident. Because of that, the whole family went into mourning and that was that for London. How she missed him!

Felicity had loved Timothy. Missing out on the frivolities of the Season was no great loss for her. Her heart would not have been in it.

But the dead were dead, and the living had to keep living, no matter how heavy the sorrow lay in their hearts. So here she was, having seen twenty summers, and looking like she would see twenty-one as a maiden.

"Unfair is hobbling my chances at any decent future simply because Grandmama wishes to take the waters."

"Your grandmother will not be gone all Season. Two or three weeks at most."

"But that's forever! She's lived her life. I have yet to start mine."

With a sigh, her mother sank into her chair. "Felicity, if we had a choice, I would have brought you out two years ago, or even last year. If we had a choice, I would have presented you the very first day." She shaded her eyes with her hands to hide her sorrow.

Jones stood back, hot tongs still in hand. Even now, Mrs. Abbot could cry at a moment's notice over the death of her son. Timothy had left a young wife and several small children who would never know their father. As he was his father's heir, his family had spared no expense for his funeral, much to their financial detriment. Mourning could be expensive.

"It is by your grandmother's generosity that we are able to present you this year at all. So yes, we wait on her." She spread her arms wide to indicate the townhouse—Grandmother's townhouse—in which they lived by her generosity. Their own had to be sold last year to cover funeral expenses. "She has a plan for you. Be grateful."

Huh. Grateful. Her parents had *gratefully* accepted Grandmama's offer to sponsor Felicity, to put them up in her townhouse and to present her at court. So they came to town, accepted invitations, went out every night, and thoroughly enjoyed themselves, leaving Felicity at home.

What good was a Season if one could not enjoy it? "At least tell me you are out scouting eligibles." If she herself could not be out, at least her mother could hasten the work along.

At that, her mother perked up. "There are always eligible men."

Felicity fell back onto the bed. "Yes, but who?"

Her mother sidestepped this question by shifting her conversation to Jones, who had finished her hair. "No, not the silver. I need the sapphire comb." Her most favorite and luckiest piece. She had inherited it from her mother, who had had it since her first debut, a gift from Felicity's great-grandmother. Felicity knew every turn and every tong of that comb, for this was the piece with which her mother had taught her magic.

That had been an exercise in frustration. When it

came to reading spells, as far as she was concerned, they might as well not be there at all. She had to have the weaves pointed out to her every time. Once someone showed her the obvious, then she could pick it out, or even pick it loose.

The disenchantment of a few silver pins had earned her mother's wrath when a younger and stupider Felicity had undone in a few seconds what had taken her mother months to create.

Maybe it was a good thing she couldn't see magic very well, otherwise, she would have gone around in her childlike innocence, undoing years of work. At least she learned to respect the magic of her mother and not disenchant anything after that.

Well, anything that belonged to her mother.

Magic was how one gained luck. Luck contributed to success. Every young lady had a few items with which she imbued with magic over the years. Many a maiden had a brooch or locket she pushed her magic into night after night. The focus of the magic influenced whatever she wanted most. Most girls enchanted their items to attract the attention of a future husband.

But Felicity's great-grandmother had been wise. Enchant an item for generalities. That way you can use it again and again. If you enchant an item for a single purpose—like finding a husband—then that item can only be used once. Thus each generation of family women were taught to focus their magic on imbuing the comb with 'Success'. Then, when she wore it, no matter what her focus was—husband, social advantage, financial advantage—the 'Success' would come through.

Felicity was destined to wear it to her coming-out

ball. "It will bring you the best of luck," her mother explained as she gave it to Felicity every night for enchantment, under supervision, of course.

She would need it. And the sapphires would look especially well in her fair curls.

But tonight, it was Mrs. Abbot's curls where the comb would rest. "Yes, definitely the sapphire. I have a few things I need to accomplish tonight."

"Yes, ma'am." Jones sighed and put away the silver comb she had selected. The sapphire comb might suit Mrs Abbot's darker hair but did not quite match her current gown. The red-blue contrast looked too sharp.

Felicity perked up. "Oh, will there be cards at the Chesters tonight?"

Their next-door neighbors, Lord and Lady Chester, were famous for their love of games. They'd held many a card party since the beginning of the Season. It was said Lady Chester had a faro bank. Her mother would never confirm this, no matter how much Felicity begged.

"No," her mother replied. "There will be no cards. The Chesters are hosting a crush. Your father and I shall stop by briefly, then we have other engagements tonight."

Multiple parties. "I wish I could go." *I would go to every single party held in London that night if I could.*

Her mother ignored her. She fussed at her gown, plucking at the ruffles, shuffling her shoulders, and picking at invisible lint.

"At least, tell me who will be there."

"I don't know who will be there."

Felicity sighed. "I meant, tell me tomorrow."

Her mother rose and shook out her skirts. "It'll all

be in the papers tomorrow."

Felicity likewise rose. "Don't you have the least bit desire to know the character of your future son-in-law?"

Her mother's hands paused. Through the mirror, her gaze settled on her daughter. "What do you mean?"

Felicity went to the window. It faced out on the square, and it looked down rather well on the neighbors' front door. What better vantage could Felicity have to see the approaching guests? Grandmama's address might not have been the best, but at least her townhouse fronted onto a decent street. Already, carriages pulled up in front of their neighbors, the Chesters.

"I am bound and determined to have a successful Season. That means marrying one of them." She pointed to a group of bucks, unloading themselves from a carriage.

Mrs. Abbot rose from the table to peer out the window. "Oh, you would not want any of that lot. Regular Corinthians, those." She twitched the curtains closed.

"See? That's what I mean." The society columns of the newspapers were all well and good about learning who was who and what they'd done and worn, but it didn't tell her what they were like. Some things could only be learned face-to-face. "Until I am presented, it's your job to scout out potential husbands for me."

Her mother steepled her fingers. Jones busied herself tidying up the dressing table.

Felicity continued. "You have been making a list, haven't you?"

Mrs. Abbot paced the floor in slow, measured steps. "If I were to find a good husband for you, I would seek him from an impeccable family of wealth and status. He himself would also be above reproach, respectable, untainted by gossip or bad habits. He would move in the best circles, be a member of the best clubs, have the best connections."

"Good conversation? How about a sense of humor?"

Her mother ignored this. "I would not advise in favor of someone with aspirations in politics. Your father is not so engaged, much to my relief."

Her grandfather was politically minded. Even held a political office. He was half the reason Grandmama's nerves were so frayed.

"So no Corinthians, no politicians." Fair enough.

"No soldiers either. You might think them dashing, but…" She shook her head. "They are not for you."

Felicity's fingers twitched at the curtains. "So that leaves…what? Gentleman farmers and vicars?"

Mrs. Abbot returned to the dressing table. "You'd consider a vicar, would you?"

Felicity's fingers played with the curtain. "Why? Do you know some?"

Her mother did not respond.

Did that mean…? Felicity bounced over to her mother. "You do know some eligible vicars!"

Jones finished Mrs. Abbot's hair and went to the wardrobe.

Felicity moved closer to give her mother a spontaneous hug. "I knew you were scouting."

"Have a care," her mother chided, pushing Felicity away. "I have not been scouting vicars for you."

Felicity's enthusiasm ebbed away. "What?"

Mrs. Abbot straightened her clothing. "Would you

kiss a vicar?"

Kiss...a vicar? Sure, they looked all noble and imposing at the lectern on a Sunday, but to kiss them? A shudder rolled through her. Wouldn't that sort of thing be a sin for them? And then Felicity would feel all guilty. "No, I suppose not."

"And that is why I shall not consider a vicar for you. If you cannot fathom kissing one, how would you ever face the marriage bed?"

Felicity gasped. How uncharacteristic of her mother to be so forward. Surely such a topic was unsuitable for her ears!

But then, was she not contemplating marriage? And didn't that mean the quiet intimacies, rarely spoken of, yet hinted to be present for all? She professed a curiosity for such things. While her mother and other ladies refused to speak of it, the servants weren't so prudish. Intimacies sounded quite fun, if their word was anything to go by. Also, being classed as sinful, it must be a rollicking good time.

Felicity conceded that her mother showed great wisdom in not considering a vicar for a husband. Everyone knew that it was lesser sons who were pushed onto the Church as a career. Vicars didn't breed vicars the way lords bred lords. Did vicars even breed? Possibly not, as intimacies led to babies, and intimacies were a sin. If a vicar fathered a baby, then how could anyone ever look upon him as a spiritual leader?

Sure, vicars had wives, but was that only so they had someone to keep house for them while they sermonized?

No. Vicars were strictly off the list.

Better off looking somewhere else for a husband.

Felicity pulled open the curtain. Who else came to the party?

She pressed her nose to the glass. "Mrs. Wyndell has arrived."

"Mmm," her mother replied while Jones sorted out gloves.

Felicity turned from the window. "I thought you liked Mrs. Wyndell." Felicity had liked her, though she had only encountered her a few times this year. Mrs. Wyndell often called on Mrs. Abbot in the mornings. Lately, Mother had let Felicity sit in when she received callers; it was the only social contact Felicity had had. But the last time Mrs. Wyndell called, her mother had chased Felicity from the room. A failed attempt at eavesdropping at the door shed no light on the mystery.

"Do give her my regards, Mama, when you see her tonight."

"I'll do no such thing." Mrs. Abbot tugged on the gloves Jones presented to her. "I do not know if we shall run into each other."

Such a flimsy excuse. Something was up between her mother and Mrs. Wyndell. Felicity had heard a few *on-dits* regarding Mrs. Wyndell's brother, as published in the paper. Maybe that's why her mother had cooled regarding Mrs. Wyndell. Mrs. Abbot eschewed scandal.

Felicity returned to the window. "Really. You will be at the same party."

"This is a crush. Lady Chester has invited every single person of whom she could possibly think. The place will be so crowded I'll be lucky to speak to anyone. Anyhow, your father and I will not be staying long."

"Why show up to a party only to leave?"

"To be seen, of course."

An idea niggled in Felicity's head. "So you'll show up, be seen, then depart, never to return to the party?"

"Indeed."

The idea swelled and blossomed. If her mother was not there, and she would be gone all night…

Felicity stared through the window, her hand on the glass. Outside, Mrs. Wyndell was not alone. "I say, who is that?" A man had emerged from Mrs. Wyndell's carriage, young and dashingly handsome. "He's got a fine pair of calves."

Her mother let out a scandalized noise. "Felicity Anne Abbot. You do not look at men's…limbs."

Felicity sniffed. The heroines in novels were not above noticing a man's fine *limbs*, as her mother had put it. They noticed quite a bit, these novel heroines.

"His coat is of fine cut." Fit his shoulders rather nicely. "I do wonder who his tailor is."

"Better," came her mother's approval.

A man's tailor spoke much of his social status. That he was with Mrs. Wyndell did not clear the matter. Felicity studied the man. Surely this was not Mrs. Wyndell's brother. He was far too young. The finely cut coat snugged a narrow waist. His shoulders were not so broad as to hint at padding.

"I am not sure I like his face. He would be far more handsome, if he didn't look so worried."

At that moment, the handsome young man looked up at her. He did not glance away but held her gaze. How interesting. One could not call it a stare so much as one would call it a study. He was studying her?

She studied him back. "Mama, does Mrs. Wyndell have a son?" Felicity turned to her mother.

13

She considered two fans. "Several, I believe." Mrs. Abbot chose the chicken skin over the lace.

Well, that was vague. "Any of them eligible?"

Her mother shrugged.

Felicity rolled her eyes. "Really, Mother! It's your job to discover these things. Until I am out, I can't."

Her mother sighed. She pushed herself up from her dressing table and came over to the bedroom window. She glanced at the young man before turning away. "He does have the look of a Wyndell about him, thank goodness. I'd hate to think he took after his mother's side of the family. In more ways than one."

Mrs. Wyndell had been a Townshend, the granddaughter of the Earl of Leicester. Her brother George was the subject of a few subtle "anonymous" gossip columns. Sure, they blanked out all but the first initial of a name, but everyone always knew whose dirty laundry was being aired. George Townshend's reputation had been nipped at by the dogs of scandal, apparently something to do with his wife.

Felicity refused to be daunted. "But is he eligible?"

Her mother returned to the dressing table. "Some of her sons are married."

"But what about that one?" Alas, his mother spoke to him, and he looked away. Pity. It might have been the most attention she had ever received from a man all Season.

"I don't know."

Felicity sighed. Was her mother really so ignorant, or was she evading the issue?

"If he is eligible, you really need to know these things." Felicity pressed her nose to the window once more, craning her neck to watch the Wyndells enter the

Chesters' residence. "Could you find out for me?"

Felicity moved from the window to the door. Jones handed Mrs. Abbot her reticule. Her mother could not leave without dealing with her.

"What if I married him?"

That got her mother's attention. "What? Why him?"

"I don't know." His face did have potential. Did he have good conversation? Did he treat a lady with respect? She had no way of finding out, trapped here as she was. "Is he suitable?"

Her mother turned away. "I'm going to be late."

That wasn't an answer. Felicity planted her fists on her hips in a most unladylike fashion. "Find out for me."

"I won't make any promises. Your father and I will not be staying long at the Chesters. We have other engagements tonight."

"I'll stay up and wait for you."

Her mother shook her fan at her. "Then you will have a very long wait." Then, as if to spite her daughter, Mrs. Abbot said to Jones, "You may retire to bed. I doubt we shall be home before dawn."

Jones gave a brief curtsey. She could not hide the little smile that tugged at her lips. "Yes, ma'am."

Felicity refused to be spited. "Jones, when my mother wakes you at three in the morning, be sure to make her tell you everything about every eligible young man she's met."

But Jones had slipped away.

Felicity returned to the window, her mind ticking over. The Chesters' party was going to be a terrible crush. "Can I at least watch the comings and goings from the window?"

Her mother pulled at her gloves, as if they threatened to slide off her hands. "I can think of better ways of spending the evening."

"You have better ways of spending the evening. I do not."

She shook her fan at her daughter. "Watch, if you must. But do not draw attention to yourself. Do not open that window nor lean outside. And by all means, do not go out the front door."

"I will not go out the front door. Nobody shall notice me at the window, either," Felicity promised.

****

Victor Wyndell attended Lady Chester's crush under great protest. His mother, Mrs. Wyndell, insisted.

She fussed and fidgeted in the carriage the whole way, gripping her hands and pinching her mouth. "I'm not happy with The Whole Situation."

Victor sighed. He flicked bits of straw off his jacket. The cursed stuff stuck to the carriage seats. Had the stable boys used the vehicle to haul straw?

"So you say." He so did not want to attend this party. He was not here to enjoy Society. He was here to protect his future, assuming there was one left.

He stared sullenly at his mother. She could natter on and on over her brother George's faults when she should be acknowledging her own social foibles.

"Practically the whole *ton* will be here tonight." Her fingers fiddled with her gown, a rather dull-looking yellow thing that failed to bring much cheer. "Look over all the pretty young things and choose one. Flirt with her. Charm her. We don't have much time." She *tsk*ed at the dour future before her youngest son. "You should have chosen a bride last Season."

"I was too young for marriage."

"You are three and twenty. That is plenty old enough."

The carriage hit a particularly nasty bump. It lurched, threatening to throw Mrs. Wyndell off her seat. He reached out a hand to steady his mother.

"Some men wait until their thirties."

His mother hissed in disagreement. "Those men had titles and money enough to do what they want. You do not have such a luxury."

No, he did not. As a younger son of a younger daughter, not much from the Leicester fortune came his way. There was enough for his needs—a simple life devoid of useless fripperies—and that was it. If it wasn't for his clock designs, his personal pockets would be rather for let.

"I am not going to pick some silly miss willy-nilly."

Her mother flicked her closed fan in his face. "No, I dare say you should not. Good fortune and family is what you need."

Victor rolled his eyes. That's what his Uncle George had done. And look at what a dog's breakfast that turned out to be. Aunt Sarah had come from good family and had brought enough dowry to make her attractive. It's a shame that was about all there was to her. She left him after a year of marriage. Oh, the scandal that followed!

Money and good connections were not enough. If he chose a wife, she would be a woman of common sense and loyalty. And not bothered by social standing. Or prone to scandal. Definitely not scandal.

"I promise I'll consider several young ladies with an eye to matrimony."

"And quickly, before our family is utterly ruined."

Victor rolled his eyes. If she wasn't so close to the truth, he'd dismiss her panic. Still, it wasn't as if he'd be able to get married before the next edition of the papers.

There was not much to be done for Uncle George. At least he had the grace to scandalize London first. Not that Victor could help him much. George's scandal had only mostly ruined the Wyndells.

No, he had scandal aplenty sitting across from him in the carriage. If it wasn't for her, he wouldn't have such a deadline for matrimony.

His mother had gone and done something foolish. What it was, he did not know. His mother had been rather tight-lipped about the details of something she called The Whole Situation while not bothering to hide how much it vexed her. It was not so much the foolishness of whatever it was she was involved in, but rather that somewhere, somehow, there was a piece of paper that documented such foolishness.

That piece of paper could mean the end of any decent social standing the Wyndells enjoyed—well, whatever was left of their social standing, after Uncle George had bulled his way through. No wonder she wanted Victor hitched before the scandal broke.

What had she done that could shake the very foundations of their reputation? Whatever it was, it rattled her enough to force him to come to this party.

Perhaps it was best he not marry. There was his Uncle Charles, happily enjoying a courtesy viscount title and accompanying wealth. As long as he didn't do anything worthy of being added to the trifecta of Leicester family scandal, there might be some hope.

Who am I bamming? What family of good connection would wish to ally themselves to his, never mind him as a person?

He had no title to defend, his fortune too small worth considering. He simply was who he was. Let his uncles and his brothers worry about begetting heirs and managing estates and wrangling in politics. He was happy to stay at home and work on a clock.

Victor loved clocks. There was something comforting about their steady ticks, their cogs and wheels matched together in a balanced choreography of precision. When the gears of a clock were sized in the perfect ratio, they kept a most admirable time.

His mother despaired of "His Little Hobby," as she put it. Wasn't politics a more suitable pastime? Politics? Too messy. Nothing fit. Therefore, nothing worked. It amazed Victor that the country managed to function at all.

"You are the last of my children. I would like to see you settled."

"Why?"

What good would he bring a wife? The simpering little misses who plagued him every Season had full pockets and empty heads. They were not interested in his good self, only what he could bring to a marriage. Right now, that wasn't much. Oh, he was fair of face, if his mother could be believed, and he enjoyed good health. Otherwise, he had little else to recommend him.

His mother laid a beringed hand on his knee. "I would see you happy."

"I like my life as it is."

"Are you happy?"

What sort of question was that? "Yes," he answered, without thinking.

He was happy, wasn't he?

His mother's response to this was a very knowing glance.

"What does that mean?"

She sighed and rolled her eyes. "I know you are not unhappy. You continue in your staid little life and never have excitement."

He folded his arms. "Excitement and happiness are not the same thing."

"And how would you know, never having any excitement in your life?"

"Everyone else has excitement enough for my satisfaction." He leaned forward in the carriage. "And what about The Whole Situation? I dare say that's been rather exciting."

She sank down, as if all the air had been let out of her. "I wouldn't call it exciting."

She didn't call it anything.

He pressed his advantage. "What about Uncle George?" His marriage had been the very example of *exciting*.

His mother was not to be cornered. "What about Frederick?"

Ah, the elder brother, his father's heir. Frederick had had a beautiful whirlwind romance full of excitement and a few mistaken adventures. That marriage almost didn't happen, if Caroline's father had had his druthers.

Yet Frederick convinced him. Victor still did not know the whole story; no one would speak of it.

Perhaps that was more scandal? Too much was kept hush-hush for it to be anything but. Frederick loved Caroline. And they'd had beautiful babies. All well and good for them.

No way he could be guaranteed such luck.

And now his mother had gotten herself into a bit of *excitement*. To be sure, like most Society scandals, it could have easily been blown over and forgotten, if it wasn't for one damning piece of paper she called The Agreement. He learned about it that afternoon.

"Why is there a document with your name on it? What is this document?"

"I can't tell you; that is what the document is about. It's an agreement that we should never speak of it." She pinched the bridge of her nose. "We should have just let it go. I see that now."

And now here they were, barreling across St. James Square in a carriage, on their way to a party neither wanted to attend all for the sake of The Whole Situation. It was bad enough his mother insisted on dragging him to the various routs and balls and other folderol that comprised the Season without a motive any stronger than marrying him off.

"So why don't you let it go?"

His mother gripped his leg so tight her nails dug in. "Oh, we can't do that now. Someone has broken The Agreement."

"How?"

She leaned in and whispered, although there was no one else in the carriage. "Someone spoke of it."

"Who?"

She shrugged. "We don't know who. But now it's out."

Victor rolled his eyes. His mother was getting tedious. "What is out?"

She whispered again. "The reason for The Agreement."

Why was she whispering? They were the only ones in the carriage.

"Which is?"

She withdrew her hand and turned from him. "I shouldn't be telling you this."

He scrubbed his hands through his hair. "Didn't you drag me along to help you?"

"Well, yes. We must find The Agreement and destroy it."

"Destroy it? Why?"

"You don't have to know what it's about."

This wasn't going well. "So how will I know if I've found it?"

"I'll know what it looks like." Mrs. Wyndell waved her hands in the air in frustration. "Just don't read it if you find it."

Like that made any sense. "Why all this subterfuge? Why not simply ask Lady Chester for it?"

Her hand gripped his leg again. "No! She must not know we've got it, or that we've destroyed it. She has to believe it still exists."

"Why?"

"Well, so she'll hold to the terms of The Agreement."

Why must she be so obtuse? "Which are?"

She shook her head. "I should not be telling you."

He stared at the window of the carriage. Darkness hadn't quite fallen yet. "So there's an Agreement between you and Lady Chester that she needs to adhere to, but you can't tell me what it is?"

"It's best you not know."

"So you want this Agreement secretly destroyed, without letting Lady Chester know about it?"

"That's the sum of it, yes."

He plucked his mother's hand from his leg. "I say that's deucedly unfair for Lady Chester."

"On the contrary. It benefits her very well. She stays out of trouble if she thinks it still exists and everyone else's reputations remain intact if it doesn't exist. Including yours."

He held up his hands. "Wait. There are others involved in The Whole Situation?"

Her hands flew to her mouth. "Oh dear. I should not have told you."

Victor folded his arms and turned from his mother. "You most certainly should not have told me in the first place." Now he was involved. "How many people?"

"It's best you don't know."

The carriage slowed. Victor poked his head out the window. Since it was a crush, naturally there were many, many people in attendance, all of whom had arrived by carriage. About a dozen of the awkward vehicles crowded the little street just off St. James Square. It would be a little while before they could disembark.

"I don't know why you got me involved."

Her hands fluttered, her face puckering up. "Because I need your help." Her hand went back to his leg. "We struck an agreement of silence to protect our honor. That agreement was broken by someone. Now all our reputations are on the line. If we destroy The Agreement, our honor will be preserved."

And maybe she would stop pushing him into a marriage too soon. "As long as Lady Chester doesn't know about it. Who else?"

But Mrs. Wyndell shook her head. "We can't afford any more scandal." She rolled her eyes and lolled her head back as she fumbled for her smelling salts.

Victor did not understand why his mother found this so pressing. "Would it destroy our family forever?"

She sniffed as she patted his leg once more. "Like poor George, it was not I who acted foolishly. Yet I must be tarred by the brush, simply because I was there." She waved her hands most dramatically. "Oh, why do these things happen to us?"

Well, Uncle George did bring it on himself in a way. He was the one who'd married his wife. Plus, she didn't desert him for no reason.

His mother, likewise, brought her own misfortunes herself. What compelled her to put her name to some mysterious agreement, one clearly so damning she could not bring herself to speak of its contents?

That alone piqued his curiosity. Had she and Lady Chester found themselves in some compromising situation? Had there been a gentleman involved? Or something even more nefarious?

He took her hands. "Mother, you must tell me the contents of the document."

Her gaze could not meet his.

"Will it utterly ruin us, should it come to light?"

She pinched her nose. "I should never have agreed."

The door to their carriage opened, startling them. They'd arrived at the party. A footman peered in and then withdrew his head.

Mrs. Wyndell recovered herself and exited the carriage without further comment. Victor followed, a frown of consternation wrinkling his brow.

Was this how his mother felt when she found herself involved in The Whole Situation? Had she been unwittingly dragged into this not of her volition?

A seed of sympathy sprouted in his gut. No wonder she wanted to get her hands on The Agreement.

Around them, several people crowded the steps of the Chesters' townhouse. Horses snorted and stamped, and coachmen shouted vulgarities. The *ton* chatted and waved to each other, sharing their gossip back and forth. Their conversations roamed over all sorts of subjects. The two men before them huffed and hawed over some deplorable conditions in Parliament whereas their wives tutted and sighed over the disappointments of a *modiste*.

The Wyndells stood on the pavement, waiting their turn for entry. Surely whatever The Whole Situation was about, it was not the prime subject on everyone's lips.

Mrs. Wyndell remained uncharacteristically silent, her eyes darting hither and yon as if afraid of accusation. Still, if it had his mother this worried, he'd help her destroy The Agreement.

But how would they find it at the party? "It would help if you gave me some kind of description."

"Not in public," she chastened him, *sotto voce*.

Victor sighed. His mother needed his help to find an agreement about which he knew practically nothing, other than it mentioned her and Lady Chester, and possibly someone else. No clue as to where in the house it could be, or even if it was in the house. Once he found it, he had to destroy it. At least the destruction was the easy part; fire was in plentiful supply.

With no one to talk to, Victor looked about. The Chesters lived in a nice little square considered fashionable yet not ostentatious. All the townhouses bore hallmarks of subtle taste: clean doorsteps, polished doorknockers, even flowers blooming at the windowsills.

As his gaze roamed upward, he discovered someone watching him.

A young lady stood at a window of the townhouse next door, her hand pressed to the glass. She watched him without ducking her head or a blush reddening her cheeks. *How bold.* Her lips moved as she spoke to someone, her eyes never leaving him. Her head tilted, and she pressed her nose to the glass. Was she studying him? With whom was she conversing? Was it about him? Or did she know his mother?

His breath caught in his throat. *Such a pretty thing.* Perhaps they were acquainted, this young lady and his mother. Introductions, then. And maybe his mother would get off his back about finding a suitable young lady.

She watched him steadily, without a single line of frown to mar her smooth forehead. If anything, she appeared intrigued.

As he regarded her further, he questioned his assumption that his mother may have been correct in her paranoia.

Mrs. Wyndell tugged at his sleeve. "Come. Let us be done with this insipid little party."

Chapter 2
How Victor Goes to the Party

Felicity sat at the window and took note of everyone who came to the Chesters. Carriages crowded the street, turning their normally quiet neighborhood into a cacophony of horse noises and coachman curses. This promised to be a smashing party if the chaos out front was any indication. Must be something spectacular if so many people were turning up. Her parents flirted with their own scandal and did not bother with a carriage. They mounted the steps of the Chesters' townhouse next door to their own and entered.

Several distinctive people arrived, whom Felicity knew by reputation—a veritable who's who of Society. But the majority of guests were unknown to her. Many a fine young man arrived, and nearly as many departed. Likewise, plenty of unmarried young ladies came, with parents or other chaperones. These did not depart as readily.

Felicity sighed. *They got to go to the crush.*

So she waited and watched for another ten minutes until her parents emerged. That was fast. Why did her parents accept the invitation if they were only going to stay for such a short time? Maybe her father had forgotten something, or maybe her mother needed a repair to her hem.

But no. Once they exited the Chesters' townhouse, they climbed into a carriage with another couple, and the Abbots were away.

Now she could leave.

Jones would be of no help to her. She'd go straight to Mrs. Abbot if she learned of Felicity's plans. But Bess in the kitchens would help. Cook had long since retired to bed, and the other servants had made themselves scarce. But Bess remained up, doing the final cleaning.

Bess had a secret; his name was James. He worked next door for Lord and Lady Chester. In exchange for various favors, Felicity wrote letters for the illiterate Bess, who could easily slip next door to deliver them.

The servants had quite the network going, Felicity had discovered. Not only were letters exchanged, but gossip and more. Some of the more clandestine goings-on Felicity did not wish to know about in the name of maidenly modesty. The rest, however, was like sugar to her porridge and filled in the gaps of the morning papers' gossip. If one wanted to know what London was truly up to, one asked a servant.

****

Felicity entered the kitchen wearing an unbuttoned gown, with a pencil and paper in her hand.

"Do me up while I write a letter for you?"

Bess, who had been banking up the fire for the evening, took one look at Felicity. "What you up to, Miss Felicity?"

She eyed the fine sprigged muslin, one of many debutante-appropriate gowns designed to present a young figure to its best advantage. It wasn't the fanciest of her Season wardrobe, but it would do. Felicity's goal was not to Be Seen.

"Never you mind. I shall not be a stone's throw away." She placed the paper on the table and bent over. "Dear James…"

Bess sighed. She dictated as she did up Felicity's buttons. "We h'ain't had any more mice, on account of that new cat we done got…"

After the letter and the dress were done, Bess paused. "I just remember'd. Cook done lock up the kitchen, as she don't trust me with keys."

Felicity gave her a smile. "Don't you worry about that. Now, how about I deliver this letter for you?"

Felicity laid a hand on the kitchen door and concentrated. Magic flowed over her skin and down her fingers. Like spells, simple things were easy to undo with her magic—knots and locks included. The tumblers clicked, and the door opened.

Felicity laid a finger over her lips as she sneaked out. The door, she locked behind her. Let Bess wonder where she got a *key*.

Only the light from a few windows illuminated the yard. As she squelched through puddles, she dreaded the state of her shoes. Too late to remove them now. At least she kept her hem high.

Through the yard she went, until she reached the back gate. This opened into a narrow alleyway that separated the townhouses from the mews, a muddy lane only big enough for small delivery carts and the night soil men. The next gate over was not a problem, nor did any servant in the yard mention the passing of a young lady, presumably out for a breath of fresh air, maybe?

The Chesters' back door was not locked. Felicity slipped in to the hot noisiness of the kitchen.

Downstairs bustled with all the party preparations and maintenance. Their cook yelled and bossed and ordered the staff about. Maids of many kinds ducked about with platters, which they handed to footmen.

As one maid returned, Felicity stopped her. "Excuse me, do—"

Her eyes grew wide. "Oh, Miss, you should not be down here."

"Do you know James?"

"Sorry. Only hired for the day."

That wasn't good luck. Still, she pulled out the letter. "Could you—"

The maid held out her arms to shoo Felicity out of the kitchen. She might be shorter than Felicity, but she was insistent. "You can't be down here." The maid corralled her into a footman's reach. "Get her outta here."

Felicity evaded the footman and tripped up the stairs. He followed, preventing her from returning down.

"You shouldn't be down here," he said, his presence encouraging her ever upward.

"Do you know James?"

He stopped. "James who?"

James who, indeed. Who was James? He worked here, and he was called James. Other than that, Felicity didn't know. "Bess's James?"

His countenance softened. "You know my Bess?"

Success! She'd found her man. Felicity held up the letter. "From Bess."

He snatched it from her fingers and read it. A smile spread across his face as he mouthed the words she'd written not five minutes prior.

As another footman bustled past them, James quickly hid the letter. "Best you get back to the party."

Felicity nodded. Before he could depart, she asked, "James, if you see me down here again tonight, could you please let me out the back door?" She smiled a winsome smile at him.

But he wasn't paying attention to her anymore. He had work to do.

Yet another footman, heavy-laden, came up the stairs. Felicity hurried before him and slipped through the wooden door into a dark corridor.

The footman went through the door and turned right.

Felicity turned left.

****

With his evening dampened even before he arrived, Victor and Mrs. Wyndell entered the Chesters' townhouse. The narrow hallway did nothing to relieve the crowded feeling. Coats and hats and more filled the little room to the side, so much that the door would not close. As Victor handed his hat to the harried maid there, he doubted he would get it back in the same condition, if he got it back at all.

Crushes were never his favorite. Nice, quiet card parties were more his thing. But this? Intolerable. His head spun from the difference in temperature from the cool outside to the stuffy, overheated inside. People of all kinds packed the entryway, steadily moving forward as they made their way to the drawing rooms. There had to be a good two hundred people here already, possibly more.

And the noise! Conversations burbled up from the crowd, each person speaking louder to raise their voice over the sound.

The Chesters' townhouse was spacious for a London residence, with high ceilings and long windows. The room itself would have been sufficient for one of the card parties the Chesters were famous for, or even a small ball. At the far end a small orchestra competed with the noise of the crowd. Surely they were not hoping to have dancing. There would be no room. He scuffed a foot across the parquet flooring. Shame there would be no dancing. Looked like there wouldn't be much of anything except getting in each other's way.

As they muddled their way from the entry into the drawing rooms, Victor saw the reason for the holdup— a receiving line as the Chesters greeted their guests. Next to Lady Chester was her daughter, Honorable Miss Chester, who had secured an engagement to a duke over the winter. He'd heard the tale several times from his mother and did not wish to suffer through it again.

He couldn't be bothered with the receiving line. Victor slipped away from his mother and pushed through the crowd. Was there anyone here he knew?

When he looked back to see if his mother had missed him, he saw her worried face bent close to Lady Chester's. She whispered fast. Lady Chester's own countenance, once beaming at the triumph of her party, dropped into darkness. What was his mother saying to her?

Lady Chester's gaze darted about. She whispered back. Then the two women parted ways, as if afraid to be caught together.

Ah. His mother had to be informing her of The

Whole Situation, or at least part of it. From the look on Lady Chester's face, she might not have known until now of the breaking of The Agreement. Someone had spoken, when all were sworn to silence.

Her work done, Mrs. Wyndell joined him. So worried was she, she did not comment on his desertion of her.

"I recommend we split up. Better chance of finding it that way." Off she went, leaving him without a plan or a hope.

Victor only sighed. Surely if The Agreement was here, it would not be in the drawing room. Possibly up in the library, or in Lady Chester's writing desk, or possibly tucked away in a bedroom? Certainly no one had any business or a good reason for going into a bedroom. Plenty of bad reasons, however. And purloining an agreement with the sole purpose of destroying it could be one of them.

So close was the company here, when Victor turned around, he bumped into someone.

"I beg your pardon," he offered automatically.

"Why, Mr. Wyndell."

Victor's skin crawled. It was not the voice itself that was unpleasant. It could have been quite lovely, if it weren't for the lady behind it.

At one of the biggest crushes of the Season yet, he had to bump into Miss Cornelia Parnell first. *Of all the rotten luck.* He'd done his best to avoid her this Season, to make up for last Season, where he'd spent far too much time in her company. Not his fault. She had pursued him with such single-mindedness he'd quickly lost any interest he might have had.

Miss Parnell had not changed over the course of a

year. This Season's high-waisted fashions did her dumpy figure and too-broad shoulders no favors. Her chins made up for what her *décolletage* lacked. At least she had all her teeth, even if they were too small for her mouth.

While it was a given that pretty much every young lady was looking for marriage, most were genteel about it. Not Miss Cornelia Parnell. She hunted a husband the way a chicken hunted a grasshopper, no grace or style, and wholly without the least bit of subtlety. Oh, at first she had been all fluttery eyelashes and hiding behind her fan last year, typical fare for new debutantes. It was easy enough to dismiss her, along with all the others who he had found shallow and dull.

But then she'd upped the stakes. She used magic.

What was it with young ladies and their magical charms? It seemed that wherever she turned up, he ended up turning out his pockets. She was always slipping something into them—a small ring, a simple brooch, even several charmed silver hairpins once. Most of the charms were rather tepid in their magic and didn't have much of an effect on him, but once she'd managed to secure a pin to the back of his jacket with a really strong 'Come Hither' charm. Slight hitch with that, as the charm was not one of her making. He figured this out when it kept drawing him to another young lady not of his acquaintance.

At least the young lady had been kind enough to recognize what had happened and had relieved him of the pin.

How it had ended up in Miss Parnell's possession, he didn't know.

"Miss Parnell." He made the obligatory bow and

looked for the best escape route.

She hooked her arm in his. "I dare say I haven't seen you at all this Season. Have you been ill?"

"No." He scanned the crowd. In a crush this large, there had to be someone else he knew.

"You remember my cousin, Miss Bitner?"

What? Victor's attention returned to Miss Parnell.

While he'd been looking away, she had been joined by the only person of his acquaintance more detestable than Miss Parnell, Miss Nora Bitner.

He remembered her, if only for the sake of his self-preservation, and to warn other men. Several times he had aided men to escape the clutches of Miss Bitner, even the Duke of Montagu himself.

She was a bit more fortunate in her face than her cousin. Could have even been considered pretty, if it wasn't for her eyes. Nasty eyes they were, sharp and cynical, so sharp they could peel the very skin off one's back, if Miss Bitner took a disliking to you.

She offered her curtsey to his bow. "My dear Mr. Wyndell. Where have you been keeping yourself?"

That unpleasant gaze raked the whole of his body as if he were for sale. And perhaps to her, he was. Nobody had been game enough last year to make her an offer, though she'd pursued many a high eligible with the same single-mindedness of her cousin. At least Victor Wyndell's social status had been low enough for him to escape her targeting skills.

"I dare say you've missed the best part of the Season. I must confess, the weather has upheld nicely."

Oh, the small talk. Like crushes, he also hated small talk. All words to fill the uncomfortable silences and empty all meaning from conversation.

Miss Parnell had also introduced the other two people in their little crowd, another tepid lady of chubby girth and some young man, "…her brother." He didn't quite catch their names and didn't bother to ask for a repeat.

Where did all these people come from? He hadn't noticed them earlier when Miss Parnell had commandeered him. He did a quick check of his pockets, in case Miss Parnell had slipped in a focus charm.

They were empty. *Thank goodness.* In hopes of avoiding being dominated by Miss Parnell, he turned to the new acquaintances.

The brother was young, only just out of short pants. This had to be his first Season, if not his first party. He sketched an awkward bow.

"Pleased," he replied, his voice cracking.

He'll charm the ladies, in about twenty years' time. Until then, the most he could expect to get out of the fairer sex was the pinching of his cheeks still chubby with puppy fat.

The sister seemed pleasant enough, at least as an acquaintance, but had this annoying habit of wiping her nose constantly with her handkerchief. Her clothes bespoke a lack of fortune. Her left hand was bare, and she looked to be very much on the shelf. She had to be six-and-twenty, if she were a day, with a puffy, moony face. She had a vague hint of magic about her, though he doubted any charm would overcome the sad little aura that drifted around her head.

Her brother looked bored. Despite Victor's attempts to engage him in conversation, the lad simply couldn't hold up his end.

He spied his mother halfway across the room, her gaze fixed very much his way. "I believe my mother requires my presence."

Miss Parnell raised her gaze, a frown creasing her forehead. It wasn't the first time he'd used such an excuse to extricate himself from her company. However, that frown eased. Mrs. Wyndell was indeed coming this way in a very determined manner.

His mother pushed through the crowd, moving past him without a glance. No, her gaze was on someone else.

Victor followed through the noisy, sharp-elbowed crowd. Miss Parnell trailed close behind, as he was unable to slip from her grasp completely. She clung to the sleeve of his jacket like a burr.

He found his mother, head bent close to another lady. Only after his mother had had a quick word in her ear and she straightened, did Victor recognize the lady as Mrs. Abbot. Was she the other party to The Whole Situation? If so, exactly what was The Agreement about? Mrs. Abbot enjoyed a good reputation. Surely she was above such scandal.

Or was she? If Mrs. Abbot was to be involved in a scandal, what kind would it be? Surely not dalliance.

The only thing that came to mind was a financial scandal. Had they invested money in some scheme that failed? He wouldn't put it above his mother to do something like that. That would also explain why they'd want to keep it a secret.

Money was both sacred and profane to the *ton*. Everyone was judged on their net worth, yet it was considered vulgar to talk about money. Young ladies were measured not only by fairness of face, but flushness of pocket as well. How much dowry would they bring? That was the question many asked before. "Is she agreeable?"

Victor didn't worry too much about money. He had income sufficient for his needs. What he lacked was decent company. He'd take a young lady in her pauperhood, if she came with a fine wit and pleasant conversation.

Miss Parnell clung to his arm. "There. She didn't need you after all."

Apparently not.

She dragged him back to her little coterie. There they found Miss Bitner spewing a quiet sort of vitriol for the benefit of the sniffly lady—a veritable ape-leader if ever he'd seen one—and her brother.

"And so I find it extremely vulgar to get engaged outside of the Season. Downright sneaky, if you ask me. I think there's something quite improper and under-the-table about it."

What was she harping on now? Was she bitter that someone else had the good fortune to find a husband and she left wanting? Miss Bitner had not taken the first two Seasons. She certainly would not take this one if her conversation and topics continued in this same poisonous manner.

But Miss Parnell's eyes livened up. "Oh, of whom are we speaking?" She'd twined her arm proprietarily in Victor's, preventing him from making a subtle escape.

"The Duke of Montagu. Such a fine specimen. Shame he'll be wasted on Miss Chester."

"Miss Chester?"

Victor did not mean to speak out loud. It took him a moment, then he recalled they were indeed betrothed.

He didn't pay too much attention to who was off the market. He'd met Miss Chester a few times. Blonde, airheaded, good pedigree, a perfect Society miss. Montagu couldn't go wrong.

He liked Montagu. A good sport, he was. Thoughtful too, according to Victor's mother and sister, both who opined it was about time His Grace had found himself a good wife. He shared this same thought with the present company.

Miss Bitner leaned closer. "But will she be a proper wife?" She gave him a knowing nod.

Victor frowned. What was she saying? "She will be a most proper wife." Her reputation was stellar. Lord and Lady Chester were well-regarded in the *ton*. Why should their daughter be any different?

Miss Bitner's eyes rolled away as if to preserve his own dignity from being soiled. Too late, if that was the case. Her mere presence made his skin crawl.

"Oh, I am not disparaging her. After all, she is young and has yet to be tarnished by the vagaries of Society." She shook her head. "One must wonder about why His Grace and Miss Chester got engaged out of Season. It is rather, how shall I say, suspect? You would think the Chesters were in a rush to get her married off. Something strange about the whole situation."

That startled him at first. He relaxed. She wouldn't know anything about The Whole Situation. Really, he had to let go of his mother's worry and focus on something else. If only he could let go of her company.

Her insinuations were leaving a nasty taste on his tongue. It was unfair of her to speak of Miss Chester in such a way.

"Every mama is in a rush to get their daughters married off. You cannot fault one for her success when your mother is probably in despair over your own failure."

Miss Bitner's jaw dropped. Miss Parnell squeaked in surprise.

Victor gave them a polite bow. "If you'll excuse me, I must go take care of some important business."

The sniffly sister spoke, for once. "You're at a party. Why would you conduct business here?"

He winked. "Every man must conduct 'business' at a party at one time or another. Thankfully, we conduct it behind the screen."

The brother guffawed. Every large party provided for the convenience of men by screening off a far corner of a quiet room and providing chamber pots, to be emptied by footmen as required. Victor had no idea what ladies did. It was not something about which one asked.

"I won't be long," he lied.

How quickly could he get away from that unfortunate company? Only the screen could save him.

He located it in a room down a hallway. It wasn't more than a closet, manned by one unfortunate footman minding three chamber pots. At least the room had a window. No doubt it was through this the footman was tossing the contents.

Nevertheless, Victor relieved himself, checked his pockets one last time, and headed back to the party with caution. No Miss Parnell or Miss Bitner to capture him. Instead, he found Jacob Goodsell, a well-met chum who enjoyed a pleasant conversation completely devoid of feminine topics.

"Demmed busy crush." Mr. Goodsell tugged at his cuffs. "If it weren't for everyone else, I wouldn't bother coming."

Victor completely sympathized. "My mother dragged me along. I take it there's nothing of interest here?"

"It's a Chesters' party; I believe there's a gaming room upstairs, though I wouldn't bother tonight."

"Oh?"

Mr. Goodsell sniffed. "Debs and their paper points. Nothing exciting. Not like last time." He scanned the crowd in a futile attempt to find a footman with a tray of drinks. The only refreshment available was a table across the room. He sighed.

"Now that was a party."

"Did I miss something interesting?" Victor wasn't at the Chesters' last party, though his mother was. When she'd returned home, she had nothing to say about it. Unusual for his mother, but nothing to which he'd given a second thought.

"And how. Mr. Marlon-Johnson lost a small house to Honorable Mr. Whiston. Honestly thought he'd win, but Whiston finessed the last trick out from underneath him. Stunning good playing."

"Indeed?"

How could his mother have failed to tell him about this? Not that he minded. Her regular reminders that he should be out more, that he should be looking for a wife, that he should make it look like he wasn't bordering on the edge of trade wore thin. Surely she would have crowed about Whiston's house, and how he was moving up in the world, and what was Victor doing?

Honorable Mr. Whiston was even younger than Victor, newly out in Society only because he'd lost enough respect for his aging father to know that the old man couldn't stop him going out of an evening. And now he had a house to his name? Lucky him. He could rent it out for a modest income or even live in it himself. That's what Victor would do, if it meant he could get away from his mother. "Where's the house?"

"King Street," he replied with some gloom.

"That's not so bad." Almack's, where exclusive subscription balls were held each Wednesday night of the Season, was on King Street.

"The far end." Indeed, the farther one got on King Street, the lower the morality of the available entertainments.

"Really? Terrible shame." *Ah well. Rental income it was. Maybe enough for bachelor's digs in a better part of town?*

"I know." Mr. Goodsell lifted up on his toes to peer over the crowd. He did not find whatever he was looking for, so he settled back down. "Interesting things always happened at the Chesters' parties. Tonight, however, I feel we are in for a very different mood. I doubt anyone will stay for long, unless you love gossip."

Victor wrinkled his nose. "Not really. I'm here under protest."

Mr. Goodsell nodded. "So you said. You plan on hiding all night?"

"I hope so." Though with his mother bound and determined to find that dratted agreement, he didn't fancy his chances. Still, best place to hide was a crowd.

Alas, his good fortune was not to last.

"Mr. Wyndell!" Miss Parnell had found him in the press of people. With great difficulty she pushed her way in his direction.

"Oh, that cursed girl," he muttered. "Do excuse me."

Mr. Goodsell rose on his toes again to peer through the crowd. "I say, still avoiding the skirts?"

"Just the unpleasant ones."

"I dare say that's most of them."

Well, not true. Earlier in the Season he had met a few with good conversation and a generally pleasant demeanor. They were rare. Once the word of their overall appeal got out, he had to compete with other men, richer, handsomer, more titled. It hurt to lose a good woman to another man, as much as it would hurt to settle for the dregs of Society. Victor had no intention on settling.

"I've encountered two of them tonight and have no desire to further the acquaintance. Excuse me."

"Quite all right, old fellow." Mr. Goodsell, a confirmed bachelor, understood.

Victor slipped away and into the quickest exit he could find, namely the service corridor.

Chapter 3
Where Felicity and Victor Meet in a Most
Awkward Manner

Felicity dashed up the servants' stairs behind the
footman. Above her she spied the door between the
downstairs world of the servants and the glittering
upstairs delights of the Season.

She imagined a thousand burning candles,
illuminating a giant ballroom like the sun. She
envisioned a thousand—no a million—people whirling
around, their jewels glittering, their gowns spectacular.
Such color! Reds and blues and greens of various hues,
plus the white that signalled that year's fresh crop of
debutantes. She even spotted a lovely pink gown that
made her heart flutter with envy. Maybe she could
convince her mother to take her back to the seamstress?
Every lady elegant, every gentleman handsome. A full
string orchestra of impeccable sound would fill the air
with musical delight.

And now, finally, she would get to see it all.

The footman opened the door just enough to slip
through.

Felicity was not far behind. She flung the door
open into a dim corridor. It hit something with a dull
thud.

"Ow!" A cry of pain echoed out, in the timbre of a
man's voice.

Oh no. Felicity grabbed the handle and pulled the door shut. She waited, hand on the knob, her heart hammering in her chest, to hear what happened on the other side.

That was not what she had been expecting. Where were the bright lights? Where was the party? She pressed an ear against the door. Yes, the murmuring of her million people was out there, but also a hiss of pain.

Carefully, she eased open the door and peeked around it. The door did not lead to a bright, open ballroom, but a dim corridor. Reflected light shone from one end, battling the gloom. Music floated her way, warring with countless conversations, still so far away.

On the other side of the door stood a gentleman, inspecting an injured hand. He shook it as if to dispel the pain.

Wait! She knew that man. He'd arrived with Lady Wyndell. Her son, wasn't he? Her heart thumped. Even close up, he looked quite handsome, if a bit scowly. Then again, she had injured him. He had reason to frown.

Felicity slunk out from behind the door. "Oh dear. I'm so sorry." How was she to know someone was standing on the other side?

He inspected his knuckles. "Quite all right." He prodded at them gingerly.

"I dare say it's not."

Felicity took his hand and inspected the injury. Whenever she got hurt, her mother would kiss it better. Always worked. Without a second thought, she lifted his hand to her lips. Her skin tingled as it pressed against his. Surely she could undo a bit of pain. It was

45

just another kind of knot.

"There. How's that?" She favored him with a broad smile.

He stared at her, his jaw slightly ajar, his gaze locked to hers. She wasn't that much shorter than he. She could almost look him in the eye. He blinked and tilted his head. Her heart hammered. For the longest time, she held his hand. He hadn't pulled away.

"How's what?" he asked, his voice vague.

"Your hand?" she replied. Was it hard to breathe? Her lips still held the taste of his skin and a faint buzz of magic.

He looked down at their connection. He pulled his hand from hers and flexed it. "Actually, that's…that's better." His gaze returned to hers. "How did you do that?"

She gave him a wry look. "Everyone knows a kiss makes things better."

He opened his fingers a few more times as if he didn't believe it.

Heavy footsteps echoed down the hall, followed by loud feminine laughter. He glanced back, his shoulders tightening.

Interesting. "You're hiding, aren't you?"

"No." His startled look confirmed a different answer.

Like she believed that. Felicity pressed her advantage. "Of course you are."

She looked up and down the corridor. It wasn't so much a corridor as an alcove, a hidden space to hide this door between the upper and lower worlds. Her grandmother's townhouse next door had one very similar. Either end of this corridor opened into the drawing rooms. In fact, if she peeked around the corner…

His hand, the uninjured one, caught her shoulder. "What are you doing?"

"Having a look." He was hiding; she knew it! "What are *you* doing?"

"W-well," he stuttered, hesitating over his next words. "Maybe I'm resting."

She surveyed his brow and his dark hair. Not a speck of sweat.

"You haven't danced once this entire evening."

He folded his arms. "And how would you know?"

"Because the night is still young. Either you would be dancing, or you would be at the punchbowl because you'd danced so much you needed a drink."

His eyes glinted and that discomfited her.

"You have not actually been out at the party, or you would know there's no dancing at all."

A self-conscious guilt flushed over her skin. "What? No dancing?"

The advantage of power had shifted. "It's a crush," he informed her. "You don't dance at a crush." He looked her over, top to toe. He leaned forward ever so slightly and inhaled.

Her hand stole to her hair. She had put it up herself and coaxed a few natural curls to cascade down her unadorned neck. No rings on her ungloved fingers, absolutely no jewelry at all. No reticule, no fan, nothing to occupy her hands. Her gown was of the first fashion; her mother had seen to that. In her rush to get to the party, she had completely forgotten to accessorize. It wasn't as if she had expected to need any charms.

He looked to the door. "You're a servant, aren't you?"

Now her flush was one of insult. "I most certainly am not!"

He folded his arms and leaned against the wall. A burst of laughter echoed from the drawing rooms. "Prove it."

Prove it? How does one prove one is not a servant? Their clothing, for one. "I'm wearing Francine." Her mother preferred this dressmaker. While one often kept her dressmaker a secret, perhaps the knowledge would serve her now.

"Dresses can be borrowed."

"And risk my being dismissed without a reference?"

All right, what else differentiated the *ton* from their servants? Family connections? Pastimes? Occupations? *Ah, of course.*

Felicity held out her hands. "I cannot borrow these."

Her hands were smooth, her nails trimmed neatly, her skin soft and pale. Servants' hands were rough and red, possibly from all the cleaning they had to do.

He let go of his breath. "So who are you?"

She froze. This was awkward. Here she was conversing with him, and they hadn't been properly introduced. She bobbed him a curtsey. "I am Miss Felicity Abbot of the Essex Colchesters. Pleased to meet you."

His expression went rigid. "Abbot…"

Oh dear. Had she said something wrong?

"Charlotte Abbot's daughter?" His gaze turned to the servants' door. "Of course," he said more to himself than to her. "It makes sense. Lady Chester, Mrs. Abbot, and my mother…"

48

His brow furrowed, very much like when she'd spied him out the window earlier. He pressed his knuckles to his lips and paced. His next comment was addressed to her.

"You're looking for The Agreement as well."

"I haven't found too much in the last five minutes to be terribly agreeable."

"Have you found anything yet?"

What on earth was he talking about? "I've found you. I've only been here a brief while." She craned to look past him. "Haven't even been out in the party yet. So if they're not dancing, what are they doing?"

"Gossiping," came his dry reply.

A footman hurried around the corner bearing empty trays. He pushed past them and went through the servants' green door. Both waited until he had passed.

"You know," she said, when the silence became uninteresting, "we have not been properly introduced."

His attention turned back to her. "We haven't? Surely we have. Unless—"

"I'm pretty sure I would have remembered you." Felicity gave him her Winning Smile. It would not do to be sprung so early in the evening.

Unlike others in her past, who had been utterly charmed by her even teeth and delicate dimples, he stiffened. "Ah. You're one of those."

Was that disappointment in his voice?

Her smile faded. "What do you mean?"

He leaned against the wall. "Let me guess: your first Season, and your only goal is to secure a titled husband with a large fortune."

She put a fist on her hip. "First, this is my first Season only because family tragedy prevented me from coming out the last two years. Second, it's my grandmother's ambition to secure a titled husband with a large fortune. Me, I don't care either way. I simply wish to sample the delights of the Season." She peered past him again. "I hear it's terribly exciting."

"You hear...?" His eyes narrowed. "Wait. Charlotte Abbot's daughter." He drew in a breath. "You're waiting on Lady Abbot to return." His stare accused her. "Are you even out?"

A lump rose in her throat. She never meant to share that information.

She evaded his question. "One could ask the same of you."

He blinked at her. "I'll have you know I've attended three Seasons."

"Three Seasons." She raised her eyebrows. "Three whole Seasons and you never took. That's a shame. I suppose you're all but on the shelf now."

"What?" He stepped backward.

That's it. Keep him off-balance.

"Surely it's not all your fault. Still, you're young-ish. I daresay three-and-twenty, maybe four?"

He stared at her without answering.

"You'd have a lot better luck if you stopped frowning so much and put on a bit of charm."

That got his back up. "Who said anything about me getting married?"

She fixed him with a determined eye. "Do you have a mother? Of course you do. Therefore, you are under pressure to get married."

He crossed his arms. "Not necessarily."

But she only shook her head at him. "Nobody has ever heard of a mother saying, 'I don't mind if you never get married, dear.'" She pitched her voice high and maternal. "'I am content for you to stay single and lonely for the rest of your life.' Go on. Tell me I'm wrong."

His arms tightened even more. "You're wrong."

She planted her fists on her hips in a most unladylike stance. "No, I'm not, and you know it."

He threw his hands in the air. "Save me from Society misses."

"Ooh. Sour grapes because I am right. Now." She looked him up and down. "You're one of the younger, if not the youngest of the Wyndell boys. Your mother, Mrs. Wyndell, is a younger daughter of the Earl of Leicester. The only way you could have been even more unfortunate in your birth is if you'd been born a girl." She reconsidered her words. "No, I take that back. Even as a girl, you would have familial value for making advantageous marriages.

"No. As a surplus boy, titles and fortunes are not in plentiful supply. Therefore you must rely on your wits and charm. Otherwise, you become a veritable family dead-end. You're the maiden uncle, tolerated, put-upon and never at the forefront of everyone's invitation list, unless desperate for an extra man to make up couples for dancing."

His arms had tightened about his chest so much, it was a wonder he didn't cut himself in half. "I don't like you very much."

"It's a good thing I'm not marrying you, then." At that, an ache fluttered through her heart. Of course she was going to marry him. He just didn't know it yet.

His jaw dropped. "I never said anything about marriage."

Ooh, had she actually offended him? For some inexplicable reason, that pleased her. "I did. Though not to you. An earlier conversation with my mother."

Before she could expand on her thought, the servants' door flew open, hitting her on the posterior.

She stumbled forward, straight into Mr. Wyndell's arms.

****

Victor found his arms full of a soft, surprised young woman. Her bosom pressed against his chest in a rather nice way. His ire melted upon contact with her arms.

"Oh, hello?" Why wouldn't his arms let go? "Are…are you all right?"

The few layers of cloth between them could not hide how her heart hammered. His hands trembled. Really, he should set her to rights. Such a position was hardly proper.

Her eyes gazed into his as her hands gripped his jacket. "I'm…fine?"

His hands slipped to her waist, then around to the small of her back. That wasn't right. Shouldn't he have been pushing her away?

Her face tilted toward his, her lips parting ever so slightly. How easy it would be to…

"My goodness!" A new voice behind him, also feminine, startled him. "I dare say, Mr. Wyndell." She sounded rather scandalized.

This would not do. He pushed Miss Abbot away, setting her properly on her feet.

She was a quick thinker.

In all innocence, she said, "Thank you, Mr. Wyndell. If you hadn't caught me, I would have fallen to the floor."

She gave him that smile of hers. It lit the room and lifted his heart. Oh, the Abbots were wise to keep her under wraps. Yet here she was, undebuted and unescorted among nearly the entire *ton*. She'd better put that smile away before she drew the wrong sort of man.

It wasn't for his benefit—all right, it was, somewhat—but more for the unwelcome interloper who'd joined them.

"Miss Parnell." Victor's back stiffened as he turned around. "I did not see you there." He bowed. "Your servant." Her looks could have been tolerable, had she a sweet disposition to go with it.

She did not. Now, she fixed Victor with a knowing look. " 'Helping' someone, were you?"

Miss Abbot slipped past him, to peer around the corner at the party, all but ignoring him. *Thank goodness for small miracles.* Had she just slipped and had he only caught her, this is exactly what would have happened next.

Perhaps Miss Abbot was not as shallow as he first thought. He watched her, hovering on the edge of the party. She did not look back. Was that disappointment in his heart? That couldn't be right.

Miss Parnell took Victor by the arm. "*We* were waiting for you."

We? Who were *we*? "You were?" It took him a moment to remember that *we* had been Miss Parnell, her cousin Miss Bitner and some other spinster whose name he'd forgotten and her younger brother, only just out of short pants.

Instead of running off, as one would have expected of a flighty young miss, Miss Abbot remained in the corridor, hidden from the party upon which she spied. What was so fascinating out in the drawing rooms? Or was she an expert in eavesdropping? *Not sure what to think about that one.* Eavesdropping was a terribly unsocial habit. However, it was one that had served him well in the past, one he might indulge in more.

Miss Abbot drew a deep breath before plunging out into the crush. Good luck to her. She knew no one and had no one to introduce her. Also, her propensity for saying exactly what was on her mind would not serve her well.

Now he was stuck with Miss Parnell. When he looked down at his companion, he wanted nothing more than to abandon her and take off after Miss Abbot.

Miss Parnell simpered, a frightening sight. "Why did you not return presently? One would think you quite ungallant."

Victor swallowed. "I'm sure I would have returned, had Miss Abbot not been struck by the servants' door."

To prove his tale, the door swung open again, nearly hitting him. He backed off, Miss Parnell following. Why wouldn't she relinquish his arm?

Miss Parnell patted his sleeve. "Well, return and be social." She dragged him back into the bright lights and too-loud noise of the party.

Clusters of people fought for standing room with their elbows. Random gentlemen nudged their way through, their hands occupied with glasses of punch. Servants didn't bother presenting trays to the crowd, but loaded the refreshments on a table at the far end. Mostly men surrounded this table, sent to brave the hordes for edibles. The Chesters had catered well. Open-faced watercress sandwiches sat piled high next to platters of frosted cake—a sight better than what one would find at Almack's. An intense heat pressed against him, a wall of warm moistness and the smells of humanity—spicy, sweaty, and not terribly pleasant.

Miss Parnell pressed close. It could have been she didn't want him to escape, or it could have been she didn't have much choice, so crowded it was.

"We missed you."

Victor didn't know why. He had contributed as little to the conversation as possible.

When Miss Parnell dragged him back to the knot of despair, they found Miss Bitner bending the spinster's ear.

The spinster did not look so keen to be keeping company with her now. Victor couldn't hear what she said, but Miss Bitner's lips flapped rapidly before the spinster's ear. She gripped the poor woman's arm so tight there was no hope of getting away.

It looked to be his role tonight to rescue every miss in need of rescue.

If only someone would rescue him.

Miss Bitner and Miss Parnell insisted on gossiping about every person they espied and in the nastiest of ways. The pudgy spinster did not contribute much. She seemed happy enough being a non-player in the group.

Victor wished there was dancing. He'd ask the spinster to dance, if only to get away from the two toxic misses.

Why did his mother insist on bringing him here?

The brother had escaped, or had he wandered off?

"Are we missing one?" Victor asked.

Only after his absence was brought to her attention, did Miss Bitner notice they were short yet another man.

"So we are."

"He went for punch," the moon-faced spinster said. She scanned the crowd. "However, I fear my brother may have deserted us."

He most likely did. Victor didn't blame him. Anywhere would be better than in the lopsided conversation from Miss Bitner and Miss Parnell.

Victor took the spinster's largish hand. "I am sorry."

She looked up into Victor's eyes and scrubbed at her nose with the handkerchief in her other hand. Victor repressed a shudder. Everyone had their faults. This was not as bad as others suffered. He glanced to Miss Bitner, who he'd interrupted.

"Well, as I was saying..." She simply carried on, now that her audience was larger.

The spinster looked relieved, somewhat. She kept a grip on Victor's hand. "Oh dear. Mother has noticed."

Victor peered over the crowd. If there was a spinster's mother out there, he couldn't see her. "So she has. Is she asking where your brother is?"

Miss Parnell also peered in the direction Victor and the spinster were staring. "I don't see her."

Victor pointed. "Over there, by Lady Cowper."

Miss Parnell stood on her toes and squinted. "Where?"

The spinster lifted her meaty hand. "Coming, Mother," she called across the crowd.

Victor tucked her arm into his. "Here. Let me escort you, as your brother so rudely deserted you."

He pushed through the crowd, forcing it to open and then close behind him. This sealed him off from Miss Parnell and Miss Bitner.

"Mr. Wyndell?" Miss Parnell called after him. He ignored her until the crush had effectively separated them.

"Thank you," the spinster said as they made their escape. "Jonathan did desert me, the rotter. I had no graceful way of extricating myself."

"You're welcome. I, too, was glad to make my escape." He scanned the crowd. "So is your mother really looking for you?"

The spinster shook her head. "She's not even here. I only brought Jonathan because he wanted to attend. I saw you use that trick and thought I'd give it a try." She gently slipped her hand from his arm. "I'm too old for this sort of thing." A wistful tone entered her voice. "I don't know anyone anymore."

Victor glanced back to see if they were being followed. "How did you end up in Miss Parnell's company?"

She shrugged. "Same as you."

Unfortunate circumstances. "Now that your brother had deserted you, what do you plan on doing now?"

"I don't know."

Her vague mooniness had returned. She stood by him, awkward and vapid. A group of young bloods behind him erupted in laughter. Glad someone was enjoying this awful gathering.

Victor was developing a distinct dislike for crushes. At least, at a ball, one could ask someone to dance. Dancing kept the body and mind occupied and reduced talking to a minimum, even nonexistent if necessary. That way one was not obliged to hold up both ends of a conversation, or suffer uncomfortable silence.

"Forgive me," he said, after the silence became too

awkward. "I've forgotten your name."

"Miss Smith." And nothing more was offered.

"Ah, yes." Couldn't get much plainer than that. "Of the Boddington Smiths?"

Miss Smith looked up. "Hmm? Oh no. We're just the Smiths."

Well. Some rescue. Yes, he'd escaped Miss Parnell and her cousin, but Miss Smith wasn't exactly enlightening company.

He looked about for an out and saw one.

He saw a familiar face by the punchbowl. Miss Abbot. She stood all alone, a glass of punch in one hand, the thumb of the other pressed against her lips. She observed the crush with studious eyes. A slight frown marred her features as if she didn't like what she saw. He couldn't blame her.

Poor thing. Here she was, hoping for an exciting introduction into the delights of the Season, and she ended up at this tedious crush of a party.

Of all the young ladies he'd conversed with tonight, she had been the most interesting, though not necessarily in a good way.

"Miss Smith, I do believe I see someone to whom I must introduce you."

"Oh?" She sounded neither excited nor dismayed.

Some subtle shoving through the crowd brought them up to the refreshment table. Victor led the way.

"Miss Abbot?"

Miss Abbot turned, her countenance brightening. "Mr. Wyndell." Not a full smile, thank goodness. He didn't know what he would have done, had she turned the full force of that smile upon him.

He pulled the spinster up. "May I introduce Miss

Smith? I do not know if you have yet made her acquaintance."

He reciprocated the introduction for Miss Smith's benefit.

At least Miss Abbot knew her manners in introductions, if not in conversation. As one, she and Miss Smith tendered their genteel curtseys.

"Pleased to meet you," Miss Abbot said.

She genuinely meant it, if her shining eyes were anything to go on. He felt a tug of sympathy. Other than himself and now Miss Smith, she truly knew no one at the party.

Immediately, Miss Abbot made conversation. "So, Miss Smith, how are you finding the party?"

Miss Smith looked around her. "I don't know."

There. Let Miss Abbot deal with Miss Smith. Frankly, he'd done them both a favor. If Miss Abbot was half as clever as she appeared to be, she'd make the best of the situation.

While Miss Abbot attempted to ply some sort of conversation from the unresponsive Miss Smith, Victor slipped away. Later he vowed he would find her and apologize most profusely. The one and only agreeable person at this whole crush, and he'd used her terribly.

Nothing more would have pleased him than to suggest they leave and find someplace far nicer to be. He was not here to enjoy the party. He was here to find that blasted agreement and see it destroyed.

But where to start?

Chapter 4
Not the Best Way to Meet the Ton

Felicity hadn't meant to stumble, much less throw herself into Mr. Wyndell's arms. One thing was for sure—she liked it. She liked it very much. To be tossed into the embrace of a man, especially this man, was like something straight from a novel. Surprise had erased his scowl for the nonce, vastly improving his countenance. If only he had smiled.

Then that other miss showed up, pinch-faced, simpering, and a tad possessive.

Ah well. There was always another woman, if stories were anything to go by. *Easy come, easy go.* Felicity was not one to steal another lady's beau.

Besides, there was the noisy promise of a full-on Season party on the other side of that wall. She abandoned Mr. Wyndell to his sour companion and crept to the edge of the corridor.

Felicity peeked around the wall.

Oh, the lights! She had never seen so many candles in her life. Dozens of them illuminated a large chandelier. Also, mirrored sconces along the walls glowed with tapers.

Alas, there was no dancing, as she expected. But the drawing rooms, about as big as Grandmama's, were positively stuffed with people.

As she moved from the darkness of the corridor,

heat flushed over her face, moist and tainted with the scent of humanity. Too bad not everyone believed in bathing. She wished she'd thought of a fan, not only to keep herself cool, but to wave away the stench of sweat.

People huddled in groups of four or five, laughing, chatting, gossiping, and flirting.

Felicity was completely unimpressed. This was fun? Nobody was doing anything interesting.

At least there were refreshments at the other end of the room. Pushing her way through with no apologies whatsoever, she reached a table of little sandwiches and a large punchbowl. The punch was an unappetizing brown color with bits of fruit floating in it. Were those chunks of apple? It was hard to tell.

A tall footman lifted a cup, filled it with a dipper, and offered it to her wordlessly.

"Ta." She took it and sipped.

Faugh! It was awful. Something nasty sat under the taste of the fruit, rotten and sharp. Would it be too rude to ask for tea, or even water? Good thing she wasn't dancing. She would rather die of thirst than sip this terrible concoction. Afraid of being rude, she slunk away, the cup still in her hand.

So nothing to drink, no one to talk to. What to do? Eavesdrop, of course.

A group of matrons stood near the refreshment table, slowly reducing its sandwich population. Felicity sidled up until her back was almost touching one portly woman. Her sprigged muslin contrasted nicely with the woman's garish sapphire-blue evening gown.

At least she wouldn't be noticed for clashing.

"If it's true," one of the women said, between swallows of a sandwich, "then I certainly wouldn't trust her tables."

"Only if she's sitting down," replied another.

"Have you seen her sit down tonight?" The blue woman's voice rumbled through Felicity, enough to make her jump. Her toxic punch sloshed over the edge of her cup. Felicity brushed the offending droplets away from her skirts. Perhaps it was time to abandon this foul brew.

"She's still receiving."

Even the gossip was dull. Where was the good, juicy stuff? Isn't that what *tonnish on-dits* were about?

A group of young, rather elegant creatures pushed their way through to the table. Like her, they took cups of that terrible punch. Unlike her, they gulped it down without a single shudder.

No accounting for taste. Felicity moved closer. Surely they would have more interesting things to talk about.

Before their conversation started, one of them saw her. She was a well-dressed young matron, the telltale glint of a gold band on her left hand. Her gown was a most flattering peacock green, highlighting her slender waist and the gentle swell of her bosom. She had to be gentry, at the very least. Possibly nobility. At the very least, her clothes screamed wealth.

When their gazes met, Felicity offered a small, polite curtsey.

The young lady did not return the courtesy. Instead, she gave Felicity a frown and a definite cold shoulder. The others, about four in number, turned to see what their compatriot was snubbing. Their laughter died, and they, too, turned from her.

Felicity's own smile faded. Snubbed.

For no reason at all.

Was this because they didn't know her, or was there another reason? Was it simply because she had not yet been properly debuted, or was there something else?

Nothing was wrong with her gown; her mother had seen to that. Was it her hair? They had jeweled pins and combs and flowers in theirs. Felicity had secured hers with a few plain hairpins. It had looked elegant at the time. But then, anything would look elegant colored by dreams in a bedroom mirror.

She was also aware of her lack of jewelry. Some of those young ladies sported quite fancy necklaces. Were they enchanted? Not that she was good at picking out magic. It often eluded her until someone pointed it out.

Felicity had not considered wearing any of her charms, other than with what God had gifted her at birth.

That might have been a mistake.

The whole party idea might have been a mistake.

As she stood there, considering her next move, Mr. Wyndell approached her.

Ah, the only bright spark in her evening. Alas, he'd been a bit of a disappointment with his standoffish wit and the frown that faded his somewhat handsome features. What a shame, for his arms were strong and his chest nicely solid. Such a waste.

Mr. Wyndell accompanied a rather plain woman, whose dull brown eyes looked about for who-knew-what.

"Miss Abbot."

Finally, something interesting. "Mr. Wyndell."

He presented the rather plain-looking woman.

"May I introduce Miss Smith?"

Of course he may. She and Miss Smith made their curtseys. This new acquaintance looked like she was no stranger to the Season, even if she was not one of its brightest diamonds.

"So, Miss Smith, how are you finding the party?"

Miss Smith looked about her as if only noticing the crush for the first time. "I don't know." She didn't seem awkward, just completely baffled.

Felicity looked at her half-empty cup. She held it out to Miss Smith. "Here. You look like you need a drink."

"Ta," Miss Smith replied, accepting the offer. She sipped it and stared off at the world around her.

Felicity made a further attempt at conversation. "First Season?"

"Oh, no. Fourth. Or fifth, I think. I forget." Miss Smith took another sip. Felicity shuddered. How could she stand the stuff?

Miss Smith wiped at her nose with a handkerchief. She offered no further explanation. When she turned to Mr. Wyndell in hopes of enlisting his aid, she discovered he was nowhere to be found.

Drat that man! No way she was marrying him now. How terrible to save her and abandon her, all in one fell swoop.

She turned her attention back to the dullish Miss Smith. How about the direct approach? "So, Miss Smith, hear any good gossip tonight?"

That seemed to be what everyone else was talking about. Surely Miss Smith couldn't have been so off with the fairies that she hadn't heard some sort of *on-dit*.

Miss Smith gathered her attention from the ether. "What kind of gossip?"

Felicity shrugged. "Anything you may have heard." *Please, anything.*

Miss Smith made vague noises while she racked her brain. "I'm not sure."

"What? Nothing?" Had the woman not spoken to anyone at all tonight? "Have you had a conversation with anyone?"

Miss Smith thought upon it. "I did say hello to Lady Chester tonight."

Finally, something. "What did she say?"

"She said welcome."

Felicity sighed. This was going to be a long night. The group of matrons she'd been listening to earlier had moved on. An older couple had taken their place. Their conversation wasn't much better than the one she was having. Something about how the dogs were running.

Miss Smith drained her cup. As they were near the punchbowl, she held it out to the footman to refill.

He obliged her. He offered another cup to Felicity. She turned it down.

Miss Smith tucked into her cup with a bit more gusto than earlier. The terrible stuff must have loosened something inside her.

"I was speaking with Miss Bitner earlier."

About time she had some conversation. "I don't believe I'm acquainted with her."

Miss Smith's attention fell to her glass. She studied the liquid in it. "This is good."

Miss Smith had no taste.

Felicity prompted her. "What did Miss Bitner say?"

65

"Nothing interesting." She held out her cup once more. The footman obliged.

"What is that stuff?" Felicity wrinkled her nose.

Miss Smith looked into her cup, half-empty once more. "Negus, I believe."

This was negus? Ah. How disappointing. For a drink made of port, sugar, lemon, and spices, she had expected something better. But then, everything she'd experienced so far had been a disappointment. She had been looking forward to giving negus a try. Now that she had, she wished she could have gone back to her dreams. She'd been expecting it to taste like the mulled punches her grandfather served at Christmas, all appley and orangey, with sticks of cinnamon floating in it. This was just foul. Was it the port or the fruit?

Miss Smith agreed. "Not the best I've had. Still." She drained her glass and offered no more opinions. At least she didn't go back for a fourth. She set the cup on the table. After perusing the food, she found a delicate little sandwich, a small triangle thing with something green sticking out. It looked impossibly small in her thick fingers.

Miss Smith had forgotten Felicity. They stood there, silent, while Felicity looked at the guests and Miss Smith stared at something unseen. She had not yet lifted the sandwich to her lips.

Felicity caved first. "Miss Smith?"

"Hmm?" She turned swimming eyes on Felicity.

Was she foxed already? What was in that negus? "What did Miss Bitner talk to you about?"

Miss Smith sniffed and scrubbed at her nose. "Oh, mostly some folderol about the Duke of Montagu."

A duke! Dukes couldn't be anything but

interesting. At least she knew something about this particular duke. He'd become betrothed to Miss Clarice Chester over the winter. She tried to remember how he looked. If Felicity wasn't occupied of a morning, as often happened, she'd sit at the window and watch callers arriving at the Chesters' door. Had she seen him?

"Is His Grace here?"

Miss Smith cast a cursory look over the crowd. "I don't know."

Felicity sighed. She was getting nowhere with this. "Is there anyone you do know?"

Miss Smith peered at her sandwich. "Miss Bitner."

Felicity's patience frayed. "For someone who's seen five or six Seasons, you don't know many people."

Miss Smith tipped that tiny little sandwich into her mouth. She chewed and swallowed. With her hands unoccupied, she looked around until she found her empty cup.

"I know. It's sad." She held her cup out to the footman, who obliged her. The full cup went straight to her lips, and the alcohol went right to her head. "I think it is more that they do not know me. I'm not good at talking to people."

"So why do you bother coming?"

"I guess I come because I was invited. I don't get invited to many parties."

That Felicity could believe. "Have you considered that if you did talk to people, you'd be more like to be invited to more parties?"

Miss Smith sniffed and wiped at her nose with her handkerchief. "I suppose so."

Felicity looked over the crowd. "Is there anyone

here you recognize?"

Miss Smith's attention was more on her cup.

"Miss Smith?"

"Hmmm?" She took another swig.

Felicity shuddered. "How can you stand that awful stuff?"

Miss Smith lifted one shoulder in a shrug. "The more you drink the better it gets."

Or the worse one got. Miss Smith had a vague sway about her person. She stuffed her handkerchief into her reticule.

"How about we go sit down?" Felicity suggested. Miss Smith did not dissuade her from taking her arm.

There were not too many chairs about the perimeter of the room. Every single one was occupied, mostly by the older set. Matrons and chaperones had plunked their ample bottoms into these chairs and refused to move for the rest of the evening.

However, in one far corner, almost hidden by a tied-up window curtain and several rather large potted plants, was a chaise longue. A man of indeterminate age occupied the end of it, thus dissuading anyone else not of his personal acquaintance from sitting down.

Felicity didn't care. She dragged Miss Smith over by her meaty hand and dropped her to the cushions right next to the man. Felicity took the chair end.

The man looked at them, a slight frown wrinkling his face.

Felicity whispered to Miss Smith, "Do you know him?"

Miss Smith swayed about and studied the man. He studied her back, possibly slightly offended at this intrusion. After all, he had been minding his own business until they came along.

"I don't know."

Not surprising. After all, this was Miss Smith. Then again, maybe nobody knew him. He was sitting all alone, his gaze on nothing in particular. Had he been scanning the crowd for familiar faces, that might have been something.

Still, it was quite rude of him to occupy an entire chaise longue to the exclusion of others.

As he had set the tone for their association, Felicity proceeded in like manner: "Who are you?"

Miss Smith turned her head, also expecting an answer.

He leaned back from them as if affronted. Still, he answered, "Thomas."

"First name or last name?"

He fixed an annoyed gaze on Felicity. "John Thomas."

Very enlightening. "Have you heard any good *on-dits* lately?"

He turned away from them. "No."

Felicity looked at his hands, folded most properly in his lap. No rings of any kind. "Are you married, good sir?"

He did not share his gaze with her. "Yes."

Felicity nodded. "Now that is a surprise. My condolences to your good wife."

Miss Smith elicited a hiccup. Finally, she fished her handkerchief out of her reticule and applied it to her nose.

The air escaped Felicity like a released balloon. "I never thought I'd say this, but this crush is frightfully dull."

"Yes," Miss Smith replied. "Yet we all come." She fiddled with her cup of negus.

Mr. Thomas said nothing.

It seemed the corner was the place to go if one wanted to conduct a conversation. A familiar pair of young ladies pushed into the plants, heads together. Felicity's jaw dropped as she recognized one of them. Immediately she rose and ducked into the curtain.

That was Miss Parnell, the lady who had wholly claimed Mr. Wyndell, and her bitter-eyed companion. Felicity didn't dare peek out, lest she be recognized. The last thing she needed was an angry Society miss thinking Felicity was poaching her beau.

Now, there was a tempting thought. If only Felicity had enough Society standing to be able to do such a thing. She would have cheerfully stolen Mr. Wyndell out from under the grip of this sallow little thing.

Miss Smith looked about with that dreamy way of hers, while Mr. Thomas frowned at Felicity hiding behind the curtain. At least he didn't say anything. Felicity remained, listening carefully, hoping Miss Parnell and her friend soon departed.

Miss Parnell ignored everyone, so focused was she on her demand.

"Please, Nora. Let me use your ribbon. He's here tonight. If I'd known, I would have brought something stronger."

The one called Nora replied, "No. I need it. And you know why."

Miss Parnell whined, "But you haven't even seen him yet."

"He'll be here. After all, this is the Chesters' party."

"I know. But—"

"Here," said Nora. "You can use this. I don't think I'll need it."

Felicity fought her curiosity. What had Nora given Miss Parnell? Alas, she never got to find out, for after a few moments of silence, she dared to peek out.

Miss Parnell and Nora were gone.

Felicity sat next to Miss Smith. "Who was that Nora with Miss Parnell?"

"Miss Bitner." Nothing more was offered.

Oh. Felicity had no desire to further the acquaintance. "What did she give Miss Parnell?"

Miss Smith shrugged. "I wasn't paying attention."

"It might have been important."

"Not really."

This was going nowhere. If Miss Smith had been around for several Seasons, she must know someone. Perhaps she could introduce Felicity to them?

Felicity scanned the crowd. Over in the corner stood a bright gaggle of young ladies, their gowns resplendent, their eyes bright, their conversation lively. It was the crowd who'd snubbed her earlier. She elbowed Miss Smith in the ribs.

"That lot over there." She indicated with her head. "Are you acquainted with any of them?"

"The shiny one in the middle in blue is the Marchioness Marque, as was Lady Deveraux, the second one. She made quite a match last Season."

Felicity had heard of the young marchioness, someday to become the Duchess of Allenbury, once her father-in-law popped his clogs. But that time was in the far future.

She'd read about how graceful, how lively the

marchioness was. No party was truly a party without her. Felicity's heart beat in her chest. Now here was some true elegance. It was people like the marchioness that Felicity longed to be around in Society. Yet her first encounter had been less than stellar.

Maybe their encounter would have been nicer, had they been properly acquainted. If that were so, then she could not blame the marchioness for snubbing someone she didn't know.

Taking Miss Smith by the arm, she dragged her over to the knot of elegant debutantes surrounding the marchioness. "You must introduce me."

The marchioness paused in her elegant monologue. A graceful hand lifted to her throat. "Yes?" Even her voice sounded like crystal.

The other young ladies surrounding her, each one more glittering than the next, turned and stared at the interlopers.

One of them sneered, "Ah, Miss Smith. Always a pleasure." Could she have shoved any more sarcasm into her words?

Perhaps this was not the best idea. Felicity elbowed Miss Smith in the ribs before she lost her courage. Miss Smith let out a whooshing breath. The marchioness gasped and raised her closed fan up to her nose.

A few of the young ladies whispered to one another. Felicity began to squirm. This was not going as well as she'd hoped.

It took a moment before Miss Smith caught her breath. She took a fortifying gulp of negus. "May I be permitted to introduce Miss Apple…"

Apple? Where on earth did she get Apple?

"Miss Apple of the…Wessex…uh, Apples?"

The Marchioness Marque laid delicate fingertips over her nose and shuddered. "No, you may not."

"What?" replied Felicity, her voice faint. That was the last thing she expected from the marchioness.

What does one say to that?

****

Victor made his way to the edge of the drawing room. The sooner he found The Agreement, the sooner he could leave this nasty assembly. His thoughts strayed to Miss Abbot. They had not been formally introduced, but if he made an offer for her to leave, would she consider it? Perhaps he should find Mrs. Abbot.

Come to think of it, had he made her acquaintance? He knew of her, as she had often spoken with his mother. Yes, they must have been introduced at some time. He'd seen Mr. Abbot here and there at social events, but as they didn't have much in common, they did not move in the same circles.

Pleasure later, business first. If he was to assist his mother, he needed more information.

Victor caught up with Mrs. Wyndell, who lurked at the edge of the drawing room. Unlike her usual self, she did not mingle with guests but stood in miserable isolation, avoiding eye contact, a loner in the crowd.

"What are you doing?" he asked her.

At the sound of his voice, she looked up and gripped his arm. "Have you found it?"

"I don't even know what I'm looking for."

"It's an agreement, signed by all of us."

All of us. Not "by me" or "by the two of us" but "all of us." That meant at least three people, possibly more. Mrs. Abbot?

"What does it look like?"

She hesitated.

"If you tell me what it looks like, I won't have to read it."

It was a lame excuse, but it worked. "It's a piece of stationery with the Chesters' crest."

Victor shook his head. Why did they choose stationery? If The Agreement had been on a plain piece of paper, it could have been claimed as a forgery. But on stationery? That was a stamp of legitimacy if ever there was one.

"If it is here, where do you think it would most likely be?"

His mother gave this some thought. "Lady Chester's writing desk? That's where we drafted it."

Victor nodded, not in agreement with his mother, but to allow time for the thoughts to tumble through his head. If Lady Chester had two thoughts to rub together, her writing desk would be the last place to keep such a sensitive document. Then again, it was drafted on her stationery. No knowing how far the thoughtlessness went.

"But it's not there," she said. "That's the first place I looked."

Where would a lady keep something she wanted to remain hidden? "If not there, then where?"

Mrs. Wyndell shrugged. "I don't know."

"Where would you have kept it?"

She fluttered her hands. "I would have burned it the moment I laid hands on it."

A few rowdy gentlemen staggered into Victor's back, knocking him into his mother. She stumbled back a step before regaining her balance. The gentlemen ignored them and moved on to knock about other guests. He and his mother moved to another, quieter corner.

"If you would have burned it immediately, why did you sign it in the first place?"

His mother sniffed and dug about in her reticule. "You wouldn't understand."

"Obviously not."

Her hand froze in the reticule. "It was a matter of honor."

"And someone broke the code of honor?"

She glanced about as if afraid of eavesdroppers. "Someone spoke of it. We said we'd never speak of it."

"How do you know?"

She leaned in even closer. "There have been rumors."

"What if they are only rumors?"

Her hand gripped his forearm. "They are very specific rumors. Nobody could have said anything unless someone spoke of The Agreement."

He tried a different tack. "I assume *you* didn't speak of it?"

She laid a hand over her bosom. "I am as silent as the grave."

"If not you, then who?"

She shook her head. "I don't know."

"Lady Chester?"

A look of terror crossed her face. "Never her. She's got the most to lose."

One piece of the puzzle fell into place. The Agreement centered about Lady Chester. "So not her and not you. Who does that leave?"

She tilted her head left and right as she considered his question, taking her time and not answering him. So there was more than three people, at least four. Mrs. Abbot most likely the third. And the rest? The more involved, the greater the chance of someone slipping up.

"I need to know."

"You do not!" The vehemence in her voice took him aback. "Someone might have broken The Agreement, but I will not make it worse."

"And yet you wish me to find it?"

"I can't do it alone. I need your help."

Victor slumped. His *help* was nothing but useless.

She placed a hand on his shoulder. "Please, Victor. You're all I've got."

"What about the others?"

But she shook her head. "Oh no. If they learned I meant to destroy The Agreement…"

He wanted to shake his mother and tell her she was singularly unhelpful. But a son's duty was to his parent.

"I'll keep looking. But I can't promise I'll be successful."

She laid her head on his shoulder. "That's all I ask."

And that's all she'd get. If she wasn't willing to be forthcoming, then he didn't have to be either.

Did Lady Chester speak of it, by accident maybe? Who knows? How about Mrs. Abbot? He was somewhat acquainted with the Abbots. Mrs. Abbot didn't strike him as one who'd act indiscreetly.

A thought ticked the edges of his mind. What about Miss Felicity Abbot? Perhaps he should ask her if she knew anything about it. This was assuming she forgave him for dumping her.

He looked about. Where was she? Not by the refreshment table where he'd left her. He squinted. So many young ladies dressed in sprigged muslin. Would he have better luck searching for large Miss Smith?

The ape-leader was easy to spot, the forlorn daisy amid the jeweled butterflies. And there was Miss Abbot. And...

Oh no.

****

Felicity blinked for a moment. "I beg your pardon." What did she say?

The marchioness completely ignored her. It was as if Felicity was invisible. Her scorn was purely for Miss Smith. "Your breath is so foul I fear it should bleach my gown and uncurl my hair."

"It...what?" replied Miss Smith, awkward.

The marchioness leaned back from Miss Smith. "Your breath stinks."

Miss Smith paused, her jaw open. It snapped shut.

Felicity blinked. "Are you serious?" She might not be out, but even Felicity knew it was totally vulgar to comment on one's shortcomings.

Miss Smith, drink in one fleshy hand, fiddled with the strings of her reticule. "I do believe I have some peppermints in—"

The marchioness smacked at the reticule with her fan. Miss Smith's drink sloshed over the rim of her cup. "Don't bother. All the peppermints in the world will not help."

The reticule slipped from Miss Smith's less-than-dexterous fingers, clattering to the floor.

"Oh." Miss Smith's countenance fell.

The glittering party of Beautiful Young Things tinkled laughter all over Miss Smith's awkwardness.

Rage rose in Felicity. She fought her desire to sink

a fist into Her Honor's face. But no, that would not do at a party. Ladies never brawled. Instead, she took her new friend by the hand.

"Come, Miss Smith. It is not your breath that taints the air, but the foulness coming out of others' mouths."

And Felicity deliberately turned her back on the marchioness. If that was the best Society had to offer, then she should be thanking her grandmother profusely for sparing her such bad company.

"Here, Miss Apple. Hold my drink?" Miss Smith bent down to retrieve her reticule.

At the same time an older man passed by, failed to see Miss Smith, and stumbled over her. He grabbed Felicity's elbow to steady himself. Not that he did a good job. He wasn't too steady to begin with.

Felicity stepped back in surprise, sloshing most of Miss Smith's terrifying negus across the ample back of a large Society matron. The marchioness and her coterie roared with laughter.

Felicity gasped. "Oh, I'm sorry!"

Miss Smith, having retrieved her reticule, stood up, right into the jaw of the man who'd stumbled against her. It surprised Miss Smith more than it hurt her. The same could not be said for the man. Howling in pain, he stepped back, right into a tight group of young bucks. What happened with them, Felicity didn't know. Her eyes were on the terrible wet stain on satin, spreading down the matron's back.

The rather large matron turned about. "I beg your pardon?"

Felicity swallowed. "Terribly sorry." *About the spill, not the punch.* It wasn't as if she was going to drink it. "Such a terrible crush."

Miss Smith, still rubbing her head, tugged at Felicity's elbow. "Our apologies, Lady Middlestone."

Lady Middlestone. It was one thing to read about someone in the society pages. It was quite another to meet them in person, especially when they had such a reputation as Lady Middlestone. The moment her ample figure had turned around, the whole silly batch of the marchioness' friends fell silent. Amazing how quickly they could melt away into the crowd.

Felicity and Miss Smith had no such luck.

Lady Middlestone had a reputation of brooking no nonsense. Even Felicity knew she had little patience for some of the antics of Society and had banned several people from her parties as a result of improper behavior, or so the newspapers had said.

Lady Middlestone lifted a lorgnette to her face. "I would never have invited so many people."

"No, of course not," replied Felicity.

And if she had, most of them would have not attended. Lady Middlestone's parties were considered frightfully dull, if the newspapers were to be believed. Was that necessarily a bad thing?

Felicity couldn't see the stain, now that Lady Middlestone had turned to face her. Was she to say anything about it? Surely the punch had soaked through by now. Felicity always felt it when her clothes got damp—rain, spilled tea, anything, really.

Lady Middlestone wasn't finished with Felicity. "I say, Miss Apple—"

"Abbot," Felicity automatically corrected. Then she snapped her mouth shut. It did not do to interrupt one's elders, especially to correct them.

Lady Middlestone didn't notice or care. "Miss

Abbot." She peered closer at Felicity. "Say, aren't you Mrs. Abbot's daughter?"

Felicity squirmed under Lady Middlestone's icy tone. "Yes."

No good denying it. She would find out eventually, assuming Grandmother ever returned from Tunbridge Wells and debuted her properly.

"Hmm." Lady Middlestone did not stop her study of Felicity. "You're one of this year's debutantes?"

Felicity bobbed her curtsey as an answer.

"I do not recall seeing your name in the papers."

Having retrieved her reticule, Miss Smith tugged on her arm. Before Felicity could use her as an excuse to get out of what looked to become an uncomfortable conversation, Lady Middlestone continued.

"Have you been presented?"

Felicity sidestepped this one. "Our name isn't that hard to miss. We'd be at the top of the list, alphabetically, of course." Felicity put a finger to her lips in thought. "Then again, I was presented later than the others, so my name might be at the bottom. Oh, I hope the newspaper editors did not accidentally cut it off."

Lady Middlestone wasn't falling for it. Her eyes narrowed. "Who is your chaperone?"

"My mother, of course."

"Really?" Lady Middlestone peered at Felicity through her lorgnette. "Your mother never mentioned the fact."

Someone who actually knew Felicity's parents. No doubt they called on each other all the time. If Lady Middlestone chose to mention this particular meeting to her mother, there would be hell to pay.

And it got worse.

"I thought your parents departed an hour ago." Lady Middlestone put down her lorgnette so her fierce Frown of Disapproval could fall upon Felicity unimpeded.

"Oh I hope not." Felicity's hand sought Miss Smith's. "It would be awfully disconcerting if they had left and not told me."

For once, Lady Middlestone did not have anything to say.

Felicity tucked tipsy Miss Smith's arm in hers. "Come, Miss Smith. I shall go find Mama and ask her if she's left without me."

****

No sooner did Victor extricate himself from his mother than he saw Miss Abbot shoving her way through the crowd, that awful ape-leader Miss Smith in tow, clearly escaping Lady Middlestone. Miss Abbot looked so small and determined compared to the larger Miss Smith.

Where were they going? So fierce was Miss Abbot's expression, he debated whether or not to follow.

They elbowed some of the highest of London's Quality out of their way and headed straight for that little servants' corridor, the same one in which he'd first made her acquaintance.

Was she angry because he'd deserted her to Miss Smith?

No, that wasn't it. If it was, she would have abandoned Miss Smith.

Hmm. She hadn't abandoned Miss Smith. What did that mean? Surely Miss Abbot wasn't so desperate for acquaintances that she'd cling to the dowdy ape-leader?

If she had been any other young lady, he would have let her go. Unfortunately, the next step in his solution involved asking her what she knew about The Whole Situation, and if she knew anything about The Agreement.

As the corridor opened on either end, he slipped through the opposite side in hopes of heading her off.

There, in the darkness, he found Miss Abbot lying against the wall, repeatedly banging her head against it.

"Stupid, stupid, stupid," she berated herself.

Miss Smith stood there, wiping at her nose and looking forlorn. "It's not your fault."

"Oh yes, it is. If I hadn't insisted on—" Felicity straightened. "You're right. It's not my fault. It's entirely hers." She spun away from the wall and paced back and forth. "Honestly. Is the marchioness the cream of Society? I think not. Oh, Miss Smith, do you know anyone who is good company?" She returned her head to the wall in exasperation.

Miss Smith fumbled with her reticule. "I know you."

Miss Abbot froze. "Oh, Miss Smith." She threw herself onto the larger woman with a big hug.

So this was Miss Abbot, was it? Perhaps he had misjudged her. A niggle of guilt tugged at his insides. He had treated Miss Smith so poorly, dismissing her because of her looks and her social awkwardness, and here was Miss Abbot defending her against who knew what sort of Society dragon. She had only known her for fifteen minutes, and already she behaved like a true friend.

Miss Smith stood there, awkward, but not resisting

the hug.

"I'm so angry with how she treated you. That was completely crass."

Victor leaned against the wall. So here was the matter that had gotten her all riled up. If she got angry over an apparent public snub, how would she ever face the true injustices of Society? A pang of sympathy tweaked at his heart.

"My breath smells," Miss Smith said, still clasped in Miss Abbot's grasp.

Miss Abbot released her. "Pish-tosh. She should never have said such a thing."

"You cannot blame her for speaking the truth. This is why I carry peppermints." She withdrew a little white pastille from the reticule and popped it in her mouth. "It's not so bad in the winter. But come spring, it gets worse." Her meaty hand wriggled back into the reticule. She offered another peppermint to Miss Abbot, who accepted it gratefully.

"Still," Miss Abbot said around the mint in her mouth, "she didn't need to be so cruel about it. If it had been me, I would have let you down easy or been far more discreet. Or better yet, say nothing at all."

Only then did her gaze light on Victor. He fought the guilt of having eavesdropped.

"What do you want?" she snapped at him.

He spread his arms. "Don't blame me. Not my fault."

Miss Abbot folded her arms in a fit of pique. "The more time I spend at this party, the worse things I see. I don't know why everyone is so enamored of the Season. All anyone is doing is standing around snubbing each other and drinking that terrible punch."

He shuddered. Miss Abbot could only be speaking about the Marchioness Marque, that two-faced, over-charmed man-eater. Last Season she'd glided into Society all light and coy glances…but only for those she deemed worthy. They said she had powerful charms, though Victor had never seen them. Maybe it was because she never used them on him. The marquess had fallen hard, and they'd been married as soon as the banns were read. His mother had exulted about the perfectness of the match, but Victor only wondered why the marquess had had such poor taste.

"I like the punch," Miss Smith added. "Sometimes it's the only decent thing at a party."

Miss Abbot stared at her, open-mouthed. "If punch like that is the best thing about a Season party, I am quite content to stay at home and never come Out at all."

She was right about this party. If one didn't know anyone, it could be frightfully tedious. Still, Victor had to defend the Season.

"It's not always this bad. You came across a poor example. That's all."

After a few more thoughtful sucks, she sighed. "If I'd known, I'd not have come. If only there had been dancing, or cards or something."

Victor pushed himself off the wall. "But there are cards. Lady Chester is famous for her card parties."

Miss Abbot perked up. "My mother has attended her card parties." Then she wilted again. "It's a shame this isn't a card party."

Miss Abbot took Miss Smith's hands. "Oh, please tell me you play cards. It would make this evening far more pleasant."

With a sad shake of her head, Miss Smith denied having any skill. "Mother never bothered to teach me."

Disappointment rolled across Miss Abbot's face. "What a shame. If only there was a deck of cards."

Victor held up a finger. "Ah, but this is Lady Chester's party. It would not be one of her parties if she didn't have a room set aside for nothing but cards. It's her passion, one could say."

Miss Abbot's jaw dropped once more. She weighed this delicious new prospect around until her eyes positively brightened from dead to delight. "Where is this card room?"

"Upstairs, I suppose."

Her anger evaporated. "Why didn't you say so in the beginning? I could have gone straight there and missed out on all this horrid socializing. I haven't even heard any good gossip worth eavesdropping on."

It was like someone opened a curtain in the room of his mind. Gossip. That was how his mother had learned that someone had breached The Agreement. If that was so, perhaps he could discover who, through the gossip.

Like the cogs of a gear, everything settled into place. Looking for The Agreement was the last thing he should be doing. Instead, he should be looking for the involved parties. Surely one of them would know where it was.

Of course there was gossip over card tables. If what his mother had said was true, and someone had disclosed the nature of The Agreement, maybe he could catch a whiff of it there.

He held out his arm to Miss Abbot. "I assume you play cards?"

She favored him with her Winning Smile and accepted. "Of course. Among other things, we learned how to play cards very well at school."

"What was your preferred game?"

"Whist."

He tucked her arm in his. "Mine too." He held his hand to the doorway. "Shall we?"

Chapter 5
The Games People Play

His heart soared. If he was to help his mother at all, he had to learn as much as he could. Here in the servants' corridor, it was quiet enough they could speak. Miss Smith stood near the exit, digging through her reticule. Still, he spoke low. One never knew who repeated what they had heard.

"Miss Abbot? Have you ever heard your mother speak of something called The Agreement?"

She tilted her head in consideration. "I can't say that I have. What is it?"

Was she honest, or was she sworn to silence? That seemed to be the way of anyone who knew about The Agreement. "Several weeks ago a matter of honor came up. Several parties agreed to silence. They would never speak of the matter again. However, someone *has* spoken of the matter. Other parties are concerned. They fear The Agreement will be exposed and scandal will erupt. Certain parties would see The Agreement burned so no one would ever learn about what had happened."

Miss Abbot mulled this over. "What is The Agreement about?"

Victor shook his head. "I don't know. I am not party to it."

"But you have been tasked to find it?"

"I have."

"How noble of you."

Not really. He felt he'd been guilted into it, almost blackmailed. Certainly his mother had threatened his future, should The Agreement come to light.

"I am merely doing a favor for someone."

"Ah. So should you find it, or worse, get caught with it, that someone can disavow all knowledge?"

Victor hadn't considered that. On the other hand, he was his mother's son. To be in possession of an incriminating document with her name on it would not do him any favors. "All I know is that The Agreement is somewhere in this house. If we could find it—"

"We?"

Did he say *we*? He meant himself and his mother. Was she even looking? Or was she spending her energy on fretfulness? "I meant, if I find it—"

"So you don't want my help?"

That gave him pause. "I never considered asking for help."

"Think I can't keep a secret?"

"I never questioned your honesty. I..." He shrugged uselessly. "One does not go soliciting random help for something someone is trying to keep a secret."

She tilted her head. "Yet you asked me about The Agreement."

His face grew warm. "I thought you might know something about it," he confessed.

She blinked at him. "Me? Why me?"

His nerves called out a warning. "Random luck? If someone had spoken of it, what are the chances you heard of it?"

She wrinkled her nose. "Very slim, considering the poor quality of gossip I've heard tonight."

"Perhaps we need to listen to more gossip."

"Have you considered asking Miss Smith? She moves through Society more than I do."

Does she? That surprised Victor. But then, Miss Abbot did say this was her first party.

They turned to their companion, still standing at the other end of the hallway. Victor had to call her name several times before Miss Smith responded in her moony-eyed way, "Did you need me?"

Something wasn't quite right about her. No wonder she never *took*. Still, Victor asked, "Have you heard of something called The Agreement?"

Miss Smith rolled this question about as she would have rolled a peppermint over her tongue. "Can't say that I have."

Oh well. Not that he expected much from one such as Miss Smith.

Yet something told him that it wasn't Miss Smith but Miss Abbot who would lead him closer to The Agreement. Best to keep her close. "How about we go play cards?"

At that, Miss Abbot's countenance blossomed. "I'd love to."

****

As they reached the line between the clandestine solitude of the corridor and the glittering too-brightness of the party, Felicity froze. In her desire for something exciting, she'd forgotten Miss Smith.

"Come with us." Felicity held out her hand to her new friend. "I'll teach you how to play."

But Miss Smith waved them on. "It's all right. I'll stand here."

Oh, that would not do. "You can't stay here all night."

Miss Smith sniffed and applied her handkerchief to the end of her nose. She looked around the dark corridor, surveying its surrounds. "I don't see why not. This is the most pleasant spot I've been to this whole party."

Felicity let her hand drop. "Are you sure?"

Miss Smith nodded. "I am content to remain here."

Felicity tried again. "Come with us to the card room. You could find a comfortable chair."

"I don't play cards."

"You don't have to. You can sit and observe, and nobody will say anything."

Miss Smith did not reply. She stared at a wall. Perhaps she was truly content there.

Felicity wondered if she herself should have stayed in that corridor instead of venturing out into the party. "If you change your mind, we will welcome your company in the card room."

Thus, with a sad reluctance, she abandoned her new friend.

Mr. Wyndell took them out in the lights and over to the staircase.

Felicity followed his lead, lost in thought. "Why didn't she want to come with us?"

"Who?"

She stopped short, making him stumble. "Really?"

He gave her a puzzled look. "Oh. Miss…um?" He shook his head. "How very strange…"

"Smith. Honestly. Do you even remember my name?"

He rolled his eyes. "You are Miss Abbot." Under his breath, he uttered, "I'm not likely to forget."

"Why is that?"

He changed the subject. "I thought you wanted to play cards."

"Not at the cost of abandoning someone."

He pulled at her arm. "We are not abandoning Miss Smith. She chose to remain behind, even when presented with your most generous offer. And should she change her mind, which I doubt, she knows where to find us."

Felicity looked back to the dark doorway. "Still…"

Mr. Wyndell did not slow down. "She's lasted several Seasons. I'm sure she'll survive this."

She balked at his pulling. "You are in an awful rush to be rid of Miss Smith."

Only then did he stop. His back remained to her. "I am not ridding myself of Miss Smith." His shoulders wilted. "Please don't think poorly of me." He turned to her. "It is a shame your first party—unofficial, of course—is this travesty. Miss Smith is under no illusions. She knows this party for what it is. The only tragedy is that this is probably the most excitement that poor female has had all week."

And…there was something else on his mind. *Something about Miss Smith, maybe?* "How long have you known her?"

He had to think about it. "I don't know." He stared at the darkness. "Though I should, shouldn't I?" To himself, he muttered, "Miss Smith, Miss Smith, Miss Smith."

Now here was a thought. Most young ladies wore enchanted charms to entice men, encourage luck, and ensure success. Could Miss Smith have something that discouraged people instead? Felicity didn't know much about magic outside her own skills. She had no idea who was wearing charms and who wasn't. It wasn't as if magic had a smell.

Miss Smith wanted to be alone. Felicity did not. She turned to Mr. Wyndell. "Please tell me this is not what all Society parties are like."

He took her hand, cradling it between both of his. "I don't know what you expected for a crush, but I believe this was not it."

She trembled. He held her hand. How warm his fingers were! His thumb traced along her knuckles. She had to speak, lest she get lost at his touch.

"I confess I was expecting more. To hear everyone speak of the Season, I thought it would be wall-to-wall excitement. Not this…" She waved her free hand to the brightness at the end of the corridor. "This… Oh, I don't know what to call it."

"I do. Boring."

Felicity nodded. "Boring. I wanted dancing. I wanted glittering banquets. I wanted cards and gossip and everyone admiring everyone else's gowns. I wanted graceful manners and genteel conversation. I even wanted scandal."

He stiffened. "No. That you do not want." He gathered her hand close to his chest. "I've seen scandal. It might sound exciting when it's happening to someone else, but when you're involved, it's an entirely different matter."

"At least it would be something. Other than making yours and Miss Smith's acquaintances, there hasn't been a single redeeming feature to this horrid little crush."

A smile tugged at the corner of his lips. For a moment, Felicity thought he would drop his scowl.

Alas, it was not to be. Still, his next words were not so dour. "That is only because you have not yet discovered the card room." With that promise, he pulled her out of the corridor.

Before they disappeared, she called out a final offer to her only other friend. "Are you quite sure you won't join us, Miss Smith?"

She got an absentminded smile from her new friend, who waved her on. "I think I shall find some more negus." And off she went.

Felicity could only blink. "What a very odd creature."

Mr. Wyndell patted her hand. "Miss Smith will be fine. She's lasted several Seasons."

"So you've said." As he led her up the stairs, she couldn't help but feel a pang for Miss Smith. "I am not so sure she's lasted this long. I think she's very much a casualty."

Yes. That was it. Once upon a time, Miss Smith must have been a young, naive debutante, with eyes just as wide and eager as her own had been earlier. Something had crushed her spirit. Now she glided through the parties and routs and musicales, a ghost of the woman who might have been.

Something inside her had to care, else why would she bother coming at all? If all she wanted to do was sit and stare at walls, she could do that very well from the comfort of her own home, drinking far better punch than what was to be had here.

Mr. Wyndell guided Felicity up the staircase and down the corridor. Up here, the crush was not so bad. One could even move without having to press against others constantly.

At the far end of the corridor were double doors, thrown open to allow in some air and potential gamesters.

Felicity gasped as they entered the room. It was huge! It occupied the whole front of the house, from side to side. The parquet floor betrayed its original use as a ballroom. Her grandmother's townhouse did not boast such a room; instead the two master bedrooms resided in the similar location. Come to think of it, Grandmama's townhouse did not have a ballroom at all.

Green gaming tables crowded every square foot, each table occupied.

"Now I know where all the chairs went." Felicity wanted to throw herself into the nearest one, but they were all taken.

"I see an opening." Mr. Wyndell gestured to a table on the far side of the room.

Felicity stood on tiptoe. A couple of older ladies had risen from a table, disappointed. They moved off, their faces as stiff as their walks.

"I don't know if that's the best table."

"Right now it's the only table." Mr. Wyndell pulled her along.

Her reluctance wasn't enough to stop her from following. "If their ladyships lost, that means the other players won. They might be excellent players. We'll be fleeced."

Mr. Wyndell slowed. "Possibly. But we need to start somewhere."

"Losing was not my idea of a good start."

They'd arrived at the table. Their opponents were a couple about the same age as Felicity's mother. Mr. Wyndell gave them a brief bow. "Lord Mayfair. Lady

Mayfair. May we join you?"

Lady Mayfair, dark of coloring and sharp of features, looked up in smug triumph. She looked resplendent in a purple evening gown, although her slight bosom featured far too many ruffles. "Ah, young Mr. Wyndell. We'd be honored." Her hands fumbled in the folds of her gown.

Lord Mayfair, likewise, had dark hair, but his was streaked with silver. If he had shaved today, he'd forgotten his upper lip. Felicity couldn't quite call it a mustache. She almost mistook it for dirt. He had an appreciative eye for Felicity in a way that unsettled her from the beginning. Did he have to stare at her for so long? Still, Felicity gave him a proper curtsey while Mr. Wyndell made the introductions.

Lady Mayfair's scant eyebrows rose. "Abbot, did you say? I believe I know your mother."

Felicity bobbed another curtsey. "Quite possibly."

"Though I have not seen her tonight. Does she not come to play?"

Mr. Wyndell held out the tiny chair for her. Felicity sank into it with relief. Standing around with not much to do could be quite tiring. "She told me she had little desire to play tonight."

Lady Mayfair nodded. Now that the barest of social niceties had been observed, she turned her attention to Mr. Wyndell on her left. "And your mother, dear boy? I dare say I haven't seen her at all tonight. Is she ill?"

He seated himself, drawing the chair close to the table. "No, my mother is well and is attending. I am surprised she has not made her way here."

Actually, he didn't sound surprised at all. He flicked an invisible speck of dust from his cuff.

"You know how much she enjoys a good game of cards."

"Yes." Lady Mayfair sounded too oily.

Felicity regretted her first hand before the cards had been dealt.

"I did so wish to resume our last encounter. Recoup losses and all that."

At this, Mr. Wyndell smiled rather unabashedly. What a difference a smile made to his face. It was as if a light had been turned on in his soul. Had he finally lost his dour attitude? If she knew he'd lighten up over a game, Felicity would have dragged him to the card room first thing. Assuming she'd known there was a card room.

This Mr. Wyndell was far more promising a companion. "Perhaps my mother is doing you a favor by refusing to play. Let you fleece someone of lesser skill."

Lady Mayfair issued a dramatic sigh. "I suppose you will have to do." Then she fixed her gaze on Felicity. "And how do you fare, my dear? Are you well acquainted with cards?"

Felicity looked between Lord and Lady Mayfair. Why did she feel like the mouse between two cats? "I learned several games at school. However, I don't get to play as often as I would like."

Lady Mayfair pillowed her chin on the back of her hand. "Are you familiar with whist?"

Felicity hesitated. "Yes…" Of course she was. Who hadn't heard of whist?

"Excellent."

Lady Mayfair issued one of those tinkling little laughs that Felicity could never master at school, no matter how much she practiced. Lord Mayfair beamed in amusement as well.

Mr. Wyndell had schooled his features to a nice, safe neutral. Felicity's eyes narrowed. What was he thinking? Whist might have been the game dealt, but she felt another game was already at play.

She was at an unfair disadvantage here. It wasn't that she didn't know the rules, but that she'd never played with Mr. Wyndell. What sort of player was he? Cowardly? Aggressive?

Lord Mayfair passed the cards to Felicity. "Would you oblige us with a shuffle?"

Oh dear. Another skill Felicity never really mastered. At home with her parents, they shuffled for her, a fond parental indulgence, really. Felicity sighed at this minute's nemesis. No helping it now. She picked up the deck and did her best. She only dropped the cards once. Still, not the most graceful of moves.

When she had the cards back in some semblance of a pile, she passed them to the left. Lady Mayfair cut the deck and passed it once more to her left, to Mr. Wyndell, who dealt.

He dealt the whole deck until he ended up with the last card. Instead of dropping this to his pile, he turned it face up. "Deuce of clubs."

Felicity nodded, as did the Mayfairs. Clubs as trumps.

When Felicity fanned her cards, she discovered only two clubs, and low ones at that. She gave a sad little shake of her head. Oh well. Pray Mr. Wyndell had a better hand she could lead to.

"So," replied Lady Mayfair, ever so casual, "a shilling a point?"

Felicity, who was sorting her cards, looked up, startled. "What?" Nobody said anything about money.

Mr. Wyndell tilted his head and gave a little shake. "I thought this was a friendly game, Lady Mayfair."

"Well, we aren't in the nursery anymore."

Felicity stood her ground. "You may have been playing all evening, but we only just arrived. It will be a penny a point, as is right and proper." Something told her if she let the Mayfairs get the bit between their teeth, she would find in her rather spare pockets even more to let. "Anyhow, I don't get the rest of my pin money until Friday."

At this, Lord Mayfair chuckled as if she were the drollest little thing. Mr. Wyndell raised an eyebrow at her. She avoided his gaze.

Lord Mayfair, seated to Mr. Wyndell's left, led out, six of diamonds. Felicity looked to Mr. Wyndell. He studied his cards and avoided her gaze. She dropped the nine of diamonds. Lady Mayfair laid out the ace of diamonds, so Mr. Wyndell dumped the three. First trick to the Mayfairs.

The next two tricks were the high diamonds of Lady Mayfair. On that last trick, Lord Mayfair ruffed; he had run out of diamonds. Felicity had one left, the five.

Lady Mayfair dropped the jack, effectively conquering Mr. Wyndell's ten. Lord Mayfair trumped with the three of clubs. Felicity plunked her rather useless five on the pile. As she did it, her gaze met Mr. Wyndell's.

He only touched on her glance briefly. "So, Lady Mayfair. Have you had a chance to play with our hostess tonight?"

Lady Mayfair, her sharp nose in her cards, stopped and looked up. "Oh?" She shook her head. "No, we have not yet had the pleasure."

"Really?" Mr. Wyndell tapped his closed deck against the back of his hand. "Has she been so popular?"

Lady Mayfair shook her head. "Downstairs maybe. She hasn't set foot up here once tonight." Her cool self-assured attitude evaporated. Now she frowned at her cards.

Lord Mayfair stared at her, his thumb stroking his upper lip.

Really, if he kept that up, he might wipe off his little wispy shadow.

A couple of strokes, and he returned to his cards.

Lady Mayfair led out a low heart. Mr. Wyndell topped it with the queen. He looked directly at Felicity, his expression neither pleased nor disconcerted. How did he keep such a straight face?

Only when Lord Mayfair upped him with the king, did Mr. Wyndell frown. Still, he watched Felicity, waiting expectantly.

Felicity allowed herself a smile. Out came the ace.

"Oh!" Lady Mayfair shook her head. "I truly believed you had the ace," she said to her husband. "Truly, I did."

He gave her an indulgent smile. "You think I have every ace."

Her coy smile flirted back. "Indeed, you do."

"Please," exclaimed Felicity. "Young ladies at the table."

The Mayfairs put their game faces back on, only after sharing another coy, flirtatious glance.

Felicity stared at the two of clubs, still lying in front of Mr. Wyndell. Trumps drawn was sheer chance. She didn't have many in her hand at all. Did Mr. Wyndell? It's not like she could ask him.

She stared at the two. He couldn't play it until he'd taken a trick. Was there something she could lead in his favor? The diamonds were gone, as were the high hearts.

Her eyes flickered up. Mr. Wyndell had been watching her. The moment she looked up, his gaze averted to the table. She wished she knew what was going on in his head.

She led the ten of hearts. It was the highest in her hand. Either Mr. Wyndell had the jack, or they'd lost this hand.

Lady Mayfair went low. Mr. Wyndell dropped the eight. Alas, Lord Mayfair had the jack.

Felicity frowned at her partner. He returned her gaze and shrugged.

Lord Mayfair led out clubs, trump. His was low, hoping to force out any stoppers.

Mr. Wyndell stared at Felicity, as it was her turn. She returned an apologetic look. Her clubs were low. She dropped her higher one, in hopes of forcing Lady Mayfair to outbid her, which she did.

Mr. Wyndell also came in low, giving the trick to the Mayfairs.

Lady Mayfair's lips twitched with the smile of triumph. One more trick to draw on par. Two more tricks to win the game. Out came a low diamond.

Clever. Lord Mayfair was out, so he could trump.

Mr. Wyndell kept his eyes down, studying his cards. He laid out a high club. Only then did he look up at Felicity, a clever gleam in his eyes. Then he dropped his head once more.

Lord Mayfair sighed and ruffed. Felicity dropped her only other club.

Mr. Wyndell had control. He could play the two of clubs if he wanted to. If he did, that would spell disaster. She watched him in expectation.

He did not choose to play the club at that time, but scooped it off the table and into his hand where it belonged. His gaze firmly on hers, he dropped a low spade.

Ah, now spades! That's something with which she might gain a few tricks, assuming nobody conquered her King with the ace.

Lord Mayfair and his spade, then Felicity with her king. Lady Mayfair sighed and dumped a low spade.

"A trick!" Felicity called out, pleased that they finally won something.

Lady Mayfair let out a tolerant gasp of defeat. "I suppose."

Felicity had the lead. But what to lead? She looked to Mr. Wyndell. Before their gazes could meet, he dropped his to the table.

Something clicked in Felicity's mind. He held the ace of spades and wanted to play it. Of course. She led out a low spade.

Nobody had a chance against Mr. Wyndell's ace.

That was their moment of triumph. Lord Mayfair held nothing but clubs in his hand, their lowness notwithstanding.

At the end of the hand, Lady Mayfair tallied up the tricks. "That's four points to us. Any honors?"

Felicity shook her head. No honors there.

Despite their losing, Mr. Wyndell had a small smile on his face. He had eyes only for Felicity. "I enjoyed that. Shall we play again?"

She returned his look. Yes, there was another game going on. Had she figured it out? "I'd love to."

Lord Mayfair smiled broadly at this. "Absolutely."

They dealt the cards. Lord Mayfair turned the three of hearts for trump. His mustache spread in the smile of a pleased cat. Felicity glanced at Lady Mayfair, who frowned at the cards she sorted. Mr. Wyndell also sorted his cards, though with a far more relaxed expression on his face.

Yes, he was definitely more pleasant looking without his dark scowls. In fact, he appeared downright handsome when relaxed. This was the face one could wake up to. Now she wondered, what would he look like asleep?

Felicity shook herself out of her distraction and turned her attention to her cards. Short honors in hearts, with the exception of the missing queen. Not much else in the other suits, but if Mr. Wyndell's expression was anything to go by, he seemed pleased enough with his hand. Did he have the queen?

Time to see who had what. Felicity led out with a middling club. Lady Mayfair fretted at her cards, then looked up to her husband. Lord Mayfair gave an apologetic shrug. That was not what Lady Mayfair wanted. With an unconcealed sigh, she played a slightly higher club.

"That's the best you've got?" Lord Mayfair asked.

"You dealt the cards," came Lady Mayfair's acerbic reply.

Their minor bickering didn't faze Mr. Wyndell a

bit. He laid out the jack of spades, to the groans of the Mayfairs. Lord Mayfair had no choice but to play a low spade.

Felicity felt better about this hand. For the next three tricks, she happily played out her low spades while Mr. Wyndell pulled out all the spade honors. Lady Mayfair ruffed clubs the last two hands; she had no hearts.

So that meant, with the five hearts sitting in her hand, and the one on the table, that left seven unaccounted for. Granted, most of them were low. Should Felicity gain lead advantage, she would be able to pull them out.

She caught Mr. Wyndell staring at her. As they locked gazes, she admired how lovely his eyes were when his brow was not furrowed in a scowl. He pulled a card from his hand. She could not help but smile at him. He hesitated, before letting his whole face relax. As he played his card, the last remaining spade, he raised an eyebrow.

Lord Mayfair crowed. He scooped up the three of hearts and trumped the spade.

Fine. Felicity laid out her one low heart, beating that three. Lady Mayfair had no hearts, so the trick belonged to Felicity. The Mayfairs both groaned.

"Of course," Lord Mayfair said. "Easy come, easy go." He leaned over and gave her a charming smile. "At least I know where the rest of the hearts are."

Oh really? Felicity blinked at him. Did he just reveal his hand to her? Were the other hearts in his possession?

Anyhow, it was her lead. She returned to her cards. What to play? All she had left were heart honors. She looked to Mr. Wyndell. He lifted his gaze to the ceiling.

That wasn't much help. Felicity played the ten of hearts. Lady Mayfair ruffed a diamond.

So did Mr. Wyndell have the queen?

No. He played a low heart, which meant…

Lord Mayfair played the queen, with a look of smug satisfaction.

Lady Mayfair sighed. "Finally."

Felicity did a quick bit of calculation in her head. *Drat.* Unless Mr. Wyndell had at least two hearts in his hand, the last trick would belong to Mayfair. The question was, would he run her through her hearts, then take what's left, or could she and Mr. Wyndell finesse out at least one more trick? Regardless, they would win the hand. Only question was, by how much?

To her surprise, Lord Mayfair led out a diamond. As he did so, he stroked his mustache with his thumb, making him look ever so melodramatic.

Lady Mayfair shook her head and rolled her eyes. Felicity had no diamonds. Did Mr. Wyndell? He met her gaze, then looked down to the table. She caught her breath. Felicity knew where the high diamonds were. She ruffed a club, instead of trumping with hearts.

"That's interesting," Lord Mayfair remarked.

Felicity shrugged apologetically. "I don't have any diamonds."

"I do," said Mr. Wyndell, after he laid the queen after Lady Mayfair's Ten.

After that, it was a battle for the hearts. Mr. Wyndell laid out all his high non-trumps until Lord Mayfair was forced to trump. Then Felicity cleaned up the rest.

Lady Mayfair had absolutely nothing of value in

her hand. "I might as well have laid out my whole hand for everyone to see, so valueless it was."

Mr. Wyndell positively glowed with triumph. "I do so enjoy a good game of cards."

"Agreed." Lord Mayfair shuffled the deck. "If it wasn't for Lady Chester's game tables, I'd dare say nobody would have come to these frightfully dull little gatherings."

Felicity looked around. Lady Chester had crammed a dozen card tables into this upper room. Every seat was taken, with more people waiting about the edge of the room for a spot to free up. All the windows had been opened. Fronds of large pot plants waved gently before them, so as to prevent any strong gusts from whisking cards off tables. Yet there were not as many people as were pressed in downstairs.

"So why are there not more players?" Felicity split the deck before handing it to Lady Mayfair.

Lady Mayfair's efficient fingers send the cards spiraling out to each player. "Because most of them are as frightfully dull as this party. I don't know what possessed Lady Chester to hold a crush. She's doomed herself to spend the whole evening downstairs."

The scowl was back on Mr. Wyndell's face. He hadn't even had a look at his cards yet.

Lady Mayfair's shuffling had settled the cards in a more even balance. Felicity had a few sporadic high ones, but nothing she could truly dominate with. Lord Mayfair sorted his cards, then gave his mustache several swipes. Five, actually, as if he were wiping away a troublesome crumb of cake or trying to rub it off. Felicity turned in time to see Lady Mayfair's small nod before turning to her cards.

They were communicating! Of all the underhanded tricks.

Well, Felicity could communicate as well. Throughout the game, she kept an eye on the two of them. As the game progressed, when Lord Mayfair stroked his mustache, Lady Mayfair played low. Together, they took the first three tricks.

On the fourth hand, when it was Lady Mayfair's turn to lead out, Lord Mayfair stroked his mustache. She led low.

Felicity caught Mr. Wyndell's gaze. The moment their gazes met, she dropped hers to the table. There she kept her eyes until she saw Mr. Wyndell play low. Lord Mayfair slid out a high-ish card, and Felicity dropped the ace, one of her few high cards. Thus, the trick was hers.

And so the game went, with Felicity making them fight for every trick. In the end the game went to the Mayfairs, but only by one point.

As she shuffled the cards for another round, she saw Mr. Wyndell watching her with admiration. "I'm glad I partnered you tonight."

That deserved a Winning Smile.

Lady Mayfair's hands shook as she cut the cards. "Our luck has turned tonight."

For the rest of the game, her gaze darted from player to player. What had disconcerted her so? She missed several cues from her husband until Felicity wanted to offer him a handkerchief for his nose. Alas, she did not have one.

The Mayfairs' game fell apart. Between them both, Mr. Wyndell and Felicity pretty much cleaned them out with a small slam. Six points!

"I say, Miss Abbot," declared Mr. Wyndell. "Well played."

He gave her the biggest smile she'd ever seen on his face. Yes, he was truly handsome when he smiled. Her head spun with the beauty of it all, and drunk on victory, she fluttered her hands.

"Oh, well, once I learned early on that Lord Mayfair had a vacancy in the trumps and had played his singleton diamond, it was easy enough to ride the rest out." She turned to Lord Mayfair. "Though I do say you thought you had everything in the bag. I'm sorry your three high spades were useless. Oh, and do stop stroking your upper lip. You look dishonest." The words popped out of her mouth before she could stop them.

Everyone at the table froze. The excitement over such a win evaporated, leaving a chilly atmosphere. Lady Mayfair went terribly pale. Mr. Wyndell looked like something was strangling him from the inside out.

Lord Mayfair slowly rose from his chair. "Are you accusing me of…" It was as if he couldn't bring himself to speak the word. "Cheating?"

Cheating. That terrible, terrible accusation. To accuse a gentleman of cheating was beyond the pale. Nobody ever did that sort of thing, either cheating or accusing. Such a thing could ruin a gentleman, should he ever be caught. It was unthinkable.

Felicity's heart dropped to the bottom of her left slipper. The words had escaped her mouth before she could give them a second thought. Dishonest was the last thing she should have said. She swallowed her *faux pas* and did some fast thinking.

Had she accused him of cheating? Had he cheated?

What would cheating look like? There had been nothing dishonest in how they played out the cards, was there?

"Who said anything about cheating?" She shook her head as Miss Pimmenter, her schoolteacher, often did. It was a silent chastisement and a warning for silly little girls to stop being so silly. "A gentleman would never cheat. You are a gentleman. Therefore, I advise you not stroke your upper lip with your thumb. It makes you look like a villain in a pantomime. You have far too much honor for that."

Mr. Wyndell exhaled. He must have been holding his breath.

Lord Mayfair swallowed. What could he say to that? Lady Mayfair made a small noise.

Felicity looked at the cards scattered about the table after their last game. "Should we play again?" Her words sounded weak and inappropriate. But what else could one say?

Lady Mayfair fumbled for her reticule. "We have been at the tables a little too long. We should pay our courtesies to Lady Chester. I dare say I haven't seen her all evening." Her hands moved a little too crisply through her reticule. She extracted a small bottle. She sniffed at this and stoppered it quickly.

Funny sort of smelling salts.

Lord Mayfair rose, his hand darting to his inside pocket. "Clever set of games, old boy." His voice was not as strong as it had been earlier that evening. "I'm afraid I'm not carrying fiddly small change." He fetched a half crown from his pocket and slid it across the table to Mr. Wyndell. "But I'm a man of my word."

Mr. Wyndell laid his hand over the coin, but did not pick it up. "I never doubted."

At this, Felicity wanted to crawl under the table and hide. She'd acted awful. How could she have said such a terrible thing to Lord Mayfair? In that, she was no better than the marchioness.

"You're far more honorable than we deserve," she muttered miserably.

Lord Mayfair sniffed. Was he crying?

When Felicity looked up, she saw a gleam of amusement in his eyes. "I dare say I do not feel so bad about losing now. I see I have come up against a worthy opponent."

Lady Mayfair did not share his enthusiasm. She flapped her fingers at him to come attend her chair. She rose as he scooted it back.

"Good evening," she bade them, her voice tight.

Her husband also bade them a good evening. "We shall have to play again. I doubt we shall repeat the same mistakes?" His thumb rose to his upper lip.

Now Felicity felt like a complete heel.

Chapter 6
The Stories People Tell

Once the Mayfairs had departed, Mr. Wyndell hissed at her. "What was that?"

Felicity could only shake her head in shame. Why oh why didn't she keep her mouth shut?

He leaned over the table. "They were not cheating. That was his tell."

She peeked up at him, her head still hung low. "His tell?"

Mr. Wyndell closed his eyes and shook his head. "That was how he was communicating with his wife. Now that he knows you know their tell, he'll change it. We'll never have an advantage over them again."

Felicity thought about it. "So that's like when you look at me, or look at the table."

He threw his hands into the air. "Finally! She gets it." He leaned back in his chair, palming the half crown. "For someone who appears quite clever, sometimes you can be rather obtuse."

That stung. "Not everyone comes to Town pre-bronzed."

A new voice broke in to their conversation. "Is this seat taken?"

Felicity looked up into a startlingly handsome face with inquisitive blue eyes. She'd seen him before. But where?

Mr. Wyndell rose to his feet. "Your Grace." He sketched a proper bow.

Felicity bounced out of her chair. Of course! John Montagu, the Duke of Montagu, Miss Chester's illustrious fiancé.

She bobbed her own curtsey. "We'd be honored, Your Grace."

He turned to her. "Have we met?"

"Had we had the chance to meet last year, we could have been very well acquainted." She followed this with an excited little smile.

She admired his form. Montagu was not too tall, certainly no taller than Mr. Wyndell, but his shoulders were broader. Naturally, his clothes were of the finest cut, and he wore his hair in the latest of mussy fashions. Felicity approved.

She held out her hand. He took it and touched a kiss to her knuckles. "I'm sure we would have."

Mr. Wyndell folded his arms tightly. "He is betrothed, you know."

Felicity looked up into Montagu's eyes. They went from amused, to apologetic. She sighed, though did not reclaim her hand.

"I know. It's in all the society pages. Pity." In a fit of pique, across the table to Mr. Wyndell she fired, "I guess I'll have to stick with my plans to marry you."

Mr. Wyndell stiffened. "Wait. What?"

His Grace beamed. "Ah, congratulations!"

"What?" Mr. Wyndell exclaimed again. "It's not what you think."

Felicity agreed with him. She explained, "Mr. Wyndell hasn't quite got up the courage to propose yet."

His Grace gave Mr. Wyndell a lofty look. "It's not that difficult. Managed it myself, you know."

Mr. Wyndell's jaw gaped. Nothing came out, for he'd lost his words. Felicity took a private, smug little pleasure out of disconcerting him so.

As they settled to the table, the Duke of Montagu spoke first, as was his privilege. "Did I see you two rout the Mayfairs?" He took the cards and gave them a shuffle. "Good job."

Mr. Wyndell let out a little noise and covered his mouth.

Felicity looked at him. Was he laughing? That was a quick change from before. "Is that a good thing?"

Montagu tapped the cards on the table. "Is in my books. I dare say gaming is their only reliable source of income, their pockets are so to let. Not impressed with how Lord Mayfair manages his estate."

Felicity leaned forward, tabling her chin on her hands. Now here was the famed Society gossip for which she yearned. "Does he have a fine estate?"

Montagu lifted a shoulder in a shrug. "No. Pithy little place up north."

He raised an eyebrow at Felicity. "I never did catch your name. And forgive me for not remembering. I'm sure we've met before."

She gave him a shy little smile. A *duke* wanted to know who she was! Dukes outranked marchionesses. "I don't expect you to remember me." She held out her hand. "Miss Felicity Abbot of the Essex Colchesters."

He shook her hand. "Abbot... Ah. Earl of Colchester's granddaughter, perhaps?"

Felicity gave him her Winning Smile. He melted under her gaze. Even dukes were susceptible. If only her brother had not died, she might have come to London last year, and she might have met him in his bachelor days, and she might have won him over, and it could have been her finger that wore his ring…

Her reverie was rudely disturbed by a kick from under the table. Felicity looked up at Mr. Wyndell.

It wasn't exactly a frown on his face, but concern. *Head in the game, lass.* And there was something else. Was he…jealous? Well. That was a new development. But then, she did just suggest marriage to him. She'd not quite known him an hour, and already she'd plotted out their whole lives together.

His Grace set the cards on the table. "What are we playing?"

Mr. Wyndell folded his hands. "It was whist."

A frown creased His Grace's forehead. "Not good with three people."

Before Felicity could suggest another game—she knew plenty—he surveyed the room. Was he looking for someone in particular? Whoever it was, he found someone. Montagu waved his hand to get her attention. Felicity followed his gaze.

On the far side of the room, a young Society miss with brunette hair stood by her mother. The mother was well-indulged in a fascinating card game while her poor daughter stood by, no doubt bored out of her wits. She twisted her sprigged muslin about in her fingers. Of course he caught her eye. She'd been scanning the room looking for something—anything—to relieve the tedium.

When she pointed to herself in question, he nodded and beckoned her over. She whispered some excuse to her mother and wove her way through the tables. The girl had to be younger than Felicity. Was she even old enough to be out? Pique irked in her heart. How dreadfully unfair.

On the other hand, who knew what the future held? Perhaps it was best this young thing came out when she did. Maybe next year she would lose a brother or a parent and be stuck in mourning away from Society like Felicity had been.

She was pretty enough, slim of form, and slightly bemused. "May I help you, Your Grace?"

Montagu rose. Mr. Wyndell followed suit. "Ah, yes, Miss Pymm. I dare say you'd not refuse to join us in a game of cards?"

Miss Pymm glanced over to her mother. "I don't know."

He held out the empty chair. "Your mother would approve."

This might or might not have been the truth. Mrs. Pymm, over on the far side of the room, hadn't noticed her daughter's absence, so enthralled in her gaming she was.

Miss Pymm didn't need to think twice before occupying the seat. "Nothing serious, I hope."

Mr. Wyndell informed her, "Whist. Paper points."

Miss Pymm gave a relieved smile. "Good. I haven't any money."

Felicity shrugged. "Me neither."

Montagu tapped on the cards. "Oh, introductions." He'd quite forgotten about Felicity. "Miss Abbot, may I present Miss Pymm, debutante. Poor thing's been thrust upon Society without too many allies, except for myself and a few other unsavory souls."

Miss Pymm ducked her head. Her smile was a

pleased one. Had Felicity missed some sort of inside joke?

"Miss Pymm, Miss Abbot of Essex. A wicked card player, if rumor is anything to go by."

Felicity sat up. "Where did you hear that?"

Montagu gave a self-satisfied chuckle. "Lady Mayfair's face, for one. And I have crossed swords with Mrs. Abbot a few times. How could you be anything but skilled?"

Felicity cocked an eyebrow at Mr Wyndell. He returned a petulant frown. "Shall we play gentlemen versus ladies?"

Montagu shook his head. "No. I would like to partner Miss Abbot."

Oh, did he, now? Felicity looked to Mr. Wyndell. They'd played so well together.

Montagu rose and shooed Mr. Wyndell out of his seat. "You're no slouch at the tables either, Wyndell. I dare say you'd suit Miss Pymm very well."

Mr. Wyndell groaned, but took the chair vacated by the duke. "Miss Pymm, are you familiar with whist?"

Miss Pymm, overawed by the attention, had drawn up her shoulders in a very girlish manner. "A few times. But never serious like this."

Felicity butted in. "First game doesn't count. It's a warm-up."

"I agree," said Montagu. He deftly shuffled the cards, then handed them to Mr. Wyndell to cut.

Mr. Wyndell then gave Felicity the cards to deal. Round they went, until Felicity turned up the final card, queen of spades.

"A-ha!" Felicity clapped her hands in delight.

"You haven't looked at your other cards yet," replied Mr. Wyndell.

"I don't care. She can only be beaten by two other cards."

Mr. Wyndell ordered his cards, then tapped them on the table. "How do you know I don't have them?"

She gave him a secretive smile, subtle and coy. "Because you don't."

Only a touch of bafflement showed through his game face. "We'll see."

She kept her eye on him. "Yes. We will."

Montagu chuckled. "You might as well concede now. She's got you pegged before the first hand."

Mr. Wyndell snorted. "I think not."

"I think so."

Miss Pymm watched the exchange with wide eyes. "Can you really tell who'll win before the first hand?"

"No," replied her partner.

"Yes," countered Montagu, "if you're playing with Wyndell and I'm partnering Miss Abbot."

"Oh." Miss Pymm laid her cards face down.

"Put your cards up," Mr. Wyndell chastised her. "You must play out the game or you will never know for sure."

Miss Pymm gathered her cards once more. "But what if she wins?"

"She won't." Mr. Wyndell sounded more like he was trying to convince himself more than anyone else.

Mr. Wyndell was wrong. Felicity and Montagu thoroughly beat them, with Mr. Wyndell and Miss Pymm only taking two tricks.

Montagu could not contain his delight. "Well done, Miss Abbott!"

Felicity couldn't help but share his triumph. "I told you."

She had the queen, and Montagu held both the king and ace of spades. Along with a few minor cards and a void in a minor suit in Montagu's hand, it was practically a bloodbath.

Miss Pymm pulled out her fan. "Well, good thing that was only practice."

"Would you like to continue?"

Her eyes brightened. "Yes, please." Mother was forgotten.

"Ah, we're only playing paper points." Montagu caught the eye of a footman and beckoned him over. His Grace whispered instructions in the footman's ear and sent him off to do his bidding.

Mr. Wyndell shuffled the cards and passed them to Felicity for cutting. She did so and gave them to Miss Pymm to deal. Miss Pymm handed those cards out quick-time and turned up the five of diamonds.

Did the Duke of Montagu have any tells? If he did, Felicity didn't notice. But Mr. Wyndell had them. She watched him and read him and played him as much as they played the cards. As he sat to her right, she saw every card he laid down before she had to play hers.

The footman returned with a tray of sandwiches and a jug of lemonade.

It was the first decent drink Felicity had had all night. "Oh, bless your furry little soul." That lemonade was the most delicious thing ever. "May I have more?"

The footman fulfilled her wish and her glass.

His Grace and Miss Pymm kept up a steady stream of gossip for the benefit of all. Most of it consisted of who Miss Pymm had met. With a subtle touch, His

Grace teased out her opinions of Society. Overall, the higher a person's rank, the more impressed Miss Pymm was.

Perhaps she should meet the marchioness. It would do Miss Pymm some good to face reality.

In the end, she and the duke barely won by one point.

"Oh," cried Miss Pymm. "Still, getting better. We'll get you next time."

Felicity shook her head. "I don't think so."

But Mr. Wyndell was keeping a close eye on her. "I think we will."

His voice was low and calculating. Under the table, his foot rubbed up against Felicity's leg. She gasped, not expecting that.

Felicity studied him. He was on to something. But what? Had he figured out Montagu's tell? She hadn't picked up on it yet. So she fumbled through shuffling, and Montagu's deal turned up diamonds as trump again.

And like he'd predicted, Mr. Wyndell and Miss Pymm won the game by a landslide.

The whole game had turned on a single hand. Mr. Wyndell had led weak. He had signaled to Miss Pymm to play strong. In response to this, Felicity played weak, well under Mr. Wyndell's card, to preserve her moderately higher card for another hand.

But Miss Pymm, contrary to Mr. Wyndell's subtle signal, had played weak. Montagu was out of suit and trump, and had to ruff. Result: trick to Pymm and Wyndell.

Felicity only had the one strong card left in that suit, so when Mr. Wyndell led strong, she had no choice but to sacrifice her card. Then he led into a suit full of honors, and that was that.

As the tricks fell to Mr. Wyndell, Felicity realized she'd been played. He knew she was reading his tells, and he had tweaked that to his advantage. From how she played, Miss Pymm had no idea Mr. Wyndell was giving off signals, thus allowing him to use them for disinformation.

Even Montagu grasped the error. "Miss Abbot, why didn't you lead out with the jack?"

Felicity chided herself. "I was playing the wrong game."

"Glad we're not playing for pennies. Though maybe Miss Pymm might be regretting it after that spectacular triumph."

"I don't mind. Can't get in trouble that way." Miss Pymm, drunk on success and His Grace's company, went on. "Mother says it's best to lay low."

"Did I miss something interesting? It wouldn't do to shame oneself at the table."

Felicity caught the whiff of gossip. For all her tender years, Miss Pymm did have a few weeks' more experience in Society than she. No doubt she would have heard something interesting. "I doubt anyone's had that bad of luck tonight."

Miss Pymm was in full swing. "Oh, not tonight." She leaned in close. "Though I do hear that someone's been cheating around tables."

A lump of ice dropped into Felicity's stomach. "Cheating?" The word squeaked out. Spots appeared before her eyes.

Miss Pymm was only getting started. "I know. Can you imagine? Who'd do something that terrible?"

Felicity could only shake her head. Those sandwiches so kindly provided by the Duke of Montagu were not sitting well in her stomach. She swigged the last of her lemonade. She pleaded with her head not to pass out. Fainting might be all the rage among the more delicate ladies, but she found the notion rather silly.

Though if she did faint, it would be all her fault.

She wasn't aware she rose. "I need to go apologize to someone." If Miss Pymm had heard rumors of gossip, then maybe someone had—or worse. If she'd known such an *on-dit* had been going around, she wouldn't have spoken out of turn.

What would Lord Mayfair think of her?

"Are you all right?" Miss Pymm's voice trembled. She sounded positively frightened. "Miss Abbot? Did I say something wrong?"

"What's wrong?" Mr. Wyndell's hand took hers.

This made her feel worse. "My apologies," she stammered, before fleeing.

****

Montagu frowned. To Victor, he asked, "She all right? She looks like a goose walked over her grave."

Victor rose, watching her hasten away. Where was she going?

Ah, it was to Mayfair after all. He lounged against the far wall, not too close to a door guarded by a maid.

The ladies' withdrawing room. Lady Mayfair must be pulling herself together. Mayfair looked nonplussed. He inspected his nails, lost in his own little world. Then Miss Abbot showed up, to pour out her contrition.

Let her get it out of her system.

Victor sat back down. "She'll be fine. Stuck her foot in her mouth earlier. Seems to think she needs to apologize to him."

Montagu observed Felicity's contrition. "Does she need to?"

Victor's opinion: "Not really. She'd already apologized for her misspoken words."

"Ah."

How had His Grace put so much meaning into one little word?

Miss Pymm picked up on it. She gasped most dramatically. "So he did cheat! She was right?"

Montagu chuckled a little. "Oh, he cheats all right. Just not at cards."

This confused Miss Pymm. "I don't understand…" She mulled it over. "So what does he cheat at?"

Victor turned to her. Was she really that naive? "Private joke."

Why ruin her innocent view of the world now? That was for someone else to do later.

Montagu laughed out loud. "Oh, good one, Wyndell." He lost his humor. "I think you might want to go put a stop to things." He gestured toward Miss Abbot and Lord Mayfair. "Someone's making a move."

Victor stiffened. "What?" When he looked at Felicity, her hands were in Mayfair's. Was he leaning over for a kiss?

Victor's chair tumbled over as he leapt out of it.

Whatever you do, Miss Abbot, do not kiss Mayfair!

****

The whole room passed in a daze for Felicity. Before she knew it, she found herself standing before Lord Mayfair. Lady Mayfair was nowhere to be seen.

Felicity gasped for breath. Had she run here? "Lord Mayfair. I must apologize."

Lord Mayfair, who had been lost in thought against the wall, stood upright. "Miss Abbot, is it?"

She rushed on, heedless of any grace or decorum. "I should never have accused you of cheating. I—" How not to blurt this out and look like the naïf she was? "I did not know there was a rumor going around to that effect. If I'd known, I wouldn't have said anything about your tells." Tears filled her eyes but did not spill.

Lord Mayfair took her hand. It felt like a fall of cool water rolled over her skin. He stood very close and patted it comfortingly.

"There, there, sweet little thing. I understand. Silly little heads often run away with the veriest of fancies. Anyhow, it wasn't me."

She sniffed. "It wasn't you...what?"

"It wasn't me who was cheating. In the rumor. Had it been me, I would have fleeced you every game." His voice sounded smooth and comforting. Of course it wasn't him. A pleasant little calm fell across her shoulders. It wasn't much, but it did make her feel better. After all, they did win those two hands before she noticed him stroking his mustache far too much. No wonder she and Mr. Wyndell had won. Lady Mayfair had done a poor job of holding up her end of the silent conversation.

His hand stroked hers rhythmically. "You are newly debuted to Society, I take it?"

Felicity moved her head. Was it a nod or a shake? For some reason she couldn't lie to him, but she shouldn't tell him the truth. There was enough dishonesty about, she didn't need to add any more. The noise of the other players melted into a muted rush that sounded like either the wind or maybe the ocean.

"They must have taught you well in your finishing school. I do believe you are the first to discover my tell."

"We never learned about tells." She swallowed. "I…I should never have said anything. It's just that you started stroking your mustache, and it seemed…ridiculous." What was she doing telling him everything?

Lord Mayfair lifted her hand to press against his lips ever so gently. The coolness on her skin sharpened to a familiar tingle.

"My dear, I am even more amazed. You won those games on sheer skill alone?" He chuckled. "No wonder I could not suss your tells. You and Mr. Wyndell had none."

Not true. She had unlocked the secret to communicating with Mr. Wyndell. Granted, it had been by accident. She could not help but to have studied those fine eyes of his, hoping to get past the perpetual scowl on his face. Mr. Wyndell seemed too young to be so careworn. Why had he been so sad tonight? She would do anything to cheer him up.

The card game had gone a long way to relaxing him. Then Miss Pymm said something about cheating.

Felicity looked up at Lord Mayfair. "I should never have said anything."

He shrugged, a casual lift of one shoulder. "I've already heard the rumor. It's been circulating around for a couple of weeks now." He gathered her hand close to his chest. "That's why I wasn't surprised you said what you said."

"Is the rumor that old? I hadn't heard anything about it until tonight."

He gave another half-shrug. "That's all right, my

dear. If you were to hear it, this house is the place."

Felicity surveyed the room. "Lord and Lady Chester's?"

He nodded. "After all, this is where the cheating took place."

Something fell into place, like tumblers onto a key. This was important, far more important than it first appeared.

"I had no idea," she murmured, more to herself.

He tilted her chin up with a finger, the tingly coolness tracing along her jaw. Why was his touch so familiar?

"In fact, I'm rather glad you haven't been paying attention to any nasty rumors." His thumb stroked her cheek, leaving a trace of...something.

Shouldn't she be pulling away? He was not at all discombobulated over her accusation. Indeed, he had forgiven her rather quickly. Too quickly?

His eyes held her, mysterious, compelling. His head bent close, lingering. Her lips parted, but no words came out. Just a little farther before...

"Lord Mayfair." A woman's cold voice shattered the spell.

His Lordship's hand jerked away from her face. He stepped back. "Ah, feeling better, my dear?"

Felicity awoke from her dream. Had she been asleep? She blinked as reality came back to her. She shook herself to release the fogginess that surrounded her. Lady Mayfair stood there, hands rigid by her side, glaring daggers at them.

"No. I am ready to leave." It was her voice, sharp and full of toxin, that dissolved any illusion Lord Mayfair had spun.

Felicity put her hand to her cheek. What had happened to her?

Lord Mayfair felt too close. She stepped back, into someone's arms.

Mr. Wyndell caught her. "I say, Miss Abbot. Are you all right?"

At the sound of his voice, her head cleared as if it had been washed by a mountain stream. "I am now."

Magic. That was what that was. Lord Mayfair had used magic on her. What a fool she'd been not to recognize it sooner. Not that she'd ever been good at seeing such things in the first place. But if she had, it would have been an easy enough matter to free herself.

If she had seen it coming.

She observed Lord Mayfair. His charms, that he'd turned on her full force, were now directed at soothing his irate wife.

"Perhaps it is time to go downstairs and pay our respects to Lady Chester. Maybe convince her into a game?"

Mr. Wyndell's arm about her waist held Felicity up. Not that she needed the support. She could stand on her own two feet, now that Lord Mayfair was no longer focusing on her.

His wife, on the other hand, wasn't giving in as easily. "I doubt she's playing." She lifted a hand to her forehead. "I don't know why you…" Whatever thought she might have had seemed to have fled.

That lord now grasped his lady wife by the arm and turned her away. "Now, now, my dear. You've had a long day. Perhaps a glass of refreshment is what you need?"

At this, Lady Mayfair perked up. "Yes. That is

what I need." She shrugged off his arm and headed for the door as if she could not quit the room fast enough.

Lord Mayfair looked back over his shoulder and sent Felicity the faintest of kisses. She was not upset or amused. Instead, it became food for thought. What had happened there?

Victor's arm tightened about her waist. Now there was an interesting development. Felicity laid her hand on his arm.

What did it mean?

Chapter 7
The Mystery of The Agreement

Victor shot Mayfair a warning glance. Lord Mayfair backed off. He was more than happy to follow his departing wife rather than tangle with Victor.

Victor chided himself. Of course he knew Lord Mayfair made a sport of charming women and luring them into the darker, sensual arts. So why did he forget now? How foolish of him. Had he remembered, he would have stopped Felicity the moment she rose from her chair.

Miss Abbot was in his arms. He held her as if afraid she'd flee after Lord Mayfair.

"Are you all right?"

She looked up at him with clear eyes. "Yes." She had a pensive look. "He was going to kiss me."

"I know." There was more tension in his voice than he meant.

Her face went from pensive to calculating. "You're jealous."

Was he still holding her? He released her as if hot. "No."

A smile teased at her lips. "You are."

"Am not."

He backed off a step. She followed.

"Absolutely you are." She pressed her advantage, drawing close.

"The man is a known rake."

Montagu spoke right behind him. Victor jumped. He had forgotten about the duke.

Miss Abbot peered around Victor. "Is he?"

He nodded.

"Of course. Makes sense."

He swore he could see her head working like a clock, ticking over, adding things up. What he wouldn't have given to know what thoughts drove her cogs.

And then there was Miss Pymm, hiding behind His Grace. "Oh no! A rake? Oh, Miss Abbot, it must have been terrible."

No doubt proper Mrs. Pymm would have warned her daughter about the dangers of rakes.

Miss Abbot shrugged. "I wasn't thinking about the kiss."

Montagu chuckled. "Mayfair will be disappointed."

Victor felt relief. The near kiss hadn't fazed her.

"It was something else he said."

"What?" asked His Grace.

Miss Abbot looked from the duke to Victor. "I'm not sure yet."

She was calculating something; he knew it.

"Oh dear," exclaimed Miss Pymm. "Our game."

When they turned back to their table, it had been taken over by other guests, now several hands deep into a card game. No other spare tables were available.

"That's a shame," His Grace admitted. He offered his arm to Miss Pymm. "May I escort you back to your mother?"

Several tables away Mrs. Pymm was still well and truly ensconced in her card game. "I'd rather you not," her daughter confessed.

"Shall we go find Miss Chester? I dare say she will be as fed up with this crush as we are."

The light died in Miss Pymm's eyes when he said that. "Oh. I suppose we could."

Off they went, leaving Victor with Miss Abbot.

She took his arm and dragged him out of the games room. Eagerness shone in her eyes.

"Good, they're gone. Lord Mayfair said something to me that I believe is important."

"Oh?"

"You know that agreement you're looking for?"

He perked up. "What about it?"

She tucked her arm in his and guided him down the corridor. "Does it have anything to do with cheating at cards?"

They stopped before the top of the stairs. "What did you hear?"

"Lord Mayfair confessed he was not bothered by my accusation. Said he'd been hearing a rumor of someone cheating for a few weeks now. That it happened in this very house."

He considered this. What if The Agreement was between four card players, one of whom was caught cheating? It was a possibility.

But if that was the case, why draw up an agreement? Wouldn't one's word do?

There had to be something more.

"I don't think that's it."

Felicity halted. "I have yet to hear a better idea from you."

She had him there, but he wouldn't let her get the better of him. "All right. What's worse than cheating at cards?"

"Murder."

He dismissed that immediately. "Doesn't make any sense."

"You never said it had to make sense." She tapped her finger against his forehead. "None of this makes any sense to you. You're taking what little you know and expecting it to be the whole. You need to look for what's missing."

How could something so crazy make so much sense? "And what is that?"

Miss Abbot shrugged. "If I knew what it was, it wouldn't be missing. Oh, if only there was somewhere to sit. I need to think."

"Parlor?"

It was the first place to pop into his head regarding a place to sit. His mother used the parlor for sitting all the time. Granted, all she did was sit, and not much else. He couldn't bear sitting idly and doing nothing. A couple passed them on their way to the gaming room.

Victor looked down the stairs. He could only see the hallway, but it, like the drawing rooms, was packed with people. "I don't figure our chances of making it there."

Miss Abbot sat on the top step.

His heart beat faster. "We can't sit here."

Sitting on steps was most improper. It was an act for children, not adults. She scowled at him as he hauled her up.

"Well, where, then?" She dusted off her skirt. The light of an idea illuminated her eyes. "I think I know where." Taking his hand, she pulled him down the stairs and straight into the overcrowded drawing room.

Talk about nowhere to sit. Could it be possible

there were even more people here than before?

Miss Abbot elbowed her way through the crowd to the far corner. There, nearly hidden by a tied-up curtain and a large potted plant, was a chaise longue. It had been shoved quite out of the way to make room for more party guests and had an advantage in being banked against a window. While the window was closed, perhaps some coolness could be found.

A lone man of indeterminate age occupied the chaise. He was a rather plain-looking man who might have suited country society better than the glittering Quality of London.

Miss Abbot didn't let that stop her.

"Up you get, Mr. Thomas." She snapped her fingers in his face. "You've been there long enough."

Mr. Thomas rose, not at her bidding, but in indignation. "I beg your pardon?"

Miss Abbot shoved him out of the way. "It is entirely unsuitable for a man of your station to come to a party and sit in the corner doing nothing." Dragging Victor with her, she sat down on the chaise. With a wave of her fingers, she shooed Mr. Thomas away. "Go find your wife. No doubt she's having more fun than you."

"Well, I never!" And off in a huff went Mr. Thomas.

Victor could only stare at his companion. "Really, Miss Abbot. Was that necessary?"

She flicked at invisible dust on her sleeve. "It was. He has been sitting here all evening doing nothing, speaking to no one."

"Had it occurred to you he might have wanted to do just that?"

She fixed him with a very determined eye. "Absolutely. I had a good five minutes earlier this night to ponder just this subject. His reasons for sitting here were very poor ones. Now he has been chastised."

Victor blew out an exasperated breath. "There is nothing wrong with sitting quietly at a party."

"Oh yes, there is. One should not come to a party merely to sit and do nothing. One can do that perfectly well at home."

"What if poor Mr. Thomas had no choice but to come?"

She changed her position on the chaise to face him. "And what choice would that be?"

Victor was here under protest. His mother insisted he come and help her look for The Agreement.

"Perhaps he is chaperoning someone, or maybe he is waiting for his wife. Maybe he has the headache."

"If he is chaperoning, he should be off doing just that, and not sitting here. What is his wife doing that he must wait for her here for two hours? If he has a headache and cannot leave the party, the last place he'd want to be is in the noisiest room of the house. Perhaps he is better off somewhere else. Do men have a withdrawing room?"

He leaned back against the chaise. "Are you going to shoot down every suggestion I have?"

"Only the unreasonable ones." She shook out a fold of her skirt. "Your idea of his being here under protest? That I believe. Someone has brought him here, and he cannot leave. They brought him here for a reason. Whatever that reason is, he's not fulfilling it. Therefore, he must get out of this corner and attend to his purpose."

Victor threw his hands in the air. How on earth did she come up with such convoluted logic? Couldn't she have let the man be? "We could have sat somewhere else."

Miss Abbot glanced about the room. The curtain pretty much hid them from most of the party, as did the potted plant. Their only egress was blocked by a group of middle-aged matrons, with backs to Victor and Miss Abbot, as they observed and commented on the party.

"This is perfect for now." She turned back to Victor. "We need to take stock of what we know, so we can identify what we don't know and then figure out what to do next."

She waved her fingers as if fanning herself. It was hot in here, the draft off the window not quite sufficient to give relief from the heat.

"Let me see if I have this correct: you are here to find The Agreement?"

"Yes."

"We don't know what The Agreement is, but we do know the nature of The Agreement, namely, not to talk about The Agreement."

"Correct."

She tapped her finger along her jaw line. "If it was important enough to draw up an agreement never to speak of whatever it was, then whatever happened has the potential to ruin someone. What could ruin someone?"

Good question. Lots of things could ruin a man. Financial disaster, gambling losses. Insulting someone and not apologizing. Not honoring one's debts. Being caught with another man's wife.

Oh, that was a good one. What if one of the

women had been caught with a man? Of all the women he suspected involved, every one was married.

His mother? Surely not. Lady Chester? Possible. He regarded Miss Abbot. Her mother? He couldn't mention that possibility. "I don't know."

Miss Abbot *tsk*ed and shook her head. "Really, Mr. Abbot. You've spent how many Seasons in Society, and you can't think of a single shameful thing? Because shame is what this agreement is all about. If someone wasn't ashamed over what happened, they would never have needed an agreement to protect their honor."

He stiffened. "I would not presume to speak of such things in front of a lady."

A light dawned in her eyes. "A lady. This agreement is about a lady. Who is being protected?" Tap, tap, tap went her finger. "Now, what is more important: who or what? Who needs protection, or what can't be revealed?"

Her logic was all over the place, spilled milk on the floor without a glass to contain it. Couldn't she simply stick to one line and work it through?

"Why would they need protecting?"

"Ladies need protecting." She sat up straighter as another thought popped into her head. "What if someone was compromised? She was discovered, and her reputation would be in tatters unless everyone agreed to keep it quiet so that…what?" Her fingers toyed absently with his. "What if it was a young, unmarried lady, maybe a debutante? Got caught in a bit of trouble. So everyone vowed to remain quiet so as not to ruin her chances of the Season?"

That was a possibility. That there were at least four people involved in The Agreement, he was sure of. He knew one—his mother—and suspected two more, Lady Chester and Mrs. Abbot. These were the only two ladies his mother had spoken to tonight, of which he knew. He didn't know for sure they were involved, but Lord Mayfair had said something about rumors of cheating here. That would implicate Lady Chester, if only by proximity. Also, The Agreement was written on her stationery.

Who was the fourth? A debutante? Was it her honor they were protecting? His mother didn't have any eligible daughters at the moment; his sisters were all safely married. She strongly hinted that should the nature of The Agreement come out, it was of such dire nature that Victor's own reputation could be damaged. Surely no one suspected *him* of compromising anyone.

His gaze fell to Miss Abbot. He drew her hand into his, fighting to keep his own fingers from trembling. "Miss Abbot?" He drew a deep breath. "I am sorry to be so forward, but do you know anything…personal…about The Agreement?"

She shook her head.

Should he believe her? After all, she'd sneaked out, completely unchaperoned, her parents ignorant as to her whereabouts. Surely she'd done this sort of thing before.

But then, there was the moment he'd first met her. She'd hidden in that corridor, practically bouncing with excitement. She'd said this was her first party. He completely believed her.

Was she prone to scandal? Absolutely.

Had she been subjected to it? No way of telling, except to ask his mother.

She wouldn't give away the contents of The

Agreement, nor betray the other signatories, at least, not directly. But ask the right question, and her face would betray all.

He changed his tact. "Have you met my mother?"

Miss Abbot grew still. "Mrs. Wyndell? Oh, a few times." She put her hand on his sleeve. "But not formally or socially. She often comes calling when my mother is At Home to guests."

Ah. There was a prior connection. A tiny corner of his heart began to cry as he considered the possibility that Miss Abbot might be the subject of The Agreement, if it did involve scandal. Here was a lovely young lady who had stirred his soul, even as she was turning his night upside down. But if she was immured in scandal, she'd be removed from Society, and he might not see her again. That did not please him at all.

Her hand tightened on his arm. Her gaze pleaded with his. "Please don't tell your mother I'm here. She knows I'm not yet Out. She'll tell my mother, and I'll be in such terrible trouble."

The cogs of his own mind ticked over. Her first party… Her first…anything? "Wait. Did you say you weren't Out yet?" He drew a sharp breath. "You haven't been presented yet?"

She froze. "I…" Her gaze darted away from his.

"How old are you?"

A blush stained her cheeks so dark he felt their warmth even here in the gloom.

"Nearly one-and-twenty, and not presented," she admitted with shame.

One-and-twenty and not presented. What could possibly lead to such an oversight?

Suspicion spidered in his gut, and his heart ached

even more. He licked his lips and gathered his courage. "What if The Agreement was to protect someone's reputation?"

She tilted her head sideways, a half-shrug of embarrassment. "Makes sense."

Could she not meet his gaze anymore?

He took a fortifying breath. "What if it's to protect yours?"

She blinked. "Mine? Whatever for?"

He let go of his breath. "So, other than tonight's foray, have you done anything that might even vaguely smell of trouble?"

"I would be lying if I said no. My brother and I were notorious for getting into scrapes. Half the time we were mortal enemies and at each other's throats. The rest of the time, we were partners in crime…"

Thus she explained her childhood *peccadilloes*, nothing out of the ordinary. Certainly nothing that would scandalize Society now.

Miss Abbot, her tongue powered by her embarrassment, rambled on. "I mean, after he got married, that was the end of that. I still had another two years before my mother would present me, then I was ill for one Season and then…" Her voice trailed off. Her countenance fell.

"What?"

Sadness filled her eyes and threatened to spill out. "He died. Horse riding accident. When he died, my future died as well." She turned away. "Nobody attends the Season with a death in the family." She caught her lip between her teeth. "So I dare say I haven't had time at all for anything remotely scandalous."

She told of her grandmother's proposal and

subsequent abandonment. The sting of that colored her voice husky. He took her hand. She let him and ran the fingers of her other hand over his nails.

"Other than fittings at the *modiste*, I haven't been out." She hung her head. "Can you blame me for wanting to come to the party?"

No, he could not.

The bottoms of the plump matrons shoved up against the potted plants, nearly knocking one over. Victor's hand shot out to rescue it. Instead, his hand smacked up firm against a matron's ample bottom, keeping her from falling backward. He snatched it away as if burned.

The plump matron didn't notice. She continued her commiseration with her friends. They huddled together, wishing they had chairs and muttering on in their conversation, complaints about the crush, about their husbands, about their children, the weather. And lack of chairs, again.

And Miss Abbot, in her ignorance, wanted to be a part of all this? Victor adjusted the potted plant and settled back to the chaise.

"I'm sorry. I was grasping at straws."

"You're grasping at sunbeams. Why on earth do you think The Agreement was about me?"

He shrugged. "I didn't know if your mother had mentioned anything or not."

One of the matrons complained about the terrible food. From the look of her muslined backside, it wouldn't hurt her to miss out on a meal or two tonight.

"My mother?" Her voice rose a few notes. "Why would she have anything to do with The Agreement?" Then a light dawned in her eyes as she put two and two together. "Are you saying my mother is involved? Oh, surely not!"

He ran a hand through his hair. "Well, I suspect. I saw her earlier today speaking with my mother and with Lady Chester."

"Could have been random conversation. What else was there to do at a crush but converse?"

The matrons kept up their dour complaints, nothing of interest to him.

Victor shook his head. "I know when my mother is having 'random conversation' and when she's up to something. She wears her heart all over her sleeve. When she spoke with your mother, she was definitely nervous."

"*I* get nervous when I speak with my mother. Maybe she makes everyone nervous."

"No, my mother's been avoiding everyone. She's only spoken to your mother and Lady Chester, as well as myself."

In his eyes, that was connection enough for him. But how she featured in, who knew?

"That doesn't mean they're involved."

"No," he conceded. "It's no proof."

But he held on to his suspicions. Oh, what had his mother dragged him into? He had not wanted to come to this crush.

He regarded Miss Abbot sitting next to him, lost in thought. On the other hand, he might not have met her. She was unlike any other Society miss he had known. Such a mixed bag, she was. For someone who insisted on upholding Society's conventions, she did a very good job of throwing them away when they inconvenienced her.

The party happened out there. But here, on the chaise longue, partially hidden by the curtain and the potted plants, here was a refuge from the insanity that was the Chesters' crush. He regretted chasing poor Mr. Thomas away from this perfectly good hiding spot.

"Why did you come to the party? You're taking a big risk going about in public unchaperoned."

She shrank into herself. "I found it dreadfully unfair to be kept away from Society, simply because someone failed to realize how important it is to me."

He couldn't help but take her hand. "They're just trying to keep you safe."

"Safe from what?"

"Well, scandal."

Lord Mayfair. Bad punch. Proposing marriage to bachelors one has only met that night.

She arched an eyebrow. "Really? Tell me, Mr. Wyndell, who keeps you safe from scandal?"

That surprised him. "I…I never thought about it."

A sprinkle of feminine laughter rang out over the general miasma of human conversation. Victor frowned at that. It sounded like Miss Bitner. He hoped she would not find him here.

"So," said Miss Abbot, "why am I so valuable and you are not as much?"

What was his value? Here he was, an unmarried younger son. He was not the heir. He had no profession, though his parents had often hinted strongly in that direction. They did not consider clock making a suitable gentleman's profession. They had thrust him out in Society and told him to fetch a bride. No other assistance.

He considered his sisters, and how they had been presented to Society, dressed up, paraded about, protected, guarded, guided until they made splendid, socially proper marriages. Indeed, their value had been greater than his, with their ability to attract the best families.

But he was a son, a younger son. While his family—currently—hadn't fully fallen from good standing, his own particular value wasn't as great. He had no expectations of great wealth or social power. No wonder his mother was so worried. She completely believed The Agreement had the potential to seal their social death. While his sisters and brother were safely married, he, the youngest, was left unattached.

"My mother defends me."

She blinked. "Your mother? I suppose that makes sense. She did chaperone you to the party."

She had dragged him along to help her look for The Agreement. After all, it was to protect his interests as much as hers.

"She would see me married well."

"I doubt any of our mothers would see us married poorly. Or not at all."

A small shudder rolled through her hand. He held it tighter.

"Does marriage frighten you?"

"The actual thought? No. I've always known I'd get married. The *who* is what concerns me."

His heart ached when she said that. "Do your parents have any suitables in mind?"

She sighed. "Not really, no. My mother says it's too early in the Season. I say it's been two years too long." She waved that thought away. "Anyhow, she has already turned down every one in the Corinthian set, and I'm afraid Montagu is off the market. That leaves only you."

His heart skipped a beat. "You mean, your parents are considering me?"

She inclined her head. The babble of other people's conversation rolled over them. The matrons, tired of standing, moved off in search of somewhere to rest their sore feet. A younger circle of ladies moved into the corner. Their conversation was much louder, more intrusive.

How annoying. He was trying to learn if someone other than his mother had designs on his future.

And why wasn't Miss Abbot answering?

"Is that why you suggested marriage in the card room?"

She tilted her head the other way as if she hadn't heard his question. "My mother knows about The Agreement?"

A new voice intruded on the conversation. "It is all terribly suspicious," said Miss Bitner.

Victor jumped. His grip tightened on Miss Abbot's hand. He looked about.

Miss Bitner was ensconced in the group of young ladies near the potted plants. A chill ran over his skin. He scooted himself to the far side of the chaise and pulled the curtain about them.

Miss Abbot peeked through the plant, but he pulled her back.

"From whom are we hiding?" she whispered.

At least she understood what he was doing.

"Someone you do not want to meet."

Miss Abbot swung herself over to the far side, scooted up pleasantly close to him, and together they hid behind the curtain and indulged in some very bad manners. They eavesdropped.

****

Felicity clutched Mr. Wyndell's hand tightly. The curtain pulled about them cast the corner in semi-darkness. Would it be enough to keep them safe?

"It is all terribly suspicious," said the nasally voice, "that their engagement happened over the winter." A bitter laugh escaped her lips. "I mean, really. Who gets engaged over winter?"

Felicity might not have known who was speaking, but she agreed with Mr. Wyndell. This was someone with whom she did not wish to be acquainted. The voice alone felt like someone running a wire brush the wrong way up her back.

She leaned over and whispered, "Who's that?"

Mr. Wyndell's murmured reply: "Miss Nora Bitner."

"Ah, the nasty one we encountered earlier."

"The same."

Another, more pleasant voice said, "Surely you aren't suggesting…"

Suggesting what? Felicity twitched with the need to peek around the curtain to see what she was missing.

"That's exactly what I mean," replied Miss Bitner, her voice dripping with poison. "Why else get engaged in winter and why her?"

"Mmm," replied the other voice in agreement. "I did wonder. But if she is…then why not get married immediately? Depending on how far along she is, might even have to be special license."

At this Mr. Wyndell drew a surprised breath. Felicity perked up. "What does she mean?"

He whispered in her ear, "Mrs. Cupitt is suggesting

His Grace and his soon-to-be wife have been, shall we say, *misbehaving*."

"Oh." How terribly romantic. And at the same time, how terribly scandalous!

Felicity hadn't met Mrs. Cupitt. She wasn't sure she wanted to, if she was keeping company with Miss Bitner.

"Ah, that's the thing. They haven't been married yet." Miss Bitner's voice dropped low, but not so low she couldn't be heard above the crowded drawing room. "Because there is a question over whether or not it's his."

"No!" Mrs. Cupitt's voice carried a weight of disbelief tinged with delight over such gossip.

Mr. Wyndell gripped Felicity's hands. She drew in a breath, but he was listening too hard to notice her. Of what was Miss Bitner speaking? What was *it*, and why did it matter if it belonged to His Grace or not? His engagement? His marriage? His scandal? This gossip would make a whole lot more sense if only she had some context.

Mrs. Cupitt's voice continued. "Surely it couldn't be any but his."

"And yet they are not married." Miss Bitner made it sound like a condemnation. "His Grace is a man of honor and would do the correct thing by her, if it were his."

"Oh. But if that were so, why does he not simply put her away quietly? He has more than sufficient grounds to do so."

But Miss Bitner's nasty chortle denied such an action. "He can't."

"Whyever not?"

"He's being blackmailed."

"Is he?" Mrs. Cupitt didn't sound so sure. "By whom?"

"Her parents, of course. They're forcing him to marry her to hide her shame."

Felicity looked to Mr. Wyndell. What had they stumbled across? His frown showed he was equally concerned.

Mrs. Cupitt replied, "Yet he hasn't."

"Oh, he will, unless it can be stopped. You see, there's a certain document in the Chesters' possession, a document that exposes the whole situation."

At this, Mr. Wyndell expelled a small noise. He clapped a hand over his mouth. Felicity caught her own breath.

They'd been unnoticed.

Miss Bitner went on. "If we could find it, it would completely ruin the Chesters and free His Grace."

"What is it?" Mrs. Cupitt sounded rapt.

"They drew up an agreement—"

Felicity and Mr. Wyndell turned to each other and mouthed, "What!"

"—that says that unless His Grace marries Miss Chester, they'll expose something he does not want Society to know."

Felicity had forgotten how to breathe. The Agreement was about Miss Chester? She shook her head. It couldn't be true. Surely the Chesters wouldn't stoop so low as to blackmail the Duke of Montagu into marrying their daughter. Could they?

Mr. Wyndell was awfully pale. This must have been news to him as well. His grip on her hand was as strong as hers was on his.

Another thing was clear: someone had definitely spoken about The Agreement. Otherwise, how did Miss Bitner hear about it? Surely she was not one of the parties to The Agreement.

So who, of her acquaintances, told her of The Agreement?

"What makes you think that an agreement exists?" Mrs. Cupitt was skeptical.

"I have it on the best of authority. I heard of it from one of the involved parties."

A burst of gentlemanly laughter blocked out the rest of the conversation. Mr. Wyndell leaned closer to the curtain in hopes of hearing more.

But all Felicity caught was Miss Bitner's final words.

"—finding it tonight."

She leaned over to Mr. Wyndell and whispered, "Are they looking for The Agreement as well?"

Mr. Wyndell didn't reply. He continued to listen, but Miss Bitner and Mrs. Cupitt must have moved off. He slumped in disappointment. In a normal voice he said, "It seems we're not the only ones looking for it."

"What will we do?"

Mr. Wyndell restored the curtain to its place and rose off the chaise. "To save Miss Chester's reputation, we need to find this agreement before Miss Bitner does." He held out his hand.

Felicity took it and stood up. How warm his hand was. As soon as she touched it, she didn't feel so anxious. But that frown of worry had returned to Mr. Wyndell's forehead.

Together they pushed their way out of the drawing room.

Chapter 8
Looking For The Agreement

Victor admired how nice Miss Abbot's hand felt in his. If anyone had asked, his excuse was to guide her through the crowd. But if they ever got out of the crowd, he didn't know if he could let go of that hand.

He didn't want to let go of that hand ever.

They headed up the steps in hopes that the next floor wouldn't be so bad.

A question bothered him. If The Agreement was about the Chesters blackmailing His Grace, what did his mother have to do with it? How could that possibly ruin his reputation? And what about Miss Abbot's mother? The cogs of this conundrum were not meshing at all.

Or could it be that His Grace was involved in something shady that also concerned his mother and Mrs. Abbot? Victor quickly pushed the idea of an affair out of his mind. For one thing, his mother was too old.

But an affair... Miss Abbot did mention cheating. She thought it was at cards, but what if it really meant infidelity?

Victor sighed as they looked up and down the corridor. It was less crowded here, but random groups of Society hovered near the door to the games room.

"If I were to hide an agreement I didn't want anyone to find, I would hide it somewhere safe," Miss

Abbot said.

"Bedroom?" Victor suggested.

She agreed. "Or library." She leaned out to view the stairway leading down. "However, I suspect it might be a bit crowded at the present."

This first floor had the game room and a few salons. The bedrooms were up another level. Without further discussion, Miss Abbot took Victor's hand and led him up another flight of stairs.

He liked the feel of her hand in his. It felt natural, like it had finally come home after a long absence. Could this have been what his mother meant?

Upstairs could not have been more different than downstairs. Here only a few lamps lit the corridor, casting shadows from vases on tables and hung pictures. The doors were smaller and more recessed.

Miss Abbot went up to the first one. She laid a hand on the doorknob and an ear to the door. After a moment of focus, she opened the door into a dark room and stepped inside.

As Victor followed, she squeaked and backed into him, forcing him out once again into the corridor. She slammed the door.

"What was that?" he asked.

She put a hand to her blushing cheeks. "That room is, shall we say, *occupied*?"

"Occupied?"

She patted him on the cheek. "Not a subject for someone so young and unmarried as yourself."

Victor folded his arms and gave her a wry look.

She ignored it. Her cheeks still burned.

A smile tugged at the corners of his lips. *Poor maiden.* What had she seen to make her so bashful?

They moved on to the next bedroom. Once more, she laid her hand on the doorknob, paused thoughtfully, then eased open the door.

This time, she stuck her head in to check before moving in.

A single lamp on a dressing table lit the room. Odd, seeing that no one was in here.

Miss Abbot took a chance. "Hello?"

No response, not even from a maid. Miss Abbot moved to another door and peered inside. "Empty here as well. The Chesters must have every servant working the party tonight. Even the lady's maid is gone."

After ascertaining the vacancy of the room, Miss Abbot dusted her hands. "Right-o. Let us find ourselves an agreement."

Victor looked about. A canopied bed occupied most of the room. A glory box stood at the base of the bed, and a bureau stood next to the window. A dressing table with a large mirror dominated a wall. Other than two chairs, there was no other furniture.

Various feminine implements lay scattered on the dressing table. Miss Abbot ran her hands over them, even picking up a hairbrush to inspect its back. "Nice. This must be Miss Chester's room."

Victor opened the drawers of the bureau. "I don't know if I'd be keeping The Agreement in here."

The drawers held various frilly unmentionables of a private nature not suited for a gentleman's eyes. He quickly shut the drawer he'd opened.

"How about you check here?" He shoved away the nagging feeling that they should not be in here at all.

She drew it open again. "What?" Miss Abbot picked up an article of clothing from the drawer. It had an awful lot of lace. "Never seen a chemise before?"

Victor shaded his eyes. "Can't say I often pursue the opportunity."

Miss Abbot watched him for a moment, the chemise still in her hand. "Good. I'd hate to think you make a habit of viewing lady's underthings."

A brief image of Miss Abbot in nothing but *her* underthings flashed through his head. He shook it out as quickly as it popped in. No good dwelling on that, especially in a bedroom, considering what was going on in the chamber next door.

To distract himself, he started sorting through the dressing table. It had a few small drawers. The top drawers held little more than hair pins and ribbons. The right drawer featured lotions and potions.

The left drawer gave him a spot of trouble. "It's locked."

Miss Abbot looked up from her bottom drawer, having found nothing resembling an agreement. "Here. Let me try."

She put her hand to the drawer and drew it open. "There."

A knock rang out on the door. "Miss Chester?"

Miss Abbot jumped at the sound of the masculine voice. She slammed the drawer shut. "C'mon," she whispered, grabbing Victor by the hand.

"Are you in there?"

The voice sounded urgent. Victor recognized it as the Duke of Montagu. He and Miss Chester were betrothed. Still, should he be knocking on the lady's door?

Miss Abbot dragged Victor through the little door she'd explored earlier. No sooner had they slipped in than the door to the bedroom opened.

"Miss Chester? Clarice?" His Grace sounded worried.

The small door closed with an audible click, leaving them very much in the dark. Panic swirled in his chest. Victor couldn't help it. His heart thumped hard. They were trapped. The duke would find them in there, thus compromising Miss Abbot.

But she had another idea. "Through here," she whispered, tugging on his hand.

To his surprise, she opened another door. The light from the corridor flooded in. Of course the maid's room would have two doors.

Gratefully, he followed her out into the corridor. Escape at last.

Or not. They were not alone in the corridor. Someone leaned into the bedroom, presumably a companion of the duke's. Miss Abbot swallowed her surprise and backed down the hallway to the next door.

Victor put his hand on the doorknob.

It was locked.

Whoever leaned into the bedroom moved back into the corridor. Victor froze.

Miss Abbot had to pry his frozen fingers off the knob. "Come on," she whispered as she opened the door.

But wasn't the door locked?

Nevertheless, he followed her into yet another dark room.

****

Locked doors had never been a problem for Felicity. If it hadn't been for her talent, Montagu would have caught them in his fiancée's bedroom. Any which way you looked at it, that would have been a very awkward explanation.

So here they were in another dark room. There had been no time to check this one for occupancy. However, as no surprised voices raised any alarm, she contented herself with the vacancy of the room. The darkness lent a sense of security, of hiddenness. Just enough light from the lamps outside provided enough illumination through the uncurtained windows. Also, a wavy line shone from under the door. Whoever was out there must have had a lantern as well.

Before she gave herself over to complacency, one more important item of business. Felicity laid her hand over the lock and felt the tumblers go s*nick*. The door was locked once more.

"Oh, I say," went a voice out in the corridor. It sounded like the Duke of Montagu. "What was that?"

Felicity didn't hear the response. She laid her ear next to the door and listened.

Montagu had at least one companion, whose voice was too muffled for her to make out.

Mr. Wyndell leaned in and put his ear to the door as well.

Down the corridor, they heard a door open, then close, followed by Montagu's voice. Then another door opened and closed.

"They're checking the room." Mr. Wyndell pulled away from the door. "We've got to hide." He pulled at Felicity.

She waved him back. "We'll be fine. Now, shh." She returned her ear to the door.

Mr. Wyndell pulled at her. "They can't find you here. You'll be compromised." The light from the corridor shone beneath the door.

"Stop that," she hissed. "The door's locked."

Just as she said that, a hand rattled the doorknob. Mr. Wyndell jumped. He yanked Felicity back from the door. He pulled her close and put his hand over her mouth. The shadow of people on the other side of the door blocked the light coming underneath.

"Clarice?"

The doorknob rattled as they tried again. But the door didn't open.

"Not here," said Montagu, rather plaintively. "Where could she be?"

They moved to the next door. The light underneath the door brightened as their shadows passed.

Only then did Mr. Wyndell relax and release Felicity. "How'd you do that?"

She shrugged. "I have a talent for locks." She returned to the door and listened.

"What do you mean, *a talent for locks*?"

She waved away his question. "They're still out there."

Mr. Wyndell resumed his post.

Montagu and his companion had remained out in the hallway. Most of their conversation was audible, if only just.

Felicity dreaded they were speaking about The Agreement, or something related to it. But no. Their topic was safely on Parliament.

"Are they talking politics?" *How odd. Why would His Grace pause to talk politics when he was looking for his fiancée?*

Mr. Wyndell moved away from the door. "They are. They could be there all night."

As her eyes had grown used to the darkness, Felicity saw a small table, a comfortable sofa, and a chair—a sitting room. She flopped down on the couch with no grace or decorum whatsoever. Oh, she was tired! How could people stay up this late every single night?

"I guess we're trapped here?"

Mr. Wyndell chose the chair. "Unless you have a desire to climb out the window."

It was a possibility. But upon further inspection, the window, quite high up, faced toward the front of the house. As she peered outside, she saw guests arriving down below, even at this late hour, to the party. Any attempt to climb out the window would be seen by far too many people.

"I'm sure we can wait it out. Montagu will not wish to stand there all evening."

Mr. Wyndell slumped. "I don't know. If I were in his shoes, I'd much rather avoid the crowds."

"If you were in his shoes, you could come and go as you pleased. Go might be a better option, given the rumors about. Do you think he knows?" She went still, listening, then shook her head. "Still discussing politics. How tedious."

Felicity redirected the subject. "Have you considered a career in politics? I understand it is a most suitable occupation for a gentleman."

"Good grief, no. Can't stand politics."

That pleased her. "Ah, a military man, then?"

"Not that either."

"The glory of war is not for you?" Her heart lifted. The more she thought about it, the more she understood her mother's wisdom about avoiding soldiers.

"Our family branch is not militarily inclined."

Felicity sighed. "Oh dear. You are running out of options."

He sat up. "Options for what?"

"You can't sit around doing nothing for the rest of your life."

"I have something to occupy my hours. I work with clocks."

"You do?"

Mr. Wyndell shifted in his chair. "I've always been fond of clocks. I like their inner workings." Life entered his voice.

She fell silent for a moment. The hum of conversation outside their door continued.

Something went thump against their door, and Felicity jumped. But it was only someone leaning against the door on the other side. What little light there was dimmed, as someone settled outside their door.

Mr. Wyndell had jumped as well, straight out of his chair.

"Sit over here," Felicity whispered.

He joined her on the couch. After they listened for any signs they'd been discovered, they relaxed somewhat.

"So, a clockmaker?" With Mr. Wyndell closer, she could lower her voice and carry on a conversation. "Isn't that, well, trade?"

She felt him stiffen. "Not so much a clockmaker, but a clock designer. I am redesigning their inner workings to improve accuracy."

Clocks were never accurate, in Felicity's experience. Her mother's mantel clock had to be adjusted back ten minutes every night at six to maintain an approximate accuracy. The Abbots had been caught out a few times when someone had forgotten to reset the clock.

Likewise, the grandfather clock in the entryway had to be adjusted once a week, when it was wound. Imagine a clock that didn't need adjusting, only needed winding.

"Have you ever designed a clock that never needed winding?"

He shifted on the couch. It was hard to see his expression in the dimness of the room. "That's impossible, I'm afraid. A few men came up with ideas for self-winding pocket watches, though."

"So why not the same principle of clocks?"

"Because the watches wound themselves due to an internal weight. They needed movement, such as being carried around, to work. A clock only sits there."

The political conversation continued outside their door. Why were they still out there, instead of looking for Miss Chester?

Felicity shifted again. If only he were facing the window, she could see his expression better. "If you could make a self-winding clock, you could make your fortune."

He elicited a small chuckle. "I will make my fortune, such as it is, with accurate clocks. Too few of those about. See, it's all about mathematics." The life had returned to his voice. "If you can get the dimensions of the cogs just right and balance it against the correct tension of the springs—for a wind-up clock—or the right balance in the weights for a grandfather clock, you get a timepiece of the most elegant accuracy."

A man of independent means. That didn't sound so bad. He didn't sound terribly flush at the present, though. Would that be an issue, she wondered?

She reached out and found his hand by what little light there was. He did not pull away, but held it.

"Do you plan on making a decent living through clocks?"

"I would love to." A wry tone entered his voice. "But my mother disagrees with my chosen hobby."

"Too close to trade?"

"My mother would have me choose another profession."

"Politics or the military, I assume."

"Actually, she suggested a career in the church."

"What?" she exclaimed, louder than she meant to. She clapped a hand over her mouth.

Immediately, they hushed and listened.

The conversation outside the door also hushed.

"What was that?" someone outside asked. And then nothing more was said.

Time passed while both sides listened for something else.

Then, on the other side of the door, someone said, "Ah, well. It must have been nothing."

Felicity frowned. Montagu had said it a little louder than necessary. Did he know someone was in here? Did he know who?

"Of course," replied his companion.

Their footfalls as they retreated were far too obvious.

They weren't fooling anyone, much less Felicity. "He knows we're in here," she whispered to Mr. Wyndell.

"So we're trapped, for the nonce." He settled back,

his voice still low. "I don't think that's a bad thing. We can avoid the crush." He still held her hand.

Felicity scooted closer, to keep their conversation to a low murmur. "What about finding The Agreement?"

She was close enough to feel Mr. Wyndell's shrug. "I guess my mother is on her own for a while."

Their conversation died while they listened. Felicity watched the light under the door. Sure enough, Montagu and his companion sneaked back. Their presence was betrayed by their shadows in the light.

She whispered in his ear. "What are they doing?"

"Waiting for us to come out."

"You and me?"

"Or someone."

So they played the Waiting Game. They sat as silent as church mice on this side of the door while Montagu and his companion waited as quiet as snakes on the other side. Eventually, the shadows left. No announcements, no heavy footsteps, only a departure of the shadow underneath. They waited with beating hearts and bated breath until they were sure they were alone.

Felicity let hers out with a great sigh. "That's a relief." She moved off the couch and padded to the door.

Mr. Wyndell made no move. "I am content to remain here a while longer."

"What?" Felicity returned to the couch. "Perhaps a career in the church *is* for you."

"No."

She plunked back on the couch in a most unladylike manner and bounced somewhat. "You are running out of options for a suitable gentlemanly career."

He crossed his ankles. "I can't imagine myself caring for a flock."

She leaned close. "I don't think it's that at all."

He sat up straighter. "Oh?"

"I think the root is a lot more personal. You, dear Mr. Wyndell, are far too enamored of sin."

"What?"

"You are." She settled back on the couch and crossed her ankles. "You, most proper Mr. Wyndell, would have no objection to being a churchman if you did not have a secret little place in your heart for sin."

He stiffened and turned from her. "That is not the sort of thing a young lady should be discussing."

"See? There you go. Had you a holy destiny, you would have jumped at the chance to sermonize on the evils of sin. Any particular kind of sin? Drink? Duels? Taking the Lord's Name in vain? Many a gentleman is fond of that one. Gambling?"

"Gambling?" he echoed. It was more a thought than a confession.

But Felicity shook her head. "Not gambling, or you would have started your night at the gaming tables, The Agreement notwithstanding. Also, you would have agreed to shilling points with Lord Mayfair."

He said nothing.

"The reason you are so straitlaced is because you are hiding your sin."

He shook himself free of his reverie. "I don't see myself as a sinful sort of fellow."

"So take up a career in the church."

He hesitated.

"Hmm. Pricked by a guilty conscience?"

"Not particularly, no."

Felicity exhaled sharply. What did it take to provoke him to some sort of reaction? Something she had once read in a novel came to her.

"There is one ultimate test that would prove beyond a shadow of a doubt, whether or not you belong in the church." She stood up.

"Is there?" Wariness tinged his voice. "I am not aware of such a test."

"Oh yes, you are. Everyone knows this one."

"Enlighten me."

She stood before him. "First, you need to put your hands before you."

He held his hands straight out. "Like this?"

She widened his arms. "Out more like this. Palms up."

He let her move his hands. "Now what?"

"Now close your eyes and listen to your heartbeat."

She did not know if he closed his eyes in the darkness. He did take a deep breath, then another.

"What's your heartbeat like?"

"Slow and steady."

"Good. Remember that. We'll need it later."

He let out a breath. "Now what?"

"Step two." Felicity hiked up her skirts in a most unladylike fashion and straddled Mr. Wyndell's lap.

So surprised was he, his hands went immediately to her arms. "Miss Abbot!"

"Sssh," she admonished before thoroughly kissing him.

She kissed him like the kisses in her novels, deep, soft, and lips slightly parted. She tangled her hands in his hair and made sure his head remained close.

His hands tightened on her arms, but instead of

pushing her away, they drew her closer. Mr. Wyndell most definitely returned her kiss.

He broke their connection to gasp for air.

Felicity laid two fingers alongside his neck. "Now feel your heart."

It thumped hard.

"This is why you are imminently unsuitable to the church."

His hands, still about her arms, shook her a little. "That was not fair." He did not dismiss her from his lap.

"Well, if I had sat around here waiting for you to kiss me, we could have been here all night."

A low, familiar sound tickled at the back of her head. "Wait." She held up a finger. "Was that a—"

The door, previously locked, flew open. Light flooded the little sitting room. Mr. Wyndell and Felicity squinted.

"Ah ha!" Montagu's companion, armed with a lamp, sprang in through the door.

Behind him, in the hallway, stood Montagu and a rather surprised footman.

Mr. Wyndell leapt to his feet, forgetting about Felicity in his lap.

As she tumbled, she grabbed on to him. This unbalanced them both, and they crashed to the floor, Mr. Wyndell most inappropriately on top of her.

"Clarice!" Montagu's voice made the windows rattle. His voice rose in pitch at the end until it squeaked. "It's true?" Pain tinged his words.

Mr. Wyndell pushed himself to standing, the familiar expression of annoyance creasing his brow. Felicity squinted against the sudden bright light.

"Wyndell," bellowed Montagu. "Of all people…"

Montagu's companion guffawed. Even a dark glare from Montagu didn't dampen his mirth.

Felicity, suddenly free of her masculine burden, raised herself to sitting. "My goodness!" Then she frowned up at Montagu. "Have you no respect for a locked door?"

How did they get it open? Out in the corridor, the footman surreptitiously tucked away a key and slunk off. She did not blame him for not wanting to get involved in the games of the Quality, especially those of Montagu.

Montagu looked down at her in surprise. "Wait. You're not Clarice." All the tension that had wound up like a spring dissipated. He sagged in contrition. "I am so sorry." He held out his hand.

"I dare say so."

"Miss Abbot, I beg your pardon."

Mr. Wyndell made a show of dusting himself off and straightening his clothing. She hadn't mussed it all that much.

Montagu's companion never lost his good humor. "Well, Wyndell. I never thought you had it in you."

"Shut up, Forsythe," Mr. Wyndell muttered.

Forsythe leaned over to peer at Felicity. "I say. Who's this delightful piece of muslin?"

Felicity squeaked at such a description. She was very much *not* a piece of muslin. Delightful was the only description she would accept.

Montagu rumbled, "Manners, lad." He tendered a bow to Felicity. "Again, my apologies. I mistook you for someone else."

Forsythe lifted his lamp higher. "I don't believe we

are acquainted."

Felicity looked him up and down. He wasn't nearly so handsome as Mr. Wyndell or Montagu. Also, his slight unsteadiness didn't add to his appeal. "I do believe we're not."

Montagu mistook that for a cue. "Ah, Lord Forsythe, may I present Miss Felicity Abbot, Wyndell's soon-to-be betrothed."

Mr. Wyndell stiffened. "We are not."

Felicity gave her curtsey to Lord Forsythe. "Only because you haven't asked yet."

Mr. Wyndell spluttered. "Stop saying that."

Forsythe let out another burst of amusement. "Are you to be shackled, Wyndell? My most sincerest congratulations."

Felicity wondered if he wasn't more than a trifle foxed.

Mr. Wyndell was not amused. "I am no such thing." He turned to her. "Stop saying that."

She ignored him and addressed Montagu. "What I want to know is why you thought I was Miss Chester?"

Now that was the question. They looked nothing alike, as far as Felicity was concerned. Sure, Clarice was fair-haired as well, but not as spectacularly. For another, Felicity was naturally curly. Miss Chester was tonged or ragged.

"I've heard some unsettling rumors. I hope they are not true."

Something didn't sit right. She pressed the issue.

"Do you have a reason to suspect your betrothed of something?"

Montagu folded his arms. "I don't like where this conversation is going."

Felicity planted her fists on her hips. "You brought it up and for good reason."

"What good reason is that?" he countered.

"I don't know. You won't tell me."

Montagu hesitated. He looked to Forsythe. His companion shrugged, ignorant of Montagu's reasoning.

"Nothing," he finally answered her. "Unsubstantial gossip. I needed to find Clarice."

At that, Felicity tapped a finger along her jaw. "There has been far too much of that lately. I don't know why everyone bothers listening, when it's clear that most of it is quite incorrect."

Mr. Wyndell had put his hand to his forehead. "If you're all quite finished—"

"Not as finished as you looked to be," Forsythe quipped.

"Shut up," Mr. Wyndell told him.

A stern look from Montagu drained Forsythe's shallow wit. He backed out of the room. "I'll, uh, go look somewhere else."

"Do," Montagu replied.

As Forsythe had taken the lamp, the room darkened. The three moved out into the corridor where other lamps illuminated the area.

Once they were alone, he turned to Mr. Wyndell and Felicity. He folded his arms like he meant business. "What do you know about Miss Chester? What is she involved in?"

Mr. Wyndell and Felicity looked to each other.

"Do we know anything of Miss Chester?" she asked Mr. Wyndell.

If he was as clever as he had appeared, he would pick up on her act of innocence and play along. She certainly wouldn't repeat the awful rumors Miss Bitner dished out to Mrs. Cupitt. Such things were never repeatable by someone respectable.

Montagu loomed over her. "What do you know?"

If he was trying to intimidate her, he did a pretty good job. Felicity's heart thumped. If she let him see her frightened, she would quickly lose control of the situation. There had been plenty of that tonight already.

"Until you accused me of being Miss Chester, we had no idea she was involved in anything."

He sighed. "Tonight I have…" He shook his head. "Quite a few rumors have been circulating the party. Very strong rumors. Have you heard anything?"

Felicity confessed. "We might have heard something about it, maybe. If we have, we dismissed it quickly." She prayed he accepted that.

Montagu folded his arms. "What, exactly, is *it*?"

"We don't know," Felicity confessed as Mr. Wyndell said, "The Whole Situation."

Montagu sighed. "That doesn't help any."

Felicity turned on the full force of her smile for Montagu's benefit. "So now you know as much as we do."

"I don't know anything! I'm losing my patience."

As Felicity took a breath, Mr. Wyndell put a hand on her shoulder. "Enough. You're confusing me, and I'm not easily confused." With that hand, he moved her out of the way so he could speak directly with Montagu. "Your Grace, there are a few rumors gadding about that might ruin a few reputations."

"I've heard." Icicles hung from his voice. "I'm not impressed."

Felicity stepped forward. "Do you know who's

been spreading these rumors? Perhaps it's time to have a word with them, ask them to stop."

Mr. Wyndell frowned. "You can't stop rumor. Once it gets out, that's it."

"But you can discredit the source. Find out who's saying such things, embarrass them openly, and not only do they shrink back, but the power of their words also shrinks back. People pay attention to the words being said, but often forget who's saying them—" Or why, she was about to say when Mr. Wyndell interrupted her.

"That doesn't do you any good if you're hearing the rumor secondhand. By then, it has a life of its own."

Montagu put up his hand. "The fact is, the rumors are alive and well. What I want to know is where did you hear them?"

"We haven't heard anything specific—" Mr. Wyndell started.

"Miss Bitner," Felicity said at the same time.

Montagu drew a sharp breath. "Nora Bitner? You know her?"

Mr. Wyndell's face screwed up. "Unfortunately."

Felicity added, "I have not had the displeasure of her acquaintance, though I have had the misery of her nearby company."

"So you don't know her?" said Montagu. "Lucky you." He turned to Mr. Wyndell. "But she had spoken to you?"

"More like at me. I was in her company under protest."

Oh? When was this? Must have been early on. Mr. Wyndell must have gotten stuck in their company before she and he met. There was that pair of unpleasant ladies who commandeered him in the corridor. Was that after he'd made his initial break for freedom? If only she'd known him better, she would have aided him in evading his second capture, instead of making good her own escape.

Mr. Wyndell shared what he had heard. "They question the speed and timing of your engagement, sir."

"The... speed?" He blinked a few times.

"They say you got engaged rather suddenly, if you get my meaning."

Montagu folded his arms. "I most certainly do not get your meaning. It took me months to convince her I was sincere in my affections."

"I hardly call that speedy," Felicity opined.

"I am only repeating what I have heard," Mr. Wyndell said.

"And is there a bad time to get engaged?"

Felicity looked away. The very evening one met might be considered a bad time for an engagement. She prayed Mr. Wyndell didn't give her a stern glance, nor Montagu ask them about the timing of theirs. Not that they were engaged or anything. They'd merely spoken of the possibility. And got caught.

"What else did she say?" Montagu demanded.

Victor held up his hands. "Only to question the suitability of your future bride."

Montagu weighed this. His countenance lightened. Upon further thought, his attitude changed considerably. "I believe you have found the source of the rumors."

"What?" Felicity interjected. "Miss Bitner?"

"Miss Bitner indeed," replied Montagu. "Last year she fancied herself in love with me and made a downright nuisance of herself. In the end I had to set her straight most directly. I think it offended her." To Mr. Wyndell he said, "Remember the time when she locked me in the closet?"

Mr. Wyndell nodded. "I had to escape Miss Parnell and find the key before anyone else did."

"Two hours I was in there, fighting her off."

"It's amazing your reputation survived at all," Felicity quipped. If she'd been out that Season, she could have freed His Grace much sooner.

"If she is the source of the rumors, then they are most assuredly false," said Mr. Wyndell.

Felicity nodded. "Bitter grapes."

His Grace frowned. "Must you have something to say about everything?"

"It's not like I don't know anything."

"Hush and let the men talk."

Oh, if that didn't take the cake! Felicity shoved her way back between the two. "If you think you know so much"—and she fixed her glare on both Mr. Wyndell and Montagu—"then where is Miss Chester?"

Mr. Wyndell rolled his eyes. "Why does it matter where Miss Chester is?"

His Grace's voice was low and dangerous. "I care very much where Miss Chester is."

Felicity gestured to Montagu. "Thank you. Where Miss Chester is, is far more important than you realize." That was worth feeling smug about.

That also brought Montagu's attention fully on her. "So you do know where she is?"

That little cold spider twined its legs through her heart.

"Not yet." How to turn this around? What was missing? "I assume you know where she is not?"

The ducal patience slipped once more. "The drawing rooms, the card rooms." He glared at her. "This room."

"What. That's it? That's all you've looked?"

Montagu's hands looked to reach up and strangle her. "Where else is there?"

Really. Were all men this obtuse? "What about the ladies' withdrawing room?"

Both men blinked at her. "Where?"

Honestly! "What if she had to, you know…powder her nose?" Even this was a subject a little too delicate for her.

Mr. Wyndell rolled his eyes. Montagu folded his arms tightly. "It doesn't take a half hour to powder one's nose."

"She's been gone that long?"

"At least."

What else? "What if her hem tore? It happens quite regularly." Felicity had had more than one hem torn at church when someone had stepped a little too close to the flounce of her good Sunday dress. Accidents happened. When they did, a lady had to withdraw and get the hem stitched up. Otherwise, it would drag or get caught on something, making the tear worse.

Montagu thought about this. Mr. Wyndell didn't. He shook his head in exasperation. "I doubt that's what happened."

Felicity put her fists on her hips. "Until you can prove otherwise, I'm willing to lay wagers that's exactly what happened." The more she thought about it, the surer she was that that was the case. Felicity had a nodding acquaintance with Clarice Chester, being neighbors and all. She seemed sweet and kind and ever-so-delightful. Surely she would not be one to get caught up in a scandal, especially one involving cheating or blackmail.

As she studied Montagu in the wan light, the idea that he was being blackmailed receded. Here he was, looking for his betrothed. If he was being blackmailed into a marriage not of his choosing, why would he be seeking her out with such great concern?

"While I may have realized the falseness of the rumors, she might not." He put a hand to his forehead. "If tonight's rumors have reached her, they will break her heart." He fixed them with a firm look. "You have it straight from me. I offered for Miss Chester because I love her and want to spend the rest of my life with her. No other coercion is involved."

That eliminated Miss Chester as the subject of The Agreement. A relief to be sure. That still begged the question over its true subject.

Didn't Mr. Wyndell say her mother was involved? She would never have pegged her own mother, very proper that she was, to allow herself to be tangled in scandal.

Doubt crept into her heart. Until now, she hadn't questioned much of anything. Her life pretty much went as expected. Even when Timothy had died and her social life died with him, there was still expectations fulfilled. The Abbots retired, mourned, grew bored, and got on with their lives. Well, a fair bit poorer; good funerals cost far too much. Her parents had gone completely overboard in expressing their funereal grief for their firstborn son and heir.

Felicity pulled herself together. If Montagu and Mr. Wyndell had any inkling of the doubts plaguing her, they would never listen to her again, even when she was sure. Especially if she was sure.

Something nefarious was going on here. She would untangle this surfeit of gossip and find the truth. Now she had to do something that required a bit more courage.

"I am going to go back to that wretched party, and I will find Miss Chester for you." She stole a glance at Mr. Wyndell.

Mr. Wyndell nodded. "Then we will know the truth."

"Well," she amended, "we'll know *her* truth."

"That's all that matters to me," said Montagu.

A balloon of hope rose in her heart. "Do you love her?"

"Very much." The honesty in his voice supported this.

Felicity held her tongue. Miss Chester might not be involved in The Whole Situation, but Lady Chester most likely was. Would Montagu sing the same tune if she were?

Before her common sense could talk her out of it, Felicity headed down the corridor, alone. It had to be her to find Miss Chester. Only she could go to places Montagu and Mr. Wyndell could not.

That also meant she had to confront the party alone. Her last solo encounter made her feel naked. If Lady Middlestone spied her again, it could mean the end not only of her time at the party, but socially for the rest of the Season.

Imagine. One's life over before it had begun.

After descending the steps, she moved quickly through the crowded gaming room to the safest and most dangerous room in the house—the ladies' withdrawing room.

Chapter 9
Love Letters

The ladies' withdrawing room was the one place a gentleman would never go. At this party it was a small salon off the larger gaming room. Lady Mayfair had retreated here earlier. Several maids—ladies' maids from the look of their livery—paid attendance on several females. One older lady was having a split seam stitched while she was still in the gown. A young lady had had her foot trodden on quite terribly. She sat in a corner, dabbing at her eyes while her mother held up a shawl to hide the foot presumably soaking in a cold bath. Yet more ladies gathered before a few mirrors to have their hair set to rights.

A screen secluded one corner of the room. This, Felicity assumed, was where the close stool resided. A few older ladies stood nearby, possibly waiting their turn.

In a corner near the close stool was a familiar form with impeccable blonde hair. Felicity had guessed correctly; here was Miss Chester, hiding out. She fretted in the corner as if waiting for something. Why was she not out in the party? Felicity took two steps toward her when the door opened.

She jumped. She didn't mean to. Was she so nervous about being discovered? As she looked over her shoulder, she saw one of the marchioness's crowd enter. Felicity hung her head and sidled away, hoping not to be noticed.

The lady ignored Felicity and went straight to Miss Chester in the corner. Miss Chester perked up at her approach. The lady withdrew a bundle from her reticule.

"Here," she murmured, softly, but not so quiet Felicity could not overhear. "These will help. Threaten her with these, and then she will back off."

Now here was a new twist.

Miss Chester accepted the letters with a reluctant hand. "I don't know."

The lady looked about her. Felicity stooped in pretence of checking her shoe. One must not get caught eavesdropping. An older lady exited the close stool. It seemed she was the one upon which the other waited, because all the older ladies departed the room together.

"We've come too far," the lady said. "You know we must do something."

As the close stool freed up, Felicity took advantage of the vacancy. Felicity dared not breathe, in part because the preceding lady had not left a pleasant scent.

"I don't know about this," Miss Chester said.

"My dear Miss Chester, you are going to marry a duke. I'm afraid your days of hiding on the edge of Society are gone."

Miss Chester whimpered. "Why are you doing this?"

The question must have surprised the lady, for she did not answer right away.

Felicity got her second fright in as many minutes. A young creature not of her acquaintance dashed into the close stool, bumping into Felicity.

174

"Oh my goodness!" The girl blushed and fled.

The poor thing looked like she really needed to go. And here was Felicity taking up the only safe spot. She slunk out, hoping to tell the young lady it was free, but she was gone.

Felicity took her time fussing with her skirts so she could remain near Miss Chester's conversation. She got her answer. The lady wilted.

"I do this because I like you. You always treat me kindly. I would rather be friends with you than loyal to her. Not after what she did…"

Didn't hurt that Miss Chester would be a future duchess, assuming His Grace didn't throw her over for rumors. No, he wouldn't do that. When he'd spoken of her earlier, his eyes were too full of love.

The lady gripped Miss Chester's hands. "So few of us have enough standing to do something about this. But you will. And I would also see you safe too." Miss Chester's companion slunk off, having completed her traitorous task.

Miss Chester was involved in a scandal after all. That did not seem like her. She stared at the bundle in her hands, then slumped down.

Felicity approached gently, for a lady does not shout across a room, especially for so delicate a matter. She laid a hand on the gently sloping shoulder. "Miss Chester?"

Miss Chester jumped. She fumbled the beribboned bundle in her hands. "Oh, you startled me." She looked closer. "Wait. Do I know you? I do."

"His Grace has been looking for you."

Miss Chester ignored that. "Why, you're Miss Abbot, from next door."

Felicity shifted her feet. "Yes. The Duke of—"

"I thought you weren't out yet." Miss Chester turned her back to the room. She clutched her beribboned bundle; Felicity looked closer. There were letters in Miss Chester's hands. Miss Chester seemed to have forgotten them.

"Why are you here, if you are not out yet?"

Felicity's patience frayed on the edges. "I got sick of missing all the fun and thought I'd creep in and see what I was missing. Not terribly impressed."

Miss Chester nodded. "It's not a good party, I must admit. I don't know what my mother was thinking when she organized it. Usually, they are more fun with fewer people. And more cards." She looked up. "Still, you shouldn't be here. What will your reputation be if you are discovered?"

Felicity waved this concern away. "Nobody's noticed me."

But Miss Chester shook her head. "Everyone notices everything. Then they gossip about it." She clutched the letters even tighter. "Tonight everyone's been saying the most terrible things."

Had Felicity come across the reason for Miss Chester's disappearance? "Have you heard something?"

"About?"

"Me." *Wait. No. That was not the question to ask.* Of course she heard nothing about Felicity. However, she had heard something about herself. "Did someone say something to your face? About you?"

Her shoulders twitched in the barest of shrugs. "It's only gossip. Nobody believes gossip." Her eyes shone with emerging tears.

A few things made more sense. "Except when they

176

do. What have you heard?"

Miss Chester shook her head hard enough to shake loose a pin. It clattered to the floor. She turned her face away from Felicity.

"Nothing of interest."

Felicity put her hands on her hips. "Now, that's not true, or you wouldn't be hiding in here."

Only then did Miss Chester turn around. She hugged the letters tightly to her chest. "Oh, that's not why I'm here. I..." She looked down at the letters. "I was helping a friend." To herself, she muttered, "Oh dear."

Or rather, a friend was helping her. Felicity studied the bundle of letters. "What are those?"

"Very important," she murmured.

"Important enough to keep with you?"

At this, Miss Chester's eyes widened. "Oh, they're not mine. Really, they're not. I don't know why I have them." She gave a nervous little laugh.

"So go put them away in your room and go find His Grace."

But that only made Miss Chester cling to the letters. "Oh, I can't do that. That's far too risky."

At this, Felicity had to agree. After all, wasn't it less than half an hour ago that she herself trawled through Miss Chester's frilly unmentionables?

"Are you going to stay here all night?"

Miss Chester shook her head. "Too dangerous." She wilted once more. "I'm a fool. What am I doing with these?"

"Burn them."

"Oh, no! You can't burn these until the spell has been removed."

Spell? What spell? Felicity peered at the letters. They could have had a vague magic about them, but she was terrible at seeing that sort of thing for herself. Still, magical letters were a whole 'nother world of scandal. Time to come out bolt.

"Are you involved in The Whole Situation?"

This brought a blank look from Miss Chester. "What situation?"

"Do you know anything about The Agreement?"

The look of bafflement on Miss Chester's face gave her the answer.

Either Miss Chester was being rather obtuse, which was possible, or she was doing her best not to speak of The Agreement. Felicity abandoned that particular line of questioning. She wouldn't be getting any useful answers any time soon.

So she changed the subject. "Your betrothed has been looking for you."

Miss Chester's eyes darted from side to side. "He has?"

She nodded. "He's worried. You've been gone for quite some time."

Now Miss Chester's focus turned inward. "I have? I confess I've been a bit distracted." She looked to the letters in her hands. "Oh dear. These stupid things."

"You'd better go to him. He'll watch out for you."

"What do I do?"

What kind of question was that? "Uh, you walk out the door and into his arms?"

Miss Chester straightened up. "Is he outside?"

Felicity wanted to shake Miss Chester. Why was she being so airheaded? "Somewhere in the games room, I believe."

Miss Chester looked to the letters, then to the door, then back to the letters. "Here." She thrust the letters into Felicity's hands. "Keep these safe and don't give them to anyone. And don't let them be destroyed, either. I'll figure out what to do with them later."

Felicity could only stare at the bundle. "What are they?"

The door opened, and several brightly dressed ladies entered the withdrawing room. Miss Chester stiffened.

"Important letters. That's all you need to know. Keep them safe." Miss Chester's gaze fell upon something over Felicity's shoulder. Apprehension darkened her eyes. "I've got to go." She laid a hand over Felicity's, as if blessing the letters given into her keeping.

"Wait. If you want to keep them safe, why don't you put them in your room?"

Miss Chester did not answer. She raised her fan to cover her face and scooted out of the withdrawing room without a further word.

Felicity could only stare at the closing door. That was a rather hasty departure by Miss Chester. She had dashed off, a spooked horse in a panic.

Felicity tucked the letters into the folds of her skirts. Curse these evening gowns, not having any pockets. It didn't help that she had no reticule either. Would it be terribly gauche if she "borrowed" one from upstairs? Even a large handkerchief would do.

If she were upstairs, she could simply hide them away. Miss Chester did not want to be caught with these letters on her person. What had happened that spooked Miss Chester so?

On the other hand, had someone entered to whom Miss Chester did not wish to speak? There were the several young ladies waiting for the close stool. Only now did Felicity think it odd that there was only the one to service a party of this size. Maybe there was another withdrawing room? The young ladies had gravitated to the mirror to check hair and *décolletages*.

She knew none of them by face. Also, they all seemed occupied with matters of their own. None of them looked to be seeking letters.

Felicity scanned the random ladies. Nobody looked suspicious. Older ladies still waited for the necessary. Another lady poked at her hair in the mirror while another powdered her nose. The injured lass was still injured, but the lady with the torn gown had departed.

One young lady had a maid attending to her shoe. Probably another casualty of the crush. While the maid fussed at her foot, the young lady looked about the withdrawing room, bored. Her gaze alighted on Felicity. Just as quickly she looked away.

Felicity recognized her as one of the hangers-on of Her Honor the marchioness.

Goodness, snubbed twice in the same night by Miss Too-Big Britches and her toads.

Ah well. Didn't hurt so much the second time, possibly because everyone else in the room was too absorbed by their own business to notice.

If only Miss Chester had given her more clues. For instance, why did the letters make her nervous? Why did they need to be kept safe? Whose were they?

Or rather…Miss Chester did not wish to be discovered with these letters. Did that mean someone would be very angry to find them? Who would that be?

Now this was Society scandal at its finest!

Felicity left the withdrawing room, the letters tucked clandestinely in her skirts.

In contrast to the quieter withdrawing room, the games room was a riot of noise.

Now, where was Mr. Wyndell? He would know what to do. Had Miss Chester found His Grace? And what to do about these letters?

A quick scan of the room gave no answers to her questions, nor did a stair-top survey of the hallway. Resigned, Felicity made her way downstairs to the drawing rooms. Where was he? *Ah well. He'd show up again.*

The more important question was, what about these letters? Miss Chester had thrust this responsibility into Felicity's hands, neglecting to ask her permission.

As the drawing room was too noisy and the chaise had been taken over by a billing and cooing couple, Felicity retreated to the only quiet place she could think of: the servants' corridor by the green baize door.

Felicity rounded the corner from garish brightness into still darkness, expecting it to be deserted. Miss Smith was still there. Felicity approached her new friend.

"My goodness! You're still here?"

Indeed she was. Miss Smith had a piece of dry madiera cake with no plate in her gloveless hands. They were getting well acquainted, this cake and her. "I like it here." She took another bite.

Felicity could only watch her chew. It must have been an hour or two. Any other person would have drifted off by now, or at the very least, being sick of the party, gone home.

"But a whole hour?"

Miss Smith swallowed her cake. "Nobody bothers me. Enough people pass by so I don't get lonely. The servants are good. They give me food if I ask, and they don't frown at me like the servants at home. My mother thinks I eat too much."

Felicity regarded Miss Smith's soft, round figure and moony face. Maybe her mother had the right of it. She looked at the letters in her hands.

"Say, Miss Smith, have you heard any rumors regarding letters?"

Miss Smith paused to swallow before giving the question some thought. "No." She polished off the last of the cake in two bites.

Too bad. Felicity wasn't about to go out and start asking either. She turned the packet over in her hands. The ribbon was a dusky pink, tied in a bow. How easy would it be to loosen it? Extremely easy. She teased out the first letter.

"Hold these." She handed the bundle to Miss Smith.

She unfolded the letter. There had been no name on the front. Inside, the salutation began, "My Darling." That was no help.

I count the hours until I see you again. The paper was plain, the hand gentle and feminine. Letters to His Grace from Miss Chester? Or someone else?

She read through the letter, her lips twitching as she figured out a case of loopy, over ornate handwriting. Surely Miss Chester would not be so frivolous. *I wish I knew when you could get away next. No doubt she has you on a short leash.*

She? She who? There wasn't much to the letter,

other than a yearning for *Darling's* company, and what a pity they were separated. The letter hinted at a third party. It was signed, *Your Deepest Love*.

Felicity fanned herself while she thought. The letter didn't contain any obvious clues. Yet something about it irked her. There some mystery locked in the lines of this letter. In the back of her head something clicked into place. Felicity looked up.

"You know those rumors going around?"

"Which ones?"

"The ones about cheating happening in this house?"

Miss Smith gave her a blank look.

Felicity waved the letter. "It's not cheating at cards. It's cheating in love!"

****

By the time Victor and Montagu reached the gaming room, they found Miss Chester. She nearly passed them by, so low was her head, and shaded by her fan.

"I say," Montagu exclaimed as she brushed by him.

Miss Chester dropped her fan and looked up, her blue eyes huge. Her anguish melted into relief. She threw herself into His Grace's arms.

"I'm so glad I found you. May we leave?"

Montagu put a protective arm about his betrothed. "The drawing rooms?"

She shook her head. "No. Let's leave the party entirely." Desperation tinged her voice. "I can't stand it anymore. Everyone is saying such terrible things about me."

"I know," murmured His Grace. "Lies, of course." He pulled her closer.

Something nagged at Victor. "Where's Miss Abbot?"

Miss Chester's eyes looked sideways, rolling away and not making contact with his. She waved her hand in a vague direction. "Oh, she's over there, I think."

Victor folded his arms. "Did you see her?"

Miss Chester hesitated, then disregarded his question. "We could go to Almack's," she suggested to His Grace.

Montagu, who only had eyes for his future bride, shook his head. "It's not Wednesday. And if it were, they would have closed the doors by now."

"We could go to a play. Or an opera. Or another party. I will even go to church if it is the only place open." She tugged at his arm. "Do let us go. If I hear another terrible word of gossip, I vow I will cry."

He let her guide him out of the gaming room, tucked protectively within his arm. Victor followed. Something wasn't right.

"Where's Miss Abbot?"

Only then did Miss Chester give him some consideration. "She's fine. She's in the withdrawing room."

They departed, leaving him a lone man with few answers.

He approached the withdrawing room. How close could a man get without looking suspicious? A hand descended on his arm, startling him. With guilt, he turned to face his mother.

"Here you are." She looked around, her eyes darting back and forth. "What are you doing in the gaming room?" Her fingers plucked at his sleeve. "We shouldn't be here." She pulled him away.

He stopped, his focus entirely on his mother. "What do you mean?"

"I mean…" She hesitated. "It's just better we are not here."

Victor folded his arms. "Does this have anything to do with The Agreement?"

Her eyes darted away, and she licked her lips. Of course it had something to do with The Agreement, otherwise his mother would have told him. She did like explaining things, except when she was trying to keep a secret. Her silence was answer enough.

Victor gazed up to the withdrawing room door. *Had anyone come out?* "Could you do me a favor? Could you look in the ladies' withdrawing room for me? I was waiting for someone. Blonde debutante in a sprigged muslin dress."

His mother's countenance changed. Her eyebrows raised, a pleased smile tugged at the corner of her lips. "Ah, so you have found someone you fancy?"

He put his hands to his temples. "Just see if she's still in there."

She patted his arm. "I will." She bounced off.

When she returned, she'd left her enthusiasm in the withdrawing room. "I'm sorry. I didn't see anyone in there by that description." She patted his shoulder. "I'm sorry she abandoned you."

But he shook his head. "I don't think that's it. That's not like her."

"Oh, you know her so well already? How long have you known her?"

"I only met her tonight."

His mother sighed. "That's too bad. Well, there's a whole party of bright little things. Go find another one."

"I don't want to find another one."

"There's not much you can do if she's given you the slip. It's not like you can convince her."

Victor gave up on his mother. "Just so you know, I haven't found The Agreement yet."

She clenched her fingers. "Where have you looked?"

"Short of going through Lady Chester's drawer of personal clothing, pretty much everywhere." A thought niggled at him. "Mother, can you tell me something about The Agreement?"

"No."

Honestly... "What I meant, can you tell me what it's not about?"

She hesitated. "I really shouldn't."

"Is it about Miss Chester?"

His mother actually put her hands over her ears. "I will not tell you anything, even what's not in there. I will not have you figuring it out." She leaned closer and, with her hands still on her ears, whispered, "It is very important we keep it a secret. Don't press me further."

And that was that. She could be mindlessly stubborn if need be.

"Fine. I'll not pry. But do not blame me if I cannot find the blasted thing. I'd much rather be pursuing a young lady."

That she would listen to. "About time you changed your tune. I was beginning to worry about you."

Despite her flightiness, he loved her. Victor kissed his mother on the forehead. "I promise I shall speak to at least three other young ladies tonight." *Did Miss Parnell, Miss Smith, and Miss Pymm count?* "In fact,

I'll go find one now." *Definitely Miss Abbot.*

If he thought to get rid of his mother, he was wrong. As he left the gaming room—after a quick check to see if Miss Abbot was there—his mother followed.

"I met some lovely young debutantes earlier. The Misses Pearl. They were introduced as twins, but I suspect they're not. The elder is rather plain, but the younger's quite a beauty. Though I don't know why they didn't bring the elder out first, so she didn't have to compete with her sister."

Beauty wasn't as important to Victor as it was to his mother. It helped, but a beautiful face with nothing behind it bored him after a few minutes.

"Do they have good conversation?"

His mother hadn't expected that question. "I don't know."

"Find out for me." He hurried her along the corridor to the stairs.

"Why?"

"Because if they don't, I'm not interested."

"Really, Victor. Isn't a pretty face and good breeding enough?"

"No." He thought of Miss Bitner. She could have been lovely, if it wasn't for her soul drenched in poison.

"You really need to get your priorities straight."

He offered his elbow. When she didn't take it, he hooked her hand around his arm anyway and dragged her down the stairs.

"Also, I've already spoken with a Miss Parnell, a Miss Bitner, and a Miss Smith. If you see them, do not consider them. Plus, avoid any of the Marchioness Marque's set."

His mother beamed. "Ah, the marchioness! She's quite a diamond of the first water."

The only water Victor would compare her to was the water found in the bottom of a chamber pot. "And married."

His mother waved that away. "She's drawn quite the coterie of eligible young ladies."

"None of those." Having listened to them earlier in the evening, especially with their poor opinions of Miss Chester, doused even the remotest interest he could have had with any one of them.

As they descended into the hubbub of the crush, his mother had to raise her voice to be heard. "Really, Victor. You ask the impossible."

"I'm merely looking out for my sanity. You might think a pretty young thing will be pleasant enough to stare at across a breakfast table, but I prefer someone who is interesting."

"Anyhow, if she's a proper lady, she'll have her breakfast in bed. Nevertheless, good luck with that."

He knew his mother had great doubts for him. They were not entirely unfounded. He'd not shown sufficient interest in any young lady for the past four years. Not that he would have considered himself old enough to marry at that age. After all, he wasn't exactly a man of wealthy means.

Was Miss Abbot wealthy? She was interesting and interested. He had to give her that. And when she turned on that smile of hers, it could melt even the most hardened of bachelor hearts.

Victor frowned as he thought of Montagu, who'd also melted under that smile during the game. Unfair. He already had a future bride.

Victor rose on his toes to scan the crowd. Where had Miss Abbot gone? How could she have kissed him like that, then disappeared? His lips hungered for hers. His lap warmed at the memory of her presence there.

"Well, Mother, you dragged me here to accomplish two things. Since I have not had any luck finding that dratted agreement of yours, I shall set off to find a lovely young lady instead."

"Wait!" she called at his retreating back. "I need your help!"

He glanced over his shoulder. "You've had my help. Until you can provide a few more clues as to the location of The Agreement, I'm not of much use to you at the present. I'm sure you can agree that finding a suitable wife before our reputations are utterly ruined by this damned agreement is of a higher priority."

She slumped at this. He left her in the middle of the frivolous crowd and set off to find that very compelling young lady who insisted on turning him upside down, throwing the pastor's shackles in his path, and stirring something else deep within him.

His Grace and Miss Chester had made a hasty departure; they were nowhere to be found. Likewise, he couldn't find Miss Smith either.

Miss Parnell and Miss Bitner stood by the refreshments table. Had the marchioness abandoned the party? He scanned the salon, but he couldn't spy her or her hangers-on anywhere. If she'd left, then already the party looked better.

Poor Miss Parnell had wrapped her plump little arms about her form and looked around with pitiful, desperate eyes. Miss Bitner battered her sad form with more vitriolic opinion as she wrinkled her nose at the dry little sandwiches on the table. Victor was far enough away to be spared whatever noxious monologue Miss Parnell suffered.

Should he rescue her? He didn't feel any particular desire to save her from her cousin. On the other hand, she did look pretty miserable. But then, she'd leech on to him, and he'd be stuck once more.

This whole social affair of the Chesters' was miserable. The only bright point had been Miss Abbot. Now she'd gone missing, taking all the sunshine with her.

"I say, Wyndell, are you still here?" Mr. Goodsell pushed his way through the crowd. He might not have much chin, but his elbows worked fine. "I thought you would have departed this dreary little funeral."

Victor clasped hands with his friend. "That would have suited me fine, had I not to account for someone." His mother would never countenance his abandoning her here. After all, he had promised to help her.

And then there was Miss Abbot. If he left now, what would she think of him?

"Ah, yes. I'd heard. Congratulations." Goodsell beamed.

Now that was unexpected. "What for?"

Mr. Goodsell slapped Victor on the back. "On your betrothal. I had no idea, you sly dog. My commiserations."

He groaned. "Who told you this?"

"Speaking earlier with Forsythe." Mr. Goodsell tugged at his cuffs, neatening them in his coat sleeves.

He should have known. "Forsythe has a big mouth, a bottomless cup, and the wrong end of the stick."

"Oh, I certainly hope not." Mr. Goodsell sucked on

his teeth. "Though I do agree with you on the first two points. He also said something about you and the lass in a compromising position?" He leaned over, presumably for more gossip. "So yes, I would prefer to believe the best about you, old chap. I would never have taken you for one to compromise a young lady's reputation. That's normally my job."

And there was the crux of it. Truth be told, he had compromised her reputation by letting her kiss him in that most shocking manner, then allowing them to be caught. He could rely on His Grace for discretion, but Forsythe in his cups had been an entirely different matter.

He found himself in a tight corner. He couldn't lie to his friend. He liked Jacob Goodsell. He enjoyed his company whenever he came to town. But he couldn't tell the truth and betray Miss Abbot, despite the fact that it was she who came on to him. Whatever happened to meek little misses who guarded their reputation closely? If he denied their betrothal, she'd be ruined before she even came out. If he acknowledged it, he'd have been tricked into a corner.

He didn't know what to say. If Miss Abbot was here, what would she say?

It was like the morning sun rose over the hills of his mind. She'd already said it.

"The lady in question herself informed Lord Forsythe of her marital prospects." He spied a blonde head in the distance, but it was not her.

This was good enough for Mr. Goodsell. He slapped Victor on the back once more. "I knew it! I knew you wouldn't have done anything so low-handed."

Victor felt a little sick to his stomach. "I would ask that you keep mum on this for now. There's been no official announcement. I'm sure her parents would appreciate not being pipped at the post."

Goodsell swallowed his enthusiasm. "Of course, old bean. Wouldn't dream of it."

Before they could move the conversation on to more comfortable topics, Mr. Goodsell paled. "Oh no. Marky Marque is here." He ducked down.

Victor rose up to peer over the crowd. Sure enough, the Marquess Marque, future Duke of Allenbury, had made his appearance at the party. "What's he doing here? I thought he'd chosen to stay in the country for the Season."

Mr. Goodsell kept his head well down. "Some say he's here to drag his errant wife back with him. Others say he's here to have it out with her lover."

Victor coughed. "Lover? Surely it's too early in the marriage for that sort of disaffection." They'd only been married a year. The rather young and rather lovely marchioness had yet to bear him an heir. She had no business dallying so soon in a marriage.

Mr. Goodsell spread his arms. "I'm only repeating what the gossips say."

"And we know how reliable gossip isn't." Victor pushed down the thought that he'd once fancied the marchioness before she'd made such a splendid match—for all of five minutes. She had been Lady Amelia Raston, daughter of the Earl of Sotherby, then. He'd spied her during a ball. His mother had pushed him in that direction. He'd stood on the periphery of her galaxy of admirers, hoping for an introduction, until she'd opened her mouth.

She might be a glittering jewel with a large fortune, but that jewel had some very sharp edges. He had once watched her very carefully shoot down a good friend of his, Johnston—in public no less—for failing to have a well-tied cravat.

Johnston's cravat had been perfectly tied. Knowing Johnston, he'd spent hours on it. It had crushed him.

His friend had been born with an unfortunate face. At least he had a good name and a minor fortune to make up for it. Johnston countered his overlarge nose and protruding teeth by sporting the finest of clothes.

Lady Amelia could not have chosen a better barb by which to pierce his heart. Victor had lost any romantic interest that had eked its way into his heart. Johnston withdrew from Society for weeks.

"Still," said Victor, "I am not surprised if it might have a grain of truth in it."

Mr. Goodsell turned them so their backs were to a fierce Marquess Marque. "They say she's been dallying with the Duke of Cambridge."

"Oh, surely not." Prinny's brothers, the royal dukes, were notorious for their indiscretions and regular antics. For highborn men, their reputations could not sink any lower. "When would they have time for an affair? Dolph's mostly out of the country." As a military man, Adolphus, Duke of Cambridge, spent more time defending England than living on her august shores. Hanover was more a home to him than here.

But if the marchioness was setting her sights high, the youngest of George's multitudinous offspring was not her best choice. There were plenty of royal dukes willing to wrinkle her sheets, and more conveniently located geographically. "I doubt she's having an affair with one of them. She'd be a fool to so early on."

Mr. Goodsell considered this. "You're right, old bean." Some bored young bucks jostled them before moving off to disturb someone else. "I say, have you heard about the Bramleys?"

No, he had not. As Mr. Goodsell filled him in on the Bramleys' financial woes, he questioned whether or not he should be listening to gossip. Didn't gossip nearly ruin Montagu's almost-marriage? And then there was this fiasco with The Agreement. Other people's stories didn't fascinate him. It was as if something was missing from their tales. That could have been facts missing or the entire truth. He peered over the heads of the crowd. Where was she?

Yet here he was listening to rumors. His mother listened to rumors. That's how he ended up here in the first place.

"...and not like the Chesters." Mr. Goodsell leaned closer. "But I'm not sure if that's true."

Victor dragged his attention back to his friend. "What about the Chesters?"

"Haven't you heard a word I said?"

Guilty. "Financial woes," he offered and hoped it was correct.

"You wouldn't have thought it of them, not with this magnificent party. Though I would not have expected it."

"What, financial woes?"

"That, and the party. This is an awful expense, considering the failure of the Dalston financial scheme. He had an awful lot of dosh tied up in it. If they're trying to fool us into thinking they're not hurting, they're failing. Should have stuck to card parties."

That made sense. The Chesters were famous for their card parties. No doubt they came away with more in their pockets than they spent. His mother often accepted an invitation when it came her way.

So why this enormous, rather tedious crush? These were hotbeds of gossip and scandal—the last thing Lady Chester, or any lady of good reputation, wanted under her roof.

Again, he scanned the crowd. It seemed Miss Abbot had completely disappeared.

"I say, where is your head?"

Mr. Goodsell had ended, or paused, his story. Victor hadn't been paying enough attention to really notice.

"Forgive me." Victor looked over the crowd once more. "I really do need to find someone."

"The future Mrs. Wyndell?"

How did he know? "Something like that. We have gotten separated. It really is important I locate her."

He happened upon the dark sliver leading to that servants' corridor where they had first met. A familiar form winked in and out of his view. Then she stepped more into the light. Miss Smith. Had she not moved since they'd abandoned her there several hours ago? She did not appear alone, for she nodded her head as if listening. Only one person had the good presence to speak to Miss Smith.

"I do believe I have found my wayward miss."

"Good luck to you." Mr. Goodsell gave his shoulder a friendly pat. "Say, I was thinking of heading out. I hear there's some dreadfully dull musicale at the Rothbury's. Gotta be better than this."

Victor failed to listen to the rest of his friend's

conversation. With a singular mind, he pushed his way through the crowd, which was now smelling quite ripe. He rounded the corner. There he found Miss Smith listening to Miss Abbot. Miss Abbot's voice was raised somewhat, to compensate for the noise of the party. Granted, it was a bit less here, but still, one needed greater volume if one was to be heard.

"I yearn for the day when I embrace your naked flesh to mine," she said to Miss Smith.

Chapter 10
Whose Love Letters?

"My goodness!" Miss Smith clutched her hands to her chest. "How shocking!"

Mr. Wyndell stepped around the corner and froze. "What?"

Felicity nearly dropped the bundle. The moment she saw who it was, her face brightened.

"I knew you'd find me."

Mr. Wyndell could only blink.

"You'll never guess what Miss Chester gave to me." Felicity held up the bundle of letters. "She entrusted them to my care and told me not to give them to anyone. Although, if she doesn't want anyone to have them, why not hide them away in her room or something? Anyhow, they are not hers by her hand, merely in her possession."

"They're scandalous," Miss Smith added.

Mr. Wyndell looked at Miss Smith, with her wide eyes and pale complexion. Her hands still clutched at her chest as if to guard her already well-guarded virtue. He recovered his capacity for speech.

"Why are you reading someone else's scandalous letters?"

"We're trying to figure out whose they are. Also, I understand they're enchanted, though I'm not sure how." Felicity turned the letter over. "Nobody ever uses names. It's worse than the newspapers. They at least offer titles and first initials, so it's easy to figure of whom they're speaking. But no further clues than that, so they can't be sued for slander. Or is it libel? Anyhow, both blatant and subtle. Got to admire them for that."

She shoved this letter to the bottom of the stack and selected another, opening it without hesitation.

"I don't think you should be reading someone else's post, especially if it's enchanted." He folded his arms and glanced over his shoulder.

Was he afraid of being seen?

A servant hurried by with an empty tray in his hands and disappeared behind the green baize door.

"Can it be considered post if it wasn't delivered by the postman?" She checked the front of the letter again, just in case. No names, no appellations, no franking, nothing. Maybe they came in envelopes, and those were destroyed. "I'm not reading all of the letters, just enough to ascertain identity." She scanned the letter. " 'To my darling boy'…whatever. 'Yours always, your deepest love.' And look here." She held the letter up for Mr. Wyndell's benefit. "Is that not a most feminine hand? Do you recognize the writing?"

Sadly, he shook his head. "Still, you should not be reading them."

She sorted through the rest. "About twenty or so." She tapped one of the unopened letters against her jaw line. "I guess the question to ask is, what are they doing here at the party?"

Miss Smith blinked. "Uh, why are they here at the party?"

Felicity looked at the unfolded letter in her hand. It

was a fine paper, thick and smooth. "They're here because someone needs them." She turned the letter over. "Why?"

Mr. Wyndell made a grab for them. Felicity jerked them back from his grasp.

"Now, now. Miss Chester told me not to give them to anyone."

His hand stilled in mid-air. "They're Miss Chester's?" His voice was thin.

Two more servants burst through the green baize door, their trays full of small sandwiches. They hurried on their way to the drawing room. Miss Smith's gaze followed them. She sighed wistfully.

"You said they were a feminine hand. Did she write them to someone?" asked Mr. Wyndell.

"Who? Miss Chester isn't dallying with another man."

Oh, that would not be good at all. Felicity lost all interest in the contents of the letters. Their weight pressed heavily on her heart.

"But it makes sense. She had a dalliance. Now, engaged to the Duke of Montagu, she broke it off with this other man, and he's returning her letters."

"No wonder she looked so unhappy." Miss Smith sighed.

Was her sigh for Miss Chester, or the sandwiches that had made their escape unscathed?

Felicity studied the letter. She sniffed it. Then she shook it next to her ear, as if it could make a noise. "No. Someone entrusted them to her. They're not hers at all." That made sense. Otherwise, the lady who had given them to Miss Chester in the withdrawing room would not have said what she said. "They are not by

Miss Chester, but rather for her use. 'I would rather be your friend than loyal to her.' That's what the lady who gave these to her said."

Mr. Wyndell shook his head as if trying to knock his brains loose. "What lady?"

"I don't know her name. However, she does support Miss Chester." What else had she said? Felicity tapped the letters against her forehead. "These were given to Miss Chester to…threaten someone, I think."

Miss Smith blinked. "But who?"

"What lady?" repeated Mr. Wyndell.

Felicity briefly explained how she had found Miss Chester in the middle of a conversation with someone else. "I wonder if these were what Miss Bitner meant when she had to find The Agreement."

But Mr. Wyndell shook his head. "The Agreement is a single sheet of paper signed by several parties."

Miss Smith, still peering after the departed servants, said, "I wonder if they'll bring more sandwiches about?"

Felicity tapped the letters against her hand. "So how are these letters connected to The Agreement?"

"Are they?"

Felicity gave this some thought. "My heart says no. How disappointing."

Mr. Wyndell blinked at her. "I thought you might be relieved."

"But we are no closer to finding out anything about The Agreement."

He folded his arms. "True, but I think we can safely dismiss these as relevant to our issue."

She sighed and extracted one of the letters she had not yet read. "I suppose so."

He held out his hand. "May I?"

Felicity handed one over. Mr. Wyndell opened it. His lips twitched slightly as he read it to himself.

"Interesting," he said at the conclusion. "These are someone's life, and a significant part. Another someone procured these, possibly with the intent of mischief."

Didn't she just finish saying that? "Or blackmail," Felicity replied as Mr. Wyndell tucked the letter back in its cream-colored envelope.

He ran his fingers over the blank front.

"Oh," cried Miss Smith as a servant emerged from the green baize door, with a tray full of little cakes.

She snatched two of them, spooking the servant. He jerked the tray away from her, sending half its contents crashing to the floor. He cursed in words one should never say in front of a lady. Felicity and Mr. Wyndell jumped, Felicity nearly dropping the letters.

"Oh, no," muttered Miss Smith as she bent to help the servant pick them up. "Terribly sorry."

She piled the cakes back on the tray with no rhyme or reason. In fact, she was so intent on picking up the cakes she shoved the servant out of her way. When that was done, Miss Smith stood up, the tray in her hands and a satisfied look on her face.

"See," she mumbled, "I can be useful."

"Please, ma'am, may I have the tray?"

The servant tried to take it away from her. Miss Smith wrestled him for the tray, but in the end, he won. With a sad shake of his head and a very disapproving look for Miss Smith, he returned to the green baize door, for the tray was no longer fit to be taken out.

"Oh, drat." She pouted, leaning against the wall. "I so wanted a cake."

Mr. Wyndell placed a hand on her shoulder. "So why don't you go out and get one from the table?"

She looked up at him with her moony eyes. "Oh, I don't know if I could do that. There's ever so many people out there."

Mr. Wyndell studied her. "Forgive me for being so forward, but if you don't like crowds, why did you come?"

She looked away as she twisted her fingers about each other. "Every time I'm at a party, I ask myself that same question. But when I am at home, all I can think of is, why am I not at the party?"

Felicity asked, "Is staying at home so bad?"

Miss Smith nodded. "My mother is at home. Besides, tonight Jonathan asked if he could go out."

"Jonathan?"

Mr. Wyndell explained, "Your…brother, correct?"

Miss Smith nodded. "I think he's had enough of staying home with Mother. She's not terribly good company. I think he fears she'll do for him what she's done for me."

Felicity looked dowdy, dumpy Miss Smith up and down. She was a sorry sight.

"What has she done for you?"

Miss Smith blinked. "Who has done what?"

"Your mother. You said she's done something for you. What was it?"

Miss Smith looked positively confused. "My mother has done…?"

It was like her thoughts deliberately fled her head. Felicity and Mr. Wyndell looked at each other in alarm. Miss Smith was clearly not right. But what to do?

"Shall I find your brother for you?" asked Mr.

Wyndell.

"Mmm? I suppose so. I don't know why. I believe he's off enjoying the party. Best he should, lest anything should happen to him too."

"How about I find young Master Smith?" His gaze slid sideward to Miss Smith. "I think it's time certain ladies retired for the evening." He regarded the letters in her hands. "What are you going to do with those?"

Oh, the letters! Felicity nearly forgot. "I need to give these back to Miss Chester immediately." She moved toward the doorway.

Mr. Wyndell's arm held her back. "No good. His Grace and Miss Chester have left."

"What? Why would they leave?"

Mr. Wyndell relieved her of the letters. "Showing good taste? This is one of the more tedious parties I've been to."

A glimmer of hope sprang in Felicity's heart. "Really? I must confess I've been sorely disappointed myself."

Mr. Wyndell sorted through the letters. "Parties like this aren't for entertainment. They're purely for being seen and passing on gossip. I fear Miss Chester may have heard some terrible things regarding herself."

Felicity peered about the corner. Sure enough, the guests had clumped together to exchange the only thing they knew—each other's business.

"Certainly enough of that." She looked back over to Mr. Wyndell. "Strange that we have not heard anything about Miss Chester tonight."

"Uh, yes, we did. All that gossip about Montagu?"

Felicity sighed, disgusted with herself. "Of course. I'd forgotten."

"We weren't looking for gossip about her." Mr. Wyndell tapped the letters to straighten them in his hand. "We should put the letters back in her bedroom. They'll be safe there."

"No, they won't."

He frowned at her. "Why not?"

She gave him a nonchalant look. "If we had a snoop through her bedroom, no doubt someone else could as well." Now that she thought about it, it made more sense. "Maybe that's why she had the letters with her. She knew someone could find them—"

"Like us?" Mr. Wyndell folded his arms.

Miss Smith stared at them both with round eyes. "You snooped through her room?"

"Someone like us, or worse, was searching for something. She didn't want them to be found." His Grace, perhaps, or maybe someone else.

Mr. Wyndell tried to tuck them in his coat pocket, but they were too big. "So why give them to you?" He tried another pocket.

"She didn't want to be caught with them, silly!" Felicity held up the ribbon that had bound them earlier. "You may find this of assistance."

Mr. Wyndell took the ribbon, then studied the letters. His attempt to wrap the ribbon around failed.

"No, like this."

Felicity took the letters and the ribbon. Kneeling on the floor, she expertly bound up the letters so they would not fall apart. As she tied them up, she put her mind to the conundrum of the letters.

"So Miss Chester is in possession of a handful of rather incriminating letters, albeit, ones that don't name anyone directly. She's nervous about them and shoves them into my hands before running away. Nobody's supposed to get their hands on these letters because…?"

That was the mystery. These letters were valuable to someone, someone Miss Chester feared.

Miss Smith clapped her hands. "Because they're important."

Felicity rolled her eyes. "You think so?"

Mr. Wyndell ran his fingers along his lapel, resettling the coat on his shoulders. "She has letters she doesn't want someone to find. Why not burn them?"

Both Felicity and Miss Smith gave him very wry looks. "One does not burn correspondence unless one truly detests the author," Felicity said.

Miss Smith added, "Plus, if you burn something that's enchanted before you remove the magic, you only end up spreading the magic about. That can be disastrous."

Fire did not destroy magic the way it destroyed paper. Imagine little sooty bits of magic floating about. Spells had to have some sort of focus, but if the spell was affecting the very dust of the atmosphere, who knew what kind of mischief it could cause before it dissipated?

"Anyhow, these aren't hers. But in her hands they could be very powerful. The original owner may do anything to get them back."

"So it's to be blackmail? Is that Miss Chester's style?"

Felicity thought back to a nervous Miss Chester, her shaking hands, the abandonment of the letters into Felicity's care. "No. Definitely not her." She thumped the letters against her forehead. "What am I missing?"

Mr. Wyndell held out his hand. "Why don't you

give those to me?"

Felicity held them out of his reach. "No. She told me to give them to no one. So unless you're the author of these letters, they do not belong in your possession."

He stiffened at this. "They do not belong in your possession either."

"Better mine than yours. They were entrusted to me. And now I've got to figure out what to do with them."

Miss Smith peered closer to the letters. "Why don't you disenchant them?"

"What?" said Mr. Wyndell and Felicity.

How could one undo someone else's magic when she couldn't even see it to begin with?

Miss Smith took the packet and undid the ribbon and handed it to Mr. Wyndell, her gaze on the letters. She selected one and opened it.

"Sure. This one has enchantment imbedded in it." She peered closer. "I think it's in the ink."

That caught Felicity's imagination. "But isn't ink made from iron?" Iron couldn't hold magic at all. Sometimes it was used to negate magic.

"Not necessarily. This could be silver nitrate," said Mr. Wyndell.

"Silver what?"

Miss Smith inclined her head. "Silver can hold magic."

By anchoring magic to something like silver, or even wood, one could leave it open-ended. If one had to tie off magic, then that magic was limited and didn't have much application. Felicity snagged a letter for a closer look. The ink looked black, like any other black ink anyone would use. It didn't look silver at all.

"So how do you tell this letter has magic?"

Miss Smith pointed out a corner of the paper. "Here you can see where the spell is anchored."

"But there's no ink there."

"I know. It's anchored to the paper." Her finger traced the edge. "It goes along here, connects with the words, and ties up back at the original spot. The letter was written first, then enchanted."

"How do you know this stuff?" Mr. Wyndell asked her.

Only after Miss Smith pointed it out, did Felicity recognize the threads of magic used to create a spell. It looked as if the spell was locked to the paper. Burn the paper to ash, and the spell would be locked to the ash.

"But what does the spell do?"

Miss Smith shrugged. "Not my spell."

"But you could see it." And now Felicity could as well. Clever of Miss Smith to be able to see magic. Did she have a talent for that sort of thing?

Mr. Wyndell studied Miss Smith as if she were one of the letters. Could someone tell if someone else had magical talent? Mr. Wyndell had said there was a vague bit of magic about Miss Smith. Maybe she had a talent for seeing such things. Was that why she didn't pay much attention to the real world?

Now that she could see the magic, Felicity saw how it locked together. She might not have been able to recognize the parts of the spell, but she could see how they fit. How easy it was to take it apart, unraveling it as if stitches in a quilt. The moment she freed the last tuck, the spell evaporated forever.

"I say," remarked Miss Smith. "That is useful."

Mr. Wyndell's jaw dropped. "You can do that?"

Felicity looked from one to another. "Do what?"

"Undo other people's spells. I didn't know that was possible."

She regarded her hands. Was it such a difficult thing? It was like untying a lace, or opening a lock. Constructing them was hard. That skill had often evaded her, no matter how often her mother tried to help her. Once an item was enchanted, it wasn't that difficult to feed magic into it, thus strengthening the spell. However, that could take an awfully long time. Years, even. She pulled out another letter and released the spell upon it.

Mr. Wyndell tugged the rest of the letters from her hand. "Should you be doing that?"

Felicity folded her arms. "You tell me." She gestured to the letters in his hands.

He lifted a letter and sniffed it. Could one smell magic? She half-lifted a letter to her nose, until she remembered that the magic had been liberated. He peered at his letter and even shook it by his ear.

"Well?"

He tucked it back in its pile and selected another. This one didn't get any investigation. Rather, he tapped it against his chin. "Why would someone wish to enchant love letters?"

Miss Smith gave another vague shrug.

"To make someone fall in love with you?" Felicity ventured.

"I don't know," was all Miss Smith would say.

"Perhaps. But if these were straightforward letters between two free parties, then it wouldn't be so scandalous."

Mr. Wyndell retrieved the first one from Felicity.

Against his previous advice, he opened it and read it once more. "These letters are between two people who shouldn't be involved."

"How do you know that?" Felicity asked.

"Because it references third parties. I presume a spouse?"

Felicity straightened. Were these letters enchanted to lure away some man from his wife? Now that was despicable.

Before he could stop her, Felicity plucked the letters from Mr. Wyndell's hands. One by one, she tugged at the magic spells, freeing them. Once a letter was done, she dropped it.

"What are you doing?" Mr. Wyndell cried, stooping to pick up each falling letter.

"I am saving a marriage," she replied. Felicity tugged at the spells until the last one was gone. "There."

Mr. Wyndell gathered the last one, refolding them.

"You know I am right."

He sighed. "Now we'll never know. Now what?"

"Could burn them," Miss Smith suggested.

Felicity shook her head. "Sorry, but no. Miss Chester trusted me. I'm not going to go about shattering that trust, no matter what she's done. They may be disenchanted, but they still have blackmail potential."

A stone of disappointment sank into her gut. These were terrible, terrible letters. Whose were they, really? Maybe she should burn them after all.

"Fine." Mr. Wyndell gave up. "You keep the letters. Now what?"

"I don't know. Possibly hold them until I find Miss Chester again?"

Mr. Wyndell shook his head. "His Grace and Miss Chester have gone on to another party. I doubt we'll see them here again tonight."

"Nonsense," Felicity cried. "She lives here. She's got to come home sometime."

"What if she doesn't?" Miss Smith asked.

Both Mr. Wyndell and Felicity turned to her. Miss Smith squirmed somewhat.

"I mean, what if they choose to run off to Gretna Green or something. We might not see them for some time."

Felicity's jaw dropped. Then a big grin spread across her face. "Why, Miss Smith. You're a romantic."

But Miss Smith blinked her big cow eyes. "Not really. But it's a better fate than being run over by a carriage. That's also possible, but I didn't want to mention it."

Now it was Felicity's turn to blink. "I do believe you're correct, Miss Smith."

Mr. Wyndell simply looked heavenward and shook his head.

Felicity continued. "Still, she must come home sometime."

"I'm not waiting around here all night until she does."

Could Mr. Wyndell fold his arms any tighter? Possibly, but he would risk tearing the seams of his coat.

"Who said anything about waiting? I'll simply take these home with me and call on her tomorrow, or maybe the next day. Surely she will not need the letters until then, otherwise, why entrust them to me?"

Felicity set off for the front door and for home. As she pushed her way through the crowd, they pushed back. Holding on to a bundle of ribbon-wrapped letters was difficult.

Best to get these letters home. If Miss Chester returned and required them, it would be a simple matter to go next door—

A particular group of young ladies jostled her extra hard. If it hadn't been for the portly gentleman behind her, she would have fallen most unspectacularly on the filthy floor.

"I beg your pardon."

He didn't care. Thoughtlessly, he pushed her away, straight into the arms of the young ladies.

"Pardon me," said one of the ladies, shoving her back again.

How did she manage to put just the right sort of sneer in her voice?

She added a kick to Felicity's ankles for the insult.

"I don't think so," Felicity muttered back as she stumbled under the kick. At this, all the young ladies looked at her, if only to know who they were laughing at.

The Marchioness Marque, center of the pack, deigned to notice Felicity's presence. She cocked an eyebrow. Then her gaze fell to the letters in Felicity's arms. Her Honor froze. "Wait." She pushed through her own ladies.

Felicity hastened back as an instinct of fear urged her to run. She did her best to keep at least one person between her and the marchioness, some poor, random elderly gentleman, getting slow in his old age, and unable to avoid nimble young ladies bent on mischief.

The marchioness's eyes burned with rage. "Where did you get those?" she spat at Felicity. One long, elegant arm reached over the elderly man's shoulder.

"I don't know what you're talking about." She danced out of the marchioness's reach.

The marchioness tried to keep her voice low and failed. "Those are my letters."

Oh really? Felicity looked at the youthful marchioness. This was the authoress? Wasn't it a little early in her marriage to be cuckolding her husband? If it had been any other lady, Felicity would have handed the letters over with a minimum of fuss.

But this was snooty Marchioness Marque, who would soon learn the consequences of pushing around her lessers. One would never know when one would be dependent on said lessers' good graces. No way were these juicy letters ending up back in her hands. *Come to think of it, how'd they end up here at the party in the first place?*

The marchioness pushed around the old man. "Give me those."

Felicity danced behind another old man. "What? These letters? I don't think so." She hugged them tight. *Time to run.*

With a turn so quick and sprightly it would make her dancing master swoon, she dashed off through the crowd.

"Bring those back!"

Felicity's heart hammered. These really were the marchioness's letters, not Clarice Chester's. She sent a silent apology to Miss Chester for thinking poorly of her, even if only for a second. The deliciously scandalous thought of blackmailing the marchioness herself crossed her mind.

But no. She had no reason, other than petty spite, to

blackmail anyone. If her mother found out, Felicity would be banished to the nursery forever, to live and die an unpresented old maid. The fact that Miss Chester also balked at the thought of using the letters painted her in a somewhat better light.

Felicity pushed past one particularly glowering man.

"Wait!" he called before the marchioness slammed into him.

Or that's what Felicity imagined what happened. She didn't dare turn around, lest he hadn't slowed the marchioness down. But she certainly heard the marchioness cry out. Maybe she stumbled, tripped by a wayward foot. She wouldn't put it past some guest with a dislike of the marchioness to take advantage of the situation. Felicity certainly would have, as much as such things would have been childish.

She pushed her way out of the drawing rooms and found herself running down the hallway toward the front door.

She paused. Going out the front door wouldn't work, for her own front door would be locked up tight. If she opened it, she could get caught by the servants, then word of her truancy would certainly reach her parents.

Best to turn and head through the kitchens and go back the way she came. One thing was certain; she needed to take the letters straight home and ask Miss Chester about them on the morrow.

As she stood there debating her actions, an arm slipped about her waist, a hand clamped over her mouth, and someone yanked her backward through a door.

Chapter 11
The Possibility of Escape

Drat, but the girl was fast. Victor followed Miss Abbot out into the party, but she'd disappeared into the crowd. Best she get those letters home before anyone discovered her with them.

It would be some time before Miss Abbot returned, if return she did. For all he knew, she might choose to stay home, rather than return to this tedious little crush. That would be for the best, really.

So why was he reluctant to let her go?

He spied his mother at the bottom of the stairs in close conversation with two other ladies. One he recognized as their hostess Lady Chester. The other, whose back was to him, he couldn't identify.

Victor walked straight to his mother, hoping to overhear their conversation before they clammed up. *Too late.* She saw him well before he could draw within eavesdropping range.

The conversation halted, on sign from his mother. Probably fuelled by guilt, Lady Chester slid away, as did the other, turning enough to reveal the face of Lady Parnell. *Now that was interesting.*

Presuming Miss Chester was scandal-free, Miss Abbot a complete innocent, and with Lady Parnell being the fourth party to The Agreement, did that mean something was amiss with Miss Parnell?

Surely not. Miss Parnell was a veritable mouse, albeit a clingy one. Granted Miss Bitner had hung on her ear all evening, but surely Miss Parnell was not mired in scandal? He simply couldn't see her writing the kinds of things Miss Abbot had found in the letters. Granted, she had adhered to him with a cloying desperation suggesting she was also under the same moral geas to find a suitable match before Too Late.

Would marriage to Miss Parnell be a better fate than perpetual bachelorhood? Not by a long mile. Besides, it wasn't as if he had prospects. He couldn't help the small chuckle that rose inside him. Imagine Miss Abbot's thoughts upon learning she was a prospect!

His mother was quite alone by the time he reached her.

"So you, Lady Chester, and Lady Parnell, hmm?"

His mother paled. "How did you know?"

Victor avoided rolling his eyes. "I surmised it. This whole evening you haven't spoken to anyone who, I believe, wasn't involved with The Whole Situation. If you're trying to be subtle, you're going about it the wrong way."

At least she had the good sense to look guilty.

"Did you discover the location of The Agreement?"

To his surprise, she did not give him an answer. It was as if she didn't know what to say. "All I know is that it's safe."

"*Safe*? What does that mean?"

She leaned over as if afraid of being overheard, not that conversation could be heard at any volume at this party. "It means nobody has found The Agreement."

"How do you know?" He looked about the room, still stuffed with folk trying to see and be seen. It wasn't as if there was much else to do, other than partake in refreshments and attempt to out-talk the music. He spared a thought of pity for the poor little octet of musicians whose hard work was going largely unnoticed. At least they had some room to play, even if not much else in the way of comfort.

He hoped Miss Abbot had gotten away safely.

His mother looked about, even though they were not going to be overheard. "Because if anyone had found it, they would have used it immediately. However…"

Victor rolled his eyes. "What?"

"There have been some distressing rumors of its existence."

"I know. That's why we're here."

She leaned in. "No, I mean someone has been speaking of it here at the party. Lady Chester heard that someone overheard someone speaking of it. She came straight to me. Of course, I have spoken of it to no one."

"You told me."

"I did not," his mother retorted. "I simply spoke of a piece of paper I needed to find. I have never told you the contents."

Victor dropped his head. Such nitpickiness would not stand up under any kind of questioning.

"Wait!"

That single word, lifted up on a most piercing voice, carried out across the crowd. The susurrus of conversation dropped. His skin crawled at the sound of it. The Marchioness Marque. Only Miss Bitner's voice grated on him more. He looked up just in time to see the marchioness in vicious pursuit of Miss Abbot.

Oh no. If she caught her and learned that she'd read every one of those scandalous letters... He left his mother and shoved his way through the guests.

Miss Abbot disappeared into the hallway. He prayed that she would escape and sequester those letters safely in her home. Later, perhaps it was best that they were burned, Miss Chester be damned.

It was easy enough to follow the shimmery blue of the marchioness's gown. Nobody else at the crush sported such a vivid shade of peacock.

As he pushed through the crowd, the crowd shoved back. How could the marchioness move so fast? The marchioness cried out again, this time in surprise.

The crowd solidified, making it almost impossible for him to get through. Indeed, they were all moving back, forming a circle near the hall. Victor finally squeaked his way through to the front.

It was not Miss Abbot he saw, but a far more interesting spectacle.

The Marquess Marque had finally caught up with his errant wife. In the middle of an ever-widening circle, he held her fast by her arm.

"I've had enough of your nonsense," he roared. "Don't think I didn't see him here."

The marchioness's usual sneer slid off her face. Instead, her gaze darted to and fro. "I don't know who you are talking about."

The marquess did. He turned and, keeping a firm hand on her arm, dragged her from the crush. "I am not the fool you played me for."

She had no hope. Her husband was big enough to

throw her over his shoulder and carry her out, should he so desire. The only thing that could have been worse was if he had shouted out her sins to the world.

He didn't need to. The *ton* would do that for him.

After that rather dramatic departure, the crowd filled in the empty space with their bodies and their gossip.

"Did you see that?" a lady behind him said to her friends, perhaps a little louder than she should.

"I should never," one replied.

The spectacle over, he turned to push past them, an automatic apology on his lips. The group gossiping behind him was none other than the marchioness's own crowd. He looked from one to another, blushed, and pushed through.

Their scrutiny followed him as he moved through. He had not yet gotten out of range of their voices when another one said, "They say Marky Marque had come to confront…You Know Who."

Victor had had it with gossip. Time to find his mother and beg her to leave, agreement or no agreement.

She was where he'd left her, a fluttery hand to her chest. "My goodness," she cried. "Was that…?"

"Someone merely taking his wife home. I think she's had enough of the party." At least she would not be going after Miss Abbot.

He hoped she had escaped.

"Mother, we really need to leave." He took her by the hand.

She resisted. "We can't. Now, more than ever, we must find and destroy…" Her voice dropped so low he had to read her lips. "The Agreement."

"No. I've had it with this horrid little party. Why, of all nights, did you choose to come looking for You Know What?"

"Because if it were discovered to be missing, no one would suspect me."

A couple of gentlemen pushing past them shoved Victor against the wall.

"This is not fun at all," he declared to his mother.

"We're not here for fun."

"Can't we just pretend The Agreement doesn't exist, and carry on with our lives?"

That took his mother aback. "Absolutely not! As long as those rumors abound, we are at risk."

"What did you do that would make the knowledge of The Agreement so dangerous to us?" She had to have done something. Otherwise, The Agreement would have no hold over them, should the contents come to light.

"I have done nothing. It is bad enough I was there. There will be those who would say I should have—" She clapped a hand over her mouth.

"What? Done something?"

She only shook her head, denying the contents of The Agreement.

He took her gently by the shoulders. "Was there something you could have done?"

With sad eyes, she looked at him. "It was after the fact. Too late."

Too late for what? Before he could ask his next question, she said, "We will not be safe until either that agreement is destroyed, or you are settled enough that no scandal can ruin your chances."

"My chances of what?"

"A good marriage."

Oh, not this again. "Why does it matter if I get married or not?"

It wasn't as if an unmarried younger son was such a dreadful fate. He had his clocks to keep him occupied. A couple of filed patents brought in some money. Maybe, if his designs were well sought after, he could live off patent royalties. A self-funding gentleman. It wasn't as if he had to maintain a certain status in Society other than individual respectability.

"It. Matters." His mother gripped his arm tightly. "If we have any hope of weathering any further scandal, it will be because of our connection to an impeccable family." Her hand loosened. "Either we find and destroy The Agreement, and thus be able to deny its existence, or we find and connect with a good family." She spread her arms. "This party is the perfect place for either success."

Another pair of party guests shoved up against them on their way up the stairs. Perhaps it was time to move.

His mother's eyes narrowed. "Say, you mentioned you'd met a young lady earlier."

"I did. And now I am going to go find her again so I can learn her name. That way, I'll know to whom I am addressing my marriage proposal."

With that, he left his mother, her mouth gaping open.

****

In Felicity's grandmother's house, this room would have been the salon. Here, the Chesters used it as a kind of cloakroom, lit by a single lamp and manned by a solitary maidservant. Wraps and hats and cloaks of all kinds littered every surface. How could anyone keep anything straight? Its closeness, ripe with the funk of humanity, felt threatening.

The man released her, and she stumbled into a table full of coats. Most of them slid to the floor.

The servant, a tired maid on a chair, rose to attention. "May I help you...?" Her voice trailed off as Felicity's assailant glared at her.

"Get out," he ordered. He pointed to the door.

The maid curtseyed and hurried out of the room, closing the door behind her.

She and her assailant were alone. He grabbed her arm, and she cried out, curling in on herself and the letters.

Felicity caught the glint of gold from the lamplight. A signet ring?

Oh no! Quality. The first name to leap to her panicked head was the Duke of Montagu. But what would he want with the marchioness's letters?

Unless he was the author? A flush of disappointment rolled through Felicity's heart. That would explain why they were given to Miss Chester. If she had solid proof of her fiancé's infidelity, she could cry off before too much damage was done.

"Shh, my pretty. I'll not harm you," he murmured.

Not that that was terribly reassuring.

Upon hearing his voice, she realized he was not the Duke of Montagu. That was somewhat of a relief. The lamp was behind him, so she couldn't see his face. "Who are you?"

He froze. "Wait. You do not know who I am?"

She shook her head and pulled the letters closer.

He relaxed. "No matter. You have something of

mine."

His hand reached for the beribboned bundle of letters.

"No."

"What?"

She clutched them to her bosom. "I promised I would not give these to anyone."

The hand about her arm relaxed, but did not release her. "Who told you?"

No, she would not betray Miss Chester. "A friend. These letters frightened her."

"I do not blame her, if she has chosen to go up against the marchioness. And now, it seems you have made an enemy of her as well."

Felicity trembled, though not because of the marchioness. She imagined Her Honor had many enemies. But this man, this strange lord, had her isolated in this room and very much wanted something from her.

Without warning, the gentleman pinched her on the arm. Felicity cried out, more in surprise than pain, and dropped the letters. He caught them deftly.

"Thank you, my dear, for keeping them safe from all but their proper owner." He turned to face the lamp so he could look over the letters.

Now she could see him better. He counted through the letters, as if to ascertain they were all there. The navy blue jacket contrasted nicely with his pale skin and his dark hair, worn in the windswept style. His snowy cravat's elegant knot was held in place by a sapphire pin. She would know him if she saw him again.

He peered closer to the letters, even holding one up

to the lamp. "What have you done to these letters?" It was not so much an accusation, but an inquiry of curiosity. He checked one, then the others.

Felicity swallowed. "They've been disenchanted. I'm sorry."

A chuckle rose deep in his chest. "Do not be. In fact, I should be most grateful to you."

Long elegant fingers slipped the bundle of letters into an inside pocket. His hands moved so smoothly, she could not get a good look at his signet ring. Still no clue as to his identity, though if she had his name, she'd know him by reputation.

He offered her a bow as if they were meeting socially. "Forgive me for my abrupt manner. I'm sure such dealings are far beneath an innocent young lady like yourself." He squinted at her. "I do not recognize you. Who are your parents?"

Felicity shook her head. "I doubt we move in the same circles."

His gaze roamed her figure, studying her dress, her lack of jewelry or other accessories, and then over her unadorned hair. "No, I believe we don't." He sketched another bow. "Perhaps it is best we never meet. I have never seen you, and you have never seen me. Understand?"

Felicity nodded.

"However, do know you will forever have my undying gratitude, for helping free me from some wicked magic. I owe you a favor." He departed, as quickly as they had met.

The maid slipped in, closing the door behind her. "You all right, miss?"

Felicity, hand over her mouth, nodded.

"He didn't…" The maid's hands flapped uselessly. "You know…?"

She shook her head. Her virtue was intact.

Maybe her pride was a bit dented, as was her self-respect. She'd let him take the letters. How could she? Not that she had any choice. He'd tricked her and not in a respectable way. Even if they really were his letters, that was rather low-handed of him.

Felicity stumbled out of the cloak room. Where was Mr. Wyndell when she needed him most? The hallway of strangers ignored her. She scooted by the parlor, likewise full of more strangers.

Then a very familiar person emerged from the drawing room—the Marchioness Marque. A dark and very angry man dragged her along by the arm. She did not resist, but terror filled her eyes, focused only on him.

Was this brute the Marquess Marque, come to claim his errant wife? He certainly was not the man she just encountered. Felicity retreated into the parlor and prayed she was not seen. Had she made an enemy of the marchioness? Quite likely.

The parlor was just as crowded as the drawing room. Felicity ducked behind a couple of portly men discussing politics. Under their huffing and droning, she listened for the angry slam of a door marking the departure of the Marques. Let them go and good riddance to them.

She peeked out of the parlor. Was it safe? It was.

"There you are."

Felicity turned to a most welcome voice. Without a second thought, she flung herself into the arms of Mr. Wyndell.

Chapter 12
Scandal Aplenty

"I'm so glad to see you!"

The sudden appearance of Miss Abbot in his arms surprised Victor. "There you are." He noticed her empty hands. "Where are the letters?"

"Gone," she cried. "Their original owner, I think, has them." Her trembling hands clutched at his jacket.

She looked like she needed a good, stiff drink, preferably something stronger than that poor excuse for negus served on the table. They needed somewhere quieter. He certainly did not trust any of the rooms upstairs. Instead, they found themselves back at the chaise longue, half hidden by the plant. By some miracle, no one occupied it.

After they sat down, she spilled out the whole story. "I don't know who he was. He didn't know me either, half the miracle."

"No indeed," Victor said. "While you were off involved in that half of the scandal, the other half was unfolding nicely here. The marquess, back from his estates, came looking for his wife. He'd heard she was here and came to fetch her. So it seems you did the marchioness a favor by not giving her the letters. Had they been found by her husband, things could have gone worse for her."

Miss Abbot fretted. "Oh. How am I to feel about

that? On one hand, I am not pleased that the marchioness got away with her atrocious behavior. On the other hand, at least I did not have a hand in the eventual destruction of a marriage. Too many hands involved. Did they ever love each other? When did it go wrong?"

Several couple loitered close to the chaise, more wrapped in their conversations than anything else. Victor watched them. "When the marquess thought that beauty and money would be sufficient qualities for a wife."

Concern wrinkled Miss Abbot's brow. "And you disagree with him?" she asked in a small voice.

Victor watched her worry her lower lip with her teeth. "I value other qualities."

"Which are?" Her hands twisted in her skirts.

He caught up those nervous hands of hers. "Why do you want to know?" A buzzing filled his ears. *What was she implying?*

She swallowed. "So…" Her eyelids fluttered shut. "So later on I may understand why you have not proposed marriage. I am not accounted a great beauty, nor are we flush in the pockets. My-my brother's death dealt us very ill."

He drew a deep breath. "Isn't it a bit soon for us to be considering marriage?"

He glanced at the crowd before scooting farther down the chaise longue. Like before, he drew the curtain about them, keeping out of sight of most people. It was the best he could do for privacy, unless they wished to chance the rooms above.

Or not. The last time they slipped into an empty chamber, they had gone in hoping to escape some social awkwardness and emerged to some rather shocking and quite premature rumors of impending nuptials. Marriage had already been mentioned that night.

"Of course it is," she replied, too rapidly. "After all, we have only just met."

Yet for those few hours they had known each other, she had brightened his life in a way he would never have anticipated. Miss Abbot was so unlike the other Society misses his mother insisted on foisting on him.

"So isn't it a bit soon to be wondering why I haven't proposed yet?"

"I don't know. What is an appropriate length of courtship?" Her hands tightened in his.

"More than a few hours, I would expect."

She weighed his words, considered them, and drew a deep breath. "How long do you think we should court before you propose?"

What? How does one answer that?

She didn't give him a chance. "After all, the marquess must have had an appropriately sufficient courtship, yet look how their marriage turned out."

"They married for political reasons."

Like most people did. Victor considered this. Was that why he hadn't put much thought into marriage? As a younger son, he did not have the pressure his eldest brother had. Granted, his mother held out hopes for a marriage of good connection. What qualified as a good connection?

Were the Abbots a good connection? Felicity's grandfather was well respected in politics. Her parents, while not leaders of the *ton*, maintained a respectable standing in Society.

"That is the stupidest reason to marry." Her brow furrowed. "Marriage should be a happy event. Are the poets not always harping on about the joys of love? Why connect yourself up to someone unlikeable for the rest of your life for the sake of politics?"

"Or money. Sometimes people marry for money."

A shudder ran through her. "That's an even worse reason. Money comes and goes, often at whim."

"So does reputation."

Her brow furrowed. "And what about blood?"

He shrugged. "If one lives up to it."

If one disregarded everything except bloodlines, Miss Abbot's were quite respectable. That alone would have made her a good match.

"And what about character?" Her voice quivered at the end.

"Character is everything."

"Do you have a good character, Mr. Wyndell?"

Could she get any more direct? "I can't think of any gentleman who would say he didn't have a good character."

She frowned. "You didn't answer my question."

He threw up his hands, nearly striking a rearward-facing matron. "How can I answer that? I would say I have a good character, but my word would not matter. The only word you could trust is of those who would agree with me."

She considered this, mulling it over in her pretty little head.

"Then it is a good thing I agree with you. And what do you think of my character?"

He gaped like a fish. "Um…"

"Oh, come now. I consider us friends, well, allies,

at the very least. We could not but treat each other with honesty."

His heart quivered. Then he gathered himself together and gave her what she wanted, honesty. "You're an undebuted miss who has sneaked away without her parents' permission to attend a social function. You have gambled on cards, indulged in scandal, have been snubbed by the highest echelons of Society."

A frozen mask descended over her face. She withdrew her hands from his and clenched them tightly before her. But her gaze never left his. No matter how hard she tried to keep that stiff upper lip, the pain from her breaking heart leaked out her facade. Even now, it welled moistly in her eyes.

His voice softened. "Then you befriended a lady who very much needed you, stood up to a man who needed his comeuppance, comforted and supported your neighbor and—" His heart choked. He couldn't get out his next thought.

So there, barely hidden from the rest of Society, he pulled her to him and gave her a beautiful kiss.

****

Felicity's head floated through the clouds. A small sigh escaped her lips before she opened her eyes. "You really meant that."

Mr. Wyndell, still holding her hands, nodded. "I did. I'm sorry I doubted you before, over Miss Chester, over Miss Smith. Instead, you've shown an admirable strength of character."

She studied him further. Sure, he'd listed all her sins, with the exception of her reading the marchioness's letters, and even had encouraged her in one or two of them.

He hadn't condemned her. Rather, he'd stood by her side and even rescued her a few times. It took a man of noble spirit to stand by a lady he only just met, especially one who skirted the edges of scandal.

And here she was, foisting her dreams off on him.

"I'm sorry I've been so forward. After all, we have only met."

"Forgiven. Though I do agree it is far, far too early to be discussing marriage."

She nodded. The noise of the crowd competed with the rushing in her head. "I hope that doesn't mean you are not adverse to the possibility. In the future. Distant future." *But not too distant.*

"I am happy to visit the question again in the future." He had not relinquished her hands. "Miss Abbot, would your parents be adverse to my consideration, if, say, my family was plagued by scandal?"

She weighed his question. Wyndells. Mrs. Wyndell had been a Townshend, the daughter of the Earl of Leicester. While that, in and of itself, was considered a good thing, there was the talk of her brother George and his disaster of a marriage. No wonder poor Mr. Wyndell was so cautious. "You crave respectability as much as I do."

"I fear so."

"And if I was also tainted by scandal, would you even consider me?"

"What kind of scandal?"

Now that was a very good question. "I honestly don't know. I dare not write salacious letters to my lover, I dare not cheat at cards, and I certainly would never kiss and tell. Well, at least I wouldn't tell."

A smile twitched his lips. "But you are not above kissing."

That was something she very much wanted to do again. She did not restrain her smile. It would do her no good to deny that.

She'd never kissed a man before. After kissing Mr. Wyndell, she had no desire to kiss another. As long as she could have him for the rest of her life, she'd be content forever.

"So what do we do now? Do I tell you when I am At Home, and you drop by your calling card, and we spend afternoons sipping tea and speaking of the weather, and occasionally remembering that dreadful crush we once attended, and how nothing would ever be as horrid as that ever again, as long as we lived?"

There! That was the smile she was hoping he'd give her. Truly, he was most handsome once he relaxed.

"And how the whole of Society behaved something awful, that any little peccadilloes we might have committed would be completely overshadowed."

"And we'd tell the story to—" She almost said, "our children," but stopped herself. "—to anyone who cared to listen, not that anyone would. For if we had nothing juicy to tell, we should be considered very dull indeed."

"I have no problem with dull," he confessed.

Felicity tilted her head coyly. "I might."

Mr. Wyndell shook his head. "You might change your mind after tonight."

She wrinkled her nose. "I doubt it."

He sobered somewhat. "What about those letters? What if the marchioness had caught you with them? I do not think you would wish that kind of excitement on anyone."

Felicity shuddered. Perhaps dull wasn't so bad after all?

He sighed. "I am acquainted with the marchioness. She is not…kind to those to whom she has taken a dislike."

"I fear she never liked me from the beginning."

"Perhaps because you are someone she could not bully about? She uses people. I cannot condone that."

Mr. Wyndell might be correct. The marchioness remembered how easily a friend had turned on her, delivering her letters into the hands of Miss Chester. And then there was her lover—former lover?—who had taken back the letters. What had he said? That the reclamation of the letters had freed him from some wicked magic?

"Is she… Does she have any magic?"

"What? You don't know?"

She turned her face away. "It's not like I've been in Society. It just struck me odd how so many people could appear to like her when to me she made my skin crawl. I couldn't understand the appeal. But if she's using enchantments to her own ends… Sad, really."

She shifted to face the crowd. "I've seen more scandal here than I thought Society would have tolerated. I don't know why people give it such significant weight when it seems everyone is mired in the stuff." She looked back to him. "If your character is as true as I judge it to be, I should not be bothered if your family name is tainted with scandal, as long as you were clear of it."

"That I am," he reassured her. "I am glad you do

not judge me by association."

"Nor you, me."

He pulled her hands close to his chest. "We are both victims of our circumstances. I confess I did not want to come. My mother made me come along."

"My mother forbade me."

"Yet I am glad I came."

This lifted her spirits. "Me too. So does it matter if we don't find The Agreement?"

He gave this some consideration. "No, I suppose it does not."

Felicity rose, and Mr. Wyndell followed. "If I was properly out, I would say let us follow the example of His Grace and Miss Chester and leave this terrible crush of a party." Her gaze dropped. "But were I to go out, that would truly be scandalous, even if only in my mother's eyes, and that would truly be the end of my dreams." She looked up once more. "If I leave, it would only be to go home, and without you. If I stay, it would be in your company, albeit among what has to be one of the worst social events of the Season." She tucked her arm in his. "So as I am to stay, we might as well eat their limp food and listen to their weak music and take advantage of this opportunity to spend as much time as we can before we must part."

"Sounds like a plan."

Together they pushed their way through the crowd to the buffet table.

More people crowded around the punchbowl than raided the sandwiches, not that the sandwiches were much to look at, having been picked over.

A footman appeared at the other end of the table to refresh the dwindling supplies. Mr. Wyndell offered to fetch fresh sandwiches. How could Felicity say no? She retreated from the table, as two large matrons pushed through. Let them have the limp sandwiches and the dry cake. What did food matter at a party, when she had Mr. Wyndell?

A young lady slipped through, paused, regarded the leftovers, and sighed. "Really, with so many people about, you'd think the food would not be left behind."

It was not so much the comments of the young lady, but her gown that caught Felicity's eye. The sprigged pattern on the fabric was exactly like hers.

"Francine?" she exclaimed as the young lady turned.

"Pardon?" She eyed Felicity up and down. "Oh!"

Granted, Felicity's dress had a few more flounces about the hem, and her neckline wasn't as ruched, but from a distance, one could be hard-pressed to tell the two gowns apart.

"We should not be seen together," the young lady said. She shooed Felicity away.

Felicity complied. Last thing she needed was one more reason for people to notice her. She bumped into a guest and didn't think anything of it, until the guest said, "This negus is not as good as the last batch."

Felicity turned around. "Miss Smith!"

Indeed, it was her first acquaintance of the night, staring mournfully into a half-empty glass. She held it up to Felicity.

"Is something missing from this?"

She waved it away. If this batch was worse than the first, as Miss Smith had declared, Felicity had no interest whatsoever in sampling it.

"I'll take your word."

At this, Miss Smith nodded and drained the cup, in spite of her judgment. "You're still here?"

"So are you."

Miss Smith gazed around. She handed the empty cup to a dandy who passed by. He looked at it with some bafflement. His wavering, blinking eyes betrayed the fact that he'd probably had more than enough full cups for the evening. Nevertheless, he took it with him, no doubt to refill it.

Miss Smith dug in her reticule for a peppermint, offering one to Felicity.

Together they sucked their candies and watched the crush. At the other end of the table, Mr. Wyndell's hand sneaked through the gathered crowd to snatch away small sandwiches.

"Miss Smith, I was just reflecting on the good that has come from this party. One of those things was that I got to meet you."

Felicity meant it. Any other time, she might have dismissed Miss Smith as too uninteresting to further her acquaintance. But Miss Smith had stood by her and even stood up for her, despite her drifty, dreamlike lack of attention to reality.

"I'm glad I met you too," Miss Smith replied.

"I would like to come calling sometime soon, if you're amenable."

"Sure," replied Miss Smith.

Felicity's mint was almost melted. "May I have your direction?"

"Of course." From her reticule she pulled a calling card. "It's my mother's. She makes me carry one around, not because I ever go calling, but in case I forget where I live."

Felicity took the card. "Have you forgotten where you live?"

"A few times, but only in the company of others."

She read the address. *Not the most fashionable neighborhood, but did it matter?* "Is that the real reason your brother came with you?"

"Perhaps, though I have not seen him in quite some time. Though if he did leave the party without me, our mother would surely give him the cane."

Lacking a reticule of her own, or even a pocket, Felicity tucked the card up in her sleeve. "Did you want me to find him for you?"

"Oh no. Let him have his fun. We don't get out much, so I intend to enjoy this party as much as I can. Got to save up the good memories for the times of drought.*"

Poor, forgotten Miss Smith. There wasn't much to do except hold her hand.

"I promise if my parents ever throw a party, I shall invite you. I shall always invite you, no matter what others say."

Miss Smith sighed in her moony way. "That would be lovely." She looked up. "Do you really think I should get out more?"

"It certainly couldn't hurt." She stroked the back of Miss Smith's hand. "I know what it's like to be disappointed in one's dreams. Doesn't mean one has to pretend they never existed."

A well-dressed lady shoved past Felicity and Miss Smith.

Really, she was getting sick of this crush.

But instead of going about her way, the lady lingered, a smug look of triumph on her face. Wasn't

236

that one of the marchioness's crowd? Felicity blinked. It was! The sneer was not meant for her, but for Miss Smith. It was she who had sarcastically greeted Miss Smith when Felicity tried to finagle an introduction to the marchioness.

The lady gave an extra shove of her shoulder and passed on. Miss Smith stared after her, almost confused.

"Do you know her?" Felicity asked.

"I…"

"Miss Smith?" A gently rounded man stopped short in front of her. "My goodness, it is you." He looked her up and down. "You… You… Oh, dear. What happened to you?" His eyes welled with tears. "I'm so sorry." He pressed a hand to his mouth and shook his head.

Sorry? She was definitely missing something. Felicity looked about for Mr. Wyndell, who was navigating the crush with a tiny plate full of sandwiches. At least he didn't bear any cups of that awful negus. It took him both hands to keep the tower of food from tipping this way and that as he jostled past the many partygoers.

"Here we go," he replied. "This should give us enough fortitude to…" He noticed the man in front of Miss Smith.

"She did this to you," the man said. "I recognize her touch anywhere." The man ignored them both as he grasped Miss Smith's hands. "I can't tell you how sorry I am. If I had known, I would never have…" He pressed her hands to his lips. "I can't ever make up for what happened."

Felicity lost interest in Mr. Wyndell's sandwiches.

The best gossip of the evening, and it involved plain Miss Smith?

Miss Smith stared at the man who had her hands. She didn't pull away but returned his sad gaze. "I don't notice hardly at all."

This brought on a fresh wave of grief from him. "This is all my fault. I didn't find out until too late. Even then, I didn't know where to find you."

"We didn't go anywhere," Miss Smith replied. "I don't go much of anywhere."

The man leaned in closer. "I'm more ashamed than you know."

At this, Felicity and Mr. Wyndell turned away. "I like the watercress," Mr. Wyndell said, low enough to appear as a natural conversation.

"So do I," replied Felicity, before they turned their ears to Miss Smith and her mysterious gentleman companion.

For a gentleman he appeared. His clothes were of a fine cut, and his vowels, while not terribly plummy, spoke more of public school than trade.

And he was groveling to Miss Smith?

"I cannot leave her now, yet I feel I've wronged you."

Felicity's jaw dropped. *Did this man hold a torch for Miss Smith? Why?*

"I don't mind," Miss Smith replied.

The man took her by the chubby arms and gave her a good shake. "That's her spell talking." He rattled her again. "I promise, I'll do my best to undo what she's done." A sigh shuddered through him, turning his breath ragged. "It's too late for us, but if I can fix this terrible, terrible thing, perhaps you can find happiness somewhere else."

Felicity strained to hear the next line of the conversation, but it never came. She searched about, only to discover him gone. Evaporated.

Miss Smith stood alone, all bemused sadness. She had no tears. It was as if they forgot to come.

Mr. Wyndell, likewise, turned to face her. "Who was that?" he asked in awe.

Only then did Miss Smith bring herself together. "Mr. Manton. I wanted to marry him, once." She dropped her head.

Felicity gasped. "You were engaged?"

Miss Smith raised her head. "Oh no. Nothing had been promised. But it would have been nice…"

Mr. Wyndell licked his lips. "Did…Mrs. Manton put a spell on you?"

Felicity could have smacked her forehead. Mrs. Manton was the well-dressed snob who'd sneered at Miss Smith as she walked by, a well-dressed snob who trailed her poor, disappointed husband in her wake. It was a shame only death could part a marriage. A lifetime was a long time to regret a poor choice.

A spell on Miss Smith. *That would explain a lot.* "What did it do to you?" She looked her friend up and down. Would the effects be visible? Mr. Manton had noticed a change. What was different about Miss Smith?

But she only got a shrug in return.

"I'm sure something's different about me. I just don't know what."

Her vagueness. Her tepid acceptance of the way things were. Felicity leaned in and sniffed. Could she smell magic? There were those, she had heard, who could smell it from across the room. But all she could smell was peppermint and party and a lack of disappointment.

"Aren't you sad you didn't get to marry Mr. Manton?"

Miss Smith considered this. "I think I am."

Felicity put her hand over her heart.

Laughter rolled out from a few conversations over. Felicity frowned. Didn't they know how serious this moment was?

Miss Smith regarded them both. "You take care of your Mr. Wyndell," she said to Felicity. "Don't let anyone come between you."

Mr. Wyndell tugged at his cravat. "Isn't it a little early to be talking about such things?"

Felicity bit her lip and turned away. Hadn't they just been canoodling on the chaise only a few minutes ago?

"I don't know about too early, " said Miss Smith. "I do know there is such a thing as too late."

What would it have been like to have known Miss Smith before her curse?

All Mr. Wyndell could do was offer her a sandwich from the plate. This she took with a soft delight. Together they finished off the refreshments Mr. Wyndell had brought. When the plate was empty, Miss Smith sighed.

"You are right, Miss Abbot. Maybe I should get out more." She looked about. "I hope Jonathan is enjoying himself."

Felicity gazed about the drawing room. Not that she would know what Miss Smith's brother looked like. "Are you planning on staying until he's had enough?"

Miss Smith nodded. "It's not like we have anywhere else to go. A crush is an interesting thing. The hostess invites as many people as she possibly can, and hosts it for as long as people show up. Guests come, stay for a few minutes, maybe an hour, then they leave. No one is obliged to stay. It fills in that time between engagements." She peered at them. "I say, you've been here a long time. Have you no other parties to attend?"

Mr. Wyndell sighed.

Felicity considered Miss Smith's words. Her mother did say she was only going to stay a short while, then leave for something else. If not, Felicity would have never come.

Did she recognize anyone here, anyone from before? None of the marchioness's set had remained. She didn't see the Mayfairs, and certainly not His Grace and Miss Chester. Lady Middlestone? No. Mr. Thomas of the long suffering longue? Even he had managed his escape.

"Tonight is enough socializing for me," Mr. Wyndell said. "Indeed, I might be ready to go home."

This dropped Felicity's spirits. Still, he might be right. Felicity had achieved her purpose and then some. She'd come to see a party—a dreadfully disappointing party—but a party nonetheless. Perhaps now it would be easier to wait on Grandmama's return from Tunbridge Wells. Let her mother think Felicity had seen reason, rather than had experienced disappointment.

Also, she had met Miss Smith, played cards with a duke, and saved some mysterious peer from the clutches of the marchioness.

Quite enough adventure to cram into an evening.

And then there was Mr. Wyndell, he who looked so handsome if only he would smile. He who did not mind her little adventures into scandal, but one who also needed to learn he had to listen to her more. Perhaps her grandmama would be home soon, then Felicity could be presented and formally meet Victor Wyndell. Maybe they could have that gentle courtship they'd talked about.

Not bad for an evening's work.

Mr. Wyndell offered his hand to Miss Smith, the other hand tucking the empty plate into his pocket. "I am pleased to meet you, truly I am. Sorry about the curse."

Miss Smith took it, possibly more out of habit than any conscious effort to make a connection.

Felicity had an idea. "Mr. Wyndell, if Mr. Manton hadn't said anything, would you have been able to tell Miss Smith had a curse?"

His hand stilled on Miss Smith's while he studied her. "Um…"

He looked about her. Did magic sit over someone like an aura? Was it like a cloud of smoke, or maybe a sunbeam?

"I can tell there's some magic about her, but I wouldn't have known any difference between a charm and a curse. I only know how magic would affect me."

That was something to consider. "So Miss Smith's curse doesn't affect you?"

He shook his head, his hand still holding Miss Smith's. "Some magic has a tug, like an attraction charm. I've had a few of those pointed my direction before," he added with some disgust. "Muddle charms, vagueness charms, glamours. These are often used by young ladies to attract—no, influence men. I don't know if I find such charms attractive."

Felicity bit her lip and hid her hands behind her back. She'd been working hard on her own charms, but nothing so specific as these. While her finishing school advocated the simpler magic like 'Look At Me' charms, both her mother and her grandmother had advised for more general but stronger magic. 'Success,' 'Grace,' and any other number of subtle, non-directed magic was what they had preferred.

Only now did Felicity see the wisdom of their choices. A 'Look At Me' charm would draw every male eye, including old married men, rakes, and scoundrels. It could not distinguish between these and a desirable future husband. But 'Success' could bring better results. While it was not designed to draw a specific gentleman to a lady, if she set her cap for him, it would aid her in her specific pursuit. But the magic would be centered entirely on her.

Now here was a thought: if Felicity had been wearing her mother's sapphire comb, would Mr. Wyndell have been able to sense the magic on her?

He studied Miss Smith closer than he or anyone else would have. He leaned in as if to whisper in her ear, and paused. Miss Smith glanced about as if there was not a man leaning over her shoulder.

He didn't move but remained there. What was he looking for? Did he sense something? Did he find something? That was an awfully long time to stand there.

"Mr. Wyndell?" Felicity prompted.

He shook the fairies out of his head and withdrew.

"Oh my," he breathed. He turned to Miss Smith. "Now I understand."

"What?" Felicity asked, feeling a little left out.

He turned, as if he'd only noticed her there. "The curse. It's like an umbrella. I…got caught myself." At least he had the good sense to look embarrassed. He leaned in, then pulled out. "It starts right here." He waved his hand in front of Miss Smith's ear.

Felicity reached out, but she could feel nothing and still saw nothing.

Would the curse affect her the way it affected Mr. Wyndell? She stepped in close to Miss Smith and laid her head next to Miss Smith's ear.

The world faded into a soft murmur, almost like the wind. How nice. A gentle relaxation filled her, starting from…the back of Miss Smith's neck? What a strange place to feel relaxed. Felicity leaned in closer. Perhaps she could go to sleep on Miss Smith's neck.

Oh look, there was something faintly buzzy there. Felicity reached out and plucked at it. A loose thread popped up. It waved there back and forth, back and forth as if buffeted by the still waters of a river. She teased at it, hoping to pull more out, so it had more flow to it. *That would be pretty. Yes.*

No sooner had she pinched it to bring it out than a set of hands yanked her out of the pretty little reverie she'd been enjoying.

The cacophony of the crowd pressed on her as did their smell and a too hot humidity. Felicity looked about, a pinch of magic in her fingers.

"You almost got caught in there as well," said Mr. Wyndell.

It was his hands that had gripped her shoulder and

pulled her free. The end thread of magic was still between her fingers. It wove about Miss Smith's head like a bad kind of knitting.

Felicity pulled and pulled, unraveling the curse one stitch at a time, bringing it out, loosening it, undoing its vagueness. As she did, Miss Smith perked up, her eyes becoming brighter, her awareness of the surroundings sharpening.

As she felt the curse weaken and fall apart under her fingers, she marveled at its cleverness. Mrs. Manton had done something quite clever. Shame she was such a notch, for Felicity could almost admire how this curse was constructed.

It wasn't anything harmful, per se, but rather something to lull the mind, to keep Miss Smith unfocused and vague. A rival couldn't be a threat if a rival had no ambition.

And if said rival wasn't actually coming to harm, nobody would investigate, find the curse, and remove it before it had accomplished its purpose—namely, keeping Miss Smith out of the way until the future Mrs. Manton had a ring on her finger.

An elegant, if despicable use of a curse. Felicity could have admired it for sheer craftsmanship alone, had it not ruined the happiness of someone she now considered her friend.

One last good tug freed the thread of magic from Miss Smith. As soon as it popped free, the thread evaporated, no longer needed.

Miss Smith drew a deep breath, putting her hands over her ears. She perked up and blinked in confusion, until the realization of her situation fell upon her. "Have I been asleep this whole time?"

Felicity took Miss Smith's hands. "You're awake now."

"Miss Apple—wait, Abbot. Sorry. I'm still getting used to..." She exhaled while she took in her surroundings, then wrinkled her nose and lifted a hand to cover her mouth. "Was that me? I—" Her reticule nearly tore in her desperate effort to open it and dig for a mint.

She stopped, suddenly aware of Felicity before her. "I'm so sorry." She gathered her manners together, after they had been lying around for so long, forgotten. "Thank you. I kept forgetting."

Miss Smith looked about as if seeing the world anew. "I had no idea I was under a curse. Nobody bothered to ask until now." She pressed her knuckles against her mouth. It was as if she didn't know to cry or not.

Felicity certainly would have been crying, whether for the curse, or having been freed from it. When her head was near Miss Smith's, sharing that fuzzy, vague world of hers, it was a pleasant enough place, albeit a bit empty. Would she, or not?

"I'm free, aren't I?"

"I suppose so," Felicity replied.

"Is it my imagination, or was there a plate of sandwiches about? And wasn't there some sort of awful punch?"

Ha! She knew the punch was truly awful!

Mr. Wyndell fished the small plate out of his pocket where it had been forgotten. "Sorry, they're all gone."

"No matter," replied Miss Smith. "Just wanted to be sure I wasn't having some sort of strange dream.

However, why do you have an empty plate in your pocket?"

"Victor! There you are. I've been looking for you."

Felicity's world sank. She knew that voice.

Mrs. Wyndell had found her son.

The last thing Felicity needed was for Mrs. Wyndell to find her.

****

Victor jumped at the sound of his mother's voice, nearly dropping the empty plate. "H-ello, Mother." He turned, hoping the guilt on his face did not show.

He felt a flurry of movement behind him and hoped it was Felicity slipping away. It would not do to be caught with her, especially if Mrs. Abbot was involved in The Whole Situation.

Mrs. Wyndell, looking rather warm and wilted, fanned herself. "I dare say I've been looking for you."

Victor put his hands and the plate behind his back. "And for..." He let the implication hang in the air over The Agreement.

"Fruitlessly," she admitted. "Really, I need your help."

"And you've looked everywhere."

Miss Smith asked, "Would you like me to take that plate, Mr. Wyndell?"

His mother blinked and leaned over to peer at Miss Smith.

Miss Smith gave a gentle wave, then relieved Victor of the plate. She winked at him, ever so subtly.

His mother's jaw dropped open. She closed it as quickly, lest her manners slip for too long. "Victor?" she inquired, her tone very heavy with meaning indeed.

Introductions... "...one of many young ladies I've

met tonight, and one of the more pleasant ones."

That gentle compliment brought a genuine smile to Miss Smith's face, one entirely lacking in vague mooniness. The real Miss Smith had returned. Perhaps there was hope for her in her original state. Not that he'd want to kiss her, curse or no curse. Miss Abbot had taken quite a liking to her, though.

His mother preferred to read more into the acquaintance than he liked.

"Is she the…?"

"No." Alas for his mother, their official meeting would not be tonight, if he could help it. "Perhaps we should give up our search and leave."

His mother clutched at her bodice. "Absolutely not!"

"I cannot see why we should continue our search when we've been here for hours and nothing has come of it. There are only so many drawers we can rifle through and only so many desks to search. There comes a time when one must give up."

Miss Smith slipped away, presumably to return the plate, or to refill it.

His mother leaned forward. "Until The Agreement is destroyed, our future will always be threatened. We are safe only after it is gone."

Or he got married. His mother's obsession grated on Victor.

"And if we don't find it tonight?"

"We have to." She pulled on his sleeve.

He shook her off. "The whole reason why I came with you was to help you. Yet we've accomplished nothing. I say it's time we give things a rest and go home."

The crowd behind him surged, pushing him into his mother. They did not fall down but delivered the momentum along to the next poor souls behind her.

"Your plan didn't work as well as you'd hoped. There are far too many people here."

Another group stumbled against them.

"Oh dear," muttered a familiar voice. "I fear I shall faint."

Victor turned in time to see Miss Parnell raise her hand to her forehead, and with a rather dramatic sigh, fall straight into his arms.

"The heat is too much for her," declared Miss Bitner behind her. "You should carry her out."

Victor eased Miss Parnell to the floor as gently as he could. He resisted the temptation to simply drop her.

His mother snagged a footman by the jacket as he hurried by. Together, Victor and the footman lifted Miss Parnell off the floor.

"Really, we should take her outside," Miss Bitner suggested.

The footman ignored her. He told Victor of the salon where all the fainting ladies were being taken. Victor agreed and let the footman take the lead. At least the crowd parted enough to let the two men carry a fainted lady through. They were not so thoughtful for Miss Bitner, who pushed past them, trying to keep up. He ignored Miss Bitner's protestations that fresh air was really the best thing for her. His mother followed but did not go into the salon with them.

"I'll continue looking," she called after them.

Whatever made her happy.

The Chesters has been prepared. In the salon were several chaises, most of which were occupied by ladies in various states of faintness. Two maids attended the room. As soon as Victor and the footman entered, one of the maids waved them over to an empty chaise.

Once Miss Parnell had been deposited, the maid waved vinaigrette under her nose until she stirred. Then the maid ignored her and went back the other young ladies.

Lucky thing.

"My goodness," Miss Parnell declared. She raised her face to Victor, her eyes all soft and liquid. "You saved me."

He evaded her as she reached out for his hand. "No. I simply brought you here. You may thank the maid for restoring your senses."

He turned to leave, but Miss Bitner halted him with a hand on his arm. "Surely you wouldn't abandon her now?"

"I'm not abandoning her. She has you." He looked over them, Miss Parnell gazing at him in desperation, her hand reaching out, and Miss Bitner, holding him without looking quite as desperate. "She's always had you."

Quicker than he expected, Miss Parnell sat up and looped something about his right wrist, drawing it tight. Miss Bitner's grip tightened just as a light-headedness came over him. She eased him to sitting on the chaise, studying him closely. He gazed at her, but she wavered slightly out of focus.

"She's ever so grateful," her voice came, as if from the other side of a door.

He tried to lift his arm to wipe at his eyes, but something held it fast.

It was a silver ribbon, not terribly wide, but strong.

It wrapped about his wrist a few times, as if caught in a noose. He tugged at it but the ribbon wouldn't come free.

What was it caught on?

A face in full focus moved into his view. Miss Parnell.

"I'm ever so grateful. You've saved me." She leaned forward. Before Victor realized what she was doing, she'd planted her lips on his.

What was he supposed to do? It was a rather chaste, unpracticed kiss. Not the right one. Something tickled the back of his head. Surely, he'd had better kisses, more proper ones.

She pulled back, her eyes full of expectation.

But Victor couldn't help wondering what he was missing. He stood up, waving away something annoying that tugged at his other arm. At least he was able to free himself. But that ribbon was still there. He guessed it should be on his wrist, else, why would he wear a ribbon?

Miss Parnell rose, the other end of the ribbon in her hand. "Here," she said. "Help me with this."

Who was she speaking to? Victor turned as someone moved in front of him. Two figures fussed at his side, his arm wiggling in response. He lifted his arm to see what was pulling at him.

There was a silver ribbon tied to his wrist. Where did that come from? He raised his hand closer to his face to study it better.

Miss Parnell's hand also lifted. It, too, was tied with a silver ribbon. Was it the same ribbon?

She took his hands and stared up at him lovingly. "Shall we go?"

Go where?

A few others pushed past him. Oh yes. They were at a party. A terrible one if he recalled correctly. They left that room and moved out into a whirl of colors and clothes. He had the impression of many people, all blurry, except for Miss Parnell. At least she wasn't out of focus.

"Why are we here?" he asked.

"We should go," she replied, guiding him through the crush by the hand.

Sounded good. He recalled that had been his original idea before...? Before what?

Oh, look. There was a silver ribbon on his wrist. How could he have not noticed before? What else was he forgetting?

Something tugged at his wrist, and he followed. Whatever it was, it was important. He turned back, but didn't know what he was looking for.

Maybe it was outside. After all, they were headed to the hall and the front door. Maybe it was out there.

The Agreement. That was it. "Have we found it yet?" he asked Miss Parnell.

She didn't stop. "Find what?"

"The Agreement."

This made her pause. "How do you know about that?"

Miss Bitner lurked over Miss Parnell's shoulders. "You mean the one about Lady Chester?"

A warning voice sounded in his head.

"Who?"

He waved the fog away. It had to be fog, for Miss Bitner was rather faded. Improved her somewhat, maybe he should let the fog be.

252

"Oh, do give up," snapped Miss Bitner. "Don't think I haven't noticed your mother skulking about. Lady Parnell told us everything."

"Lady Parnell?" Victor asked. "What does she have to do with it?"

Had someone guessed Lady Parnell as one of the signatories to The Agreement? He tried to recall what he knew of it, what he and…who?…had uncovered that evening.

Miss Parnell sighed. "He doesn't know." She tried to pull him along, but he didn't move.

They had to find The Agreement first. *Can't leave without that. Mother insisted.*

"I think he does." Miss Bitner came in closer, sneering in his face. "You can't play stupid with us."

"I've agreed to nothing." This was true. He hadn't signed anything. So why did his wrist want him to leave the party? "Gotta go." He grinned at Miss Bitner as he was pulled away from her. Yes, let them leave this dreadful party and its blurry guests and the Miss Bitners behind.

Somewhere he heard the sound of a horn. It sounded like someone was calling for a fox hunt.

What was that for?

Chapter 13
Uh-Oh...

Felicity cursed Miss Parnell. She'd fainted deliberately, just to get Mr. Wyndell's attention. *What a shallow trick.* She was not impressed.

Oh, how she wished she could follow them, but Mrs. Wyndell still made her way through the crowd, her son very much in sight. She would have to be avoided.

She pushed in the opposite direction, toward the buffet table, in search of Miss Smith.

She had managed to get rid of the empty plate in her hand. At least her eyes were clear and her attention focused.

"I'm sorry, Miss Apple—wait. That's not your name." Miss Smith sighed. "Have I been calling you Miss Apple the whole evening?"

Only once, Felicity recalled. "I'm sure you remember my real name as Abbot. Not that I've minded. The marchioness only knows me as Miss Apple, so should she dare gossip about me, nobody will know to whom she refers."

Lucid humor tugged at Miss Smith's lips. "At least you get a second chance." Grief rolled into her countenance. "I don't know if I do."

Felicity caught her hands. "You get a new start. I'm sorry it's too late for Mr. Manton."

The old Miss Smith would have dismissed this. The new Miss Smith allowed herself a few tears.

"Oh no," said Felicity, taking Miss Smith's reticule and digging for her handkerchief. "This will not do. I should not have mentioned his name."

"I'm glad you did." She took the handkerchief and delicately mopped her cheeks. "I haven't been able to cry over him yet. I really should."

Her frame shuddered as she clung tightly to her new friend. A few warm drops fell onto the bare part of Felicity's neck.

Felicity could do nothing but pat her comfortingly. The crowd was too tight to push their way from the table. Anyhow, it didn't seem that anyone had noticed the little puddle of grief standing near the watercress sandwiches.

Finally, Miss Smith pulled back, sniffing. "It's very silly of me, to cry over something that happened so long ago."

Felicity disagreed. Mrs. Manton's curse might have happened five years ago, but the news was fresh to Miss Smith.

She kept an eye out while Miss Smith blew her nose and tidied up any stray tears that had clung to her skin. "How do I look?"

Maybe a little red-eyed, considering the circumstances. "Better than you'd think."

"Good." She patted at her hair, checked her dress, and sighed. She regarded her hands. "They're ever so pudgy. How did I get so plump?"

By standing at parties all by oneself and stuffing free food into one's mouth. "It was the curse. I'm sure you'll slim down in no time. You and I can go for strolls in the park next week."

Miss Smith broke out into a smile. "I'm so glad I met you. More than you know."

A rude young gentleman pushed through the crowd without remorse, his "Pardon me" and "Excuse me" hardly the buffer for his behavior they should have been. He dragged a bag across the floor, a bag that wriggled suspiciously. Felicity and Miss Smith moved well back from this strange squirming bag.

"Is that a cat?" Miss Smith wondered.

What an odd thing. "I wonder if it is time for me to leave the party," said Felicity.

Not that she would leave without saying farewell to Mr. Wyndell and extracting a promise from him that he would come calling as soon as she was officially out. Meanwhile, the thought of letters between them briefly crossed her mind.

No. Until they could carry everything above board, that would be too risky. She thought of the marchioness's letters, and all the trouble they had caused.

"Tally-ho!" cried the rude gentleman, several groups away. He ducked down into the crowd.

Somewhere outside the townhouse, a horn sounded. Immediately, it was met with the baying of hounds. Guests shouted in surprise, their cries of alarm spreading. As one, the whole party erupted into a wriggling mass of confusion. Something red and furry and fast flashed between guests' legs, desperate for escape. Many of the ladies cried out and jumped away from the creature.

"It's a fox," Miss Smith declared as she and Felicity moved back with the rustling crowd.

The baying of hounds grew louder until their belling calls came into the townhouse.

The entire party broke out in shrieks and cries as the guests scattered like mad ants.

Felicity and Miss Smith retreated as far back as they could, letting frightened guests shoved past on their panicked way to the door. It was just a pack of dogs. One would think that everyone had seen a dog before, granted, not at a Society party, not like this.

Still, did all these people have to lose their hold on their sanity?

No way would she be able to find Mr. Wyndell in this mess. Gentlemen whooped while ladies screamed. No one stayed still. She hoped he didn't think she had abandoned him. Felicity considered slipping back to the familiar dark corridor and ducking out through the servants' entrance, but it was too far away.

Hounds rushed in and around the departing guests, sniffing the floor and calling out as they caught the scent of the poor fox. They ran through, heedless of the people in their way, focused only on their prey.

Pressed back against the wall, Felicity let the chaos roll over her. While she waited to see how events would end, Miss Smith grabbed her arm.

"It's her. It's Miss Jones."

Felicity looked about. Who was Miss Jones? A frightened matron pushed her out of the way.

Miss Smith had not released Felicity's arm. "Please tell me I should not scratch her eyes out."

Before Felicity could answer, Miss Smith threw her aside and took off. Who knew she could move that fast? At least the fluidity of the crowd allowed her to push through, her aim unwavering.

Some dogs bayed while others whimpered as they were captured by intrepid gentlemen and servants. Between the disrupted crowd and the running dogs pursued by footmen, there wasn't much Felicity could do. She followed after Miss Smith, calling her name and wondering who Miss Jones was.

Ah, that Miss Jones, now known as Mrs. Manton. This victim didn't see Miss Smith bolting after her. She was too focused on her own escape.

To Felicity's secret delight, Miss Smith gave Mrs. Manton an almighty shove, and the dreadful woman sprawled forward. No way would Felicity dare stop her friend from wreaking a long-awaited vengeance. For cursing a romantic rival and essentially ruining her socially, Mrs. Manton had everything coming to her that Miss Smith could dish out.

The crowd around them pushed back, their worry over the dogs evaporating as they watched Mrs. Manton sprawl on the parquet floor and Miss Smith throw herself on her with a mighty shriek. Some of the gentlemen even shouted her on as she pummeled her rival with two meaty fists. No one was game to stop the fun too soon.

Over and over she beat against Mrs. Manton's back. Mrs. Manton could do nothing but bellow and cover her head with her arms. Miss Smith's superior weight pinned her down so she couldn't move.

Felicity stood on the edge, letting Miss Smith work out five years of frustration. She deserved it. Felicity only waited to help rescue her friend, should she need it.

And where was Mr. Manton? Felicity spied him several rows back, watching the fight with a hand over his mouth and his eyes full of fascination. Did he not see any reason to save his wife? Or had her devious ways of securing his hand in matrimony prevent him from extending that same hand to her aid?

Eventually two busybody gentlemen pulled the ladies apart, much to the audience's groans of disappointment. This was what Felicity was waiting for. She caught a disheveled Miss Smith and hurried her away. At least the crowd had thinned enough they could make their getaway without interference.

In fact, it was best they slip outside entirely. It would be harder for anyone to find them in the darkness. And should things get really bad, she would hide Miss Smith away in her own home.

Miss Smith let her lead her away. Her eyes burned with triumph. "Did you see that?"

"Wouldn't have missed it."

Miss Smith inspected her knuckles. "I'm bleeding. It was worth it, though."

Felicity hastened Miss Smith to the crowded hallway. *Hm. Maybe the front door wasn't the best way to leave.*

Miss Smith looked up as someone shouted, "Eliza!"

Her brother Jonathan came pushing through the crowd. "Did you see that?" he said, his voice squeaking from the excitement of the party. "Did you see the hounds?"

She nodded, her eyes bright. "I think the party's ending."

Jonathan studied her. "You all right?"

Miss Smith lifted her hand. "Oh, I punched someone."

His jaw dropped. "What? You?"

She shrugged. "What can I say? I feel better now." She inspected her thrashed knuckles. "Still, I should go take care of this."

Her brother flopped. "But this stupid party's only just getting interesting. I didn't know you could have an indoor fox hunt."

A footman dragged two reluctant hounds out the front door by their collars.

"You can't." She wrapped her handkerchief about her knuckles.

Felicity reached out. "I only live next door, should you wish to come calling."

Miss Smith smiled at her. "And you have my direction. So glad to have met you, Miss Apple-whoever-you-are. Escape while you can."

Felicity nodded. She watched the Smiths leave.

Perhaps it was time for her to depart as well. Felicity turned to see if it was easier to get to the back corridor. She came face-to-face with Miss Parnell leading Mr. Wyndell by the hand—no, what was that? She looked closer. A silver ribbon? Had Miss Parnell tied herself to him?

"Mr. Wyndell?" Felicity called. "Are you all right?"

Miss Bitner pushed her out of the way. "He's fine. He's just leaving."

"I don't think so," Felicity muttered.

She grabbed Mr. Wyndell's other hand and pulled, hoping to keep him from leaving the drawing room.

"Oh!" Miss Parnell tugged back.

Felicity tucked herself under Mr. Wyndell's arm. What kind of ribbon had Miss Parnell used to ensnare him? Most likely magical, though Felicity couldn't really tell about the magic.

It was looped about his wrist in a noose. Had it been a simple knot, she could have untied that easily. This hitch was more difficult. She'd have to free the other end from Miss Parnell.

But if she undid the weaving...

Felicity concentrated. Ribbons were a simple satin weave. Disconnect a few of the weft threads, and the whole thing could easily fray.

One by one the threads came loose. Felicity hooked a finger between the ribbon and Mr. Wyndell's wrist. Miss Bitner yanked at her other arm. Felicity came away from Mr. Wyndell. The ribbon loosened and detached itself from Miss Parnell. It trailed on the floor.

Job done!

She peered into Mr. Wyndell's eyes. "Are you all right?"

Chapter 14
Time to Leave the Party

Victor's head cleared. The muddled noise around him sharpened into a panicked mess of chaotic people, trying to get out of the party. He looked about. "What the—"

His gaze fell on Miss Abbot, tucked under his arm. She released a silver ribbon—the one that had recently graced his wrist—to the floor. Then she kicked it out of the way and favored him with such a bright smile he felt he would melt under its glory.

Victor lifted his wrist and rubbed it as if to dispel its treacherous magic. Only now that he was free, did he realize he'd been trapped.

"Oh, you beautiful diamond!" He pulled her closer, fully intending to scoop her up, whirl her about, and carry her off for the rest of his life.

A desperate hand pulled at his coat sleeve. "You're with me," demanded Miss Parnell.

"You are mistaken."

No matter how much he struggled, he couldn't free her hand from his sleeve. Only a new voice caused her to release her grasp. Lady Chester, the hostess herself, pushed into the circle.

"Young Miss Abbot!" she cried. "What are you doing here?"

Miss Abbot squeaked, untucking herself from

Victor's arm. "I've only just arrived. Was that hounds I heard? I have been watching the comings and goings all evening. But when I heard the baying of hounds, I could not help but come over. Hounds, Lady Chester. In Town?"

She pulled Lady Chester aside, moving through the crowds toward the door. Victor headed after them. The last thing Miss Abbot needed was to get caught out by Lady Chester. Even worse, what if she said something about The Agreement to her? Miss Abbot could be locked away for good before she had a chance to come out at all.

Drat the girl for being able to move so fast. As he attempted to push past a pair of men, they grabbed him by the arms.

" 'Pon rep, if it isn't Wyndell."

****

Lady Chester's eyes narrowed. "How long have you really been here?"

Felicity's mind rattled through any number of plausible excuses. She hesitated too long. At the merest shake of Lady Chester's head, she knew she'd been sprung.

"You head home right now, and I will disavow any and all knowledge that you were here tonight." Her firm grip on Felicity's arm brooked no nonsense.

Felicity had one last chance to assuage her curiosity before she was so unceremoniously hustled home. "One cannot help but wonder at The Whole Situation."

At this, Lady Chester stopped. "What do you know about that?" Her voice wavered.

The last piece of the puzzle fell in place. "Well,

I'm sure everyone knows. Those hounds were pretty loud."

"Hounds?"

Felicity looked up at her with wide, innocent eyes. "I presume it was some gentlemen's prank?"

Lady Chester relaxed somewhat but did not forgive Felicity. She marched her straight to the door. "Go home. Now."

"Of course, Lady Chester. Please give my regards to Miss Chester. I am fond of her, you know, and would be At Home to her anytime."

Lady Chester's only response was giving Felicity a shove out the door. Felicity went down the steps before turning. Lady Chester had disappeared.

Naturally, she hastened back up and ducked again into the party. No way was she leaving without saying goodbye to Miss Smith and Mr. Wyndell.

Especially Mr. Wyndell.

****

Victor rolled his eyes at Lord Forsythe. The gentleman, well and truly into his cups, swayed with Mr. Ragsdale by his side, equally inebriated. They needed Victor's steady frame to keep them somewhat upright. At least they appeared to be having a good time at this horrid little crush, if a bit over-friendly. Victor failed to extract himself from their arms, equally as clingy as Miss Parnell's.

She tried pushing past Forsythe, in a poor attempt to free Victor from the drunken lord. Forsythe ignored her.

"We were just *shpeaking* about you." Ragsdale gave him a very sloppy grin. His voice was louder than necessary, even considering the rumble of the crowd.

"Let me offer you my most sincerest apologies." He laughed at his gaffe. "I meant, *felishitations* on your recent betrothal-ment." He draped an arm about Victor.

He ducked out from the drunken hug. "Shouldn't you be finding a quiet corner in which to cast up your accounts?"

Victor looked out over the crowd. Miss Abbot and Lady Chester were no longer visible. *Where'd they go?*

Ragsdale dragged at his shoulder. "I never figured you to get married, old chap." His wavering gaze fell on Miss Parnell. "Oh dear. Don't tell me this green shackler is your intended."

"Her?" cried Lord Forsythe. "Hardly. He's chosen a pretty one. You should see her." He outlined the form of a woman's curvy body in the air with his hands.

"Mr. Wyndell?" Miss Parnell's voice startled him. "Is this true?"

She'd heard the whole conversation.

He schooled his features to neutral. "Is what true?" He eased himself out from under Ragsdale's arm.

Miss Parnell's eyes welled with tears. Her chest heaved with emotion. Miss Bitner, on the other hand, had him pegged. Even now, the harpy stood behind Miss Parnell, dark eyes narrowed at him in accusation. Her bitterness rolled off her in waves, washing over him. A shudder ran up his back.

She mouthed, "Bastard."

Miss Parnell sniffed. "Are you betrothed?"

"Hah!" Forsythe added his good-natured observation. "To be shackled as soon as the banns are called."

Would he never be free from that blasted rumor? "No doubt you have heard a great many things tonight.

For example, the state of my marital prospects. I have also heard rumors about the state of wedded bliss of the marquess, and also regarding Montagu and Miss Chester. Awful lot of gossip going about." He gave her a withering stare.

Miss Parnell paled. "Miss Chester? You're not supposed to know about her."

Oh? And what did that imply?

Behind Miss Parnell, Miss Bitner inhaled sharply.

Victor's gaze flickered over to her. "I recall you were rather fond of His Grace last year; am I right, Miss Bitner? Also, I recall he did not return your affections."

Forsythe added his opinion. "He thought her a rather nasty piece of work, no secret about it. Is that her there? No wonder he ran."

Victor shoved him back. Last thing he needed was a gossip-monger hearing the wrong things.

"Oh!" Miss Bitner's face flushed at the insult.

"Nora?" Miss Parnell turned to her cousin. "But you told me—"

"He made me promises and used me ill!" Miss Bitner blurted out. "He would have made me an offer if it wasn't for that conniving Miss Chester. She lured him away and tricked him into marriage. They're all like that. Every one of them. The whole family are nothing but bad apples."

"Every one of whom?" Miss Parnell asked.

"Mr. Wyndell!" Another voice, sweeter, sang in his ears.

"Every one of whom?" Miss Parnell demanded again.

Miss Abbot pushed her way through the crowd and practically threw herself into his arms. He caught her, his hands settling nicely about her waist, a smile on his face.

"I think I've figured it out."

"Who are you?" Miss Parnell demanded.

Victor released Miss Abbot, who blushed most appropriately and stepped back. She offered her apologies to the others in the circle and made to dart off.

Victor caught her hand before she fled entirely. No way she was escaping until he found out what she'd said to Lady Chester.

"I can't stay," she said. "I'm not supposed to be here. I only came to say goodbye." She pressed his knuckles to her lips in a kiss.

A sob wracked through Miss Parnell. With a noisy burst of crying, she fled, pushing guests out of her way.

Miss Bitner watched her go. She turned back to Victor with hatred in her eyes. "How could you treat her like that?"

Victor did not answer her question. As she moved to go after her cousin, he gripped her arm.

"Let me go."

"What did you mean when you said they're all like that? Are you referring to the Chesters?"

Miss Bitner's eyes darted side to side. "How could you treat her like that?"

He didn't bite. "Have you been spreading lies about the Chesters? That is a most vulgar practice, you know."

Ragsdale leaned closer to Forsythe. "What's this about the Chesters?"

Forsythe couldn't remember.

Miss Bitner's voice rose an octave. "I wasn't lying."

Miss Abbot, her hand still clasped in his, said, "Not about Lady Chester, anyhow."

"What?" Victor asked.

"That's what I came to tell you. I've figured it out." She turned her focus to Miss Bitner. As her smile could light a room, her scowl could darken it.

"She didn't lie about Lady Chester, as far as she knows. But Miss Chester, that's another story completely. And a rather barmy one at that." She pointed to Miss Bitner. "Miss Chester never stole His Grace away from you. She won him fair and square. You had a *tendre* for His Grace, one he never returned. So no, he did not break a promise, and no, Miss Chester did not steal him away. You were a nonentity. You were wallpaper. And so you thought you could get revenge by spreading false stories?" Miss Abbot shook her head. "Poorly done, Miss Bitner. Poorly done."

Victor turned to Miss Bitner. "You were the one who spread the rumor about Lady Chester?"

His mouth pinched as if he'd sucked a sour lemon. Miss Bitner's company grated on him.

Miss Bitner's shoulders shook. She drew in a sharp breath. Then Miss Bitner slapped Miss Abbot squarely across the face, knocking her to the floor.

That got the attention of the crowd. Everyone within earshot of that resounding slap stopped mid-conversation and turned around.

"I say," declared Ragsdale. "That is not the done thing!"

Miss Abbot picked herself off the floor, her cheek burning an angry red. That must have hurt. The slap could have knocked a tooth loose.

But Miss Abbot did not cry. Her eyes were cold

and disapproving, her voice loud and clear. "You, *mam'zelle*, are a pox on Society. You attempted to destroy a good lady's name because of jealousy. And you dare strike me for defending her?"

She drew back her fist and returned the blow, full and hard, directly on Miss Bitner's nose. Everyone gasped. A few ladies cried out at the violence of her action. The crunch was most audible. A few of the men, forgetting themselves, applauded the blow.

"Good show," one of them called.

Miss Bitner sank down with a very loud cry. Blood spurted from the hand she clenched to her face. "You bitch!"

The ladies were not as appreciative. Several declared *they'd never,* and a few ladies in the crowd fainted, though whether from the sight of blood or Miss Bitner's profanity, Victor was not sure.

One thing was sure; he had to get Miss Abbot out of there as quickly as he could. He took her by the shoulders and shoved his way out of the throng.

"Congratulations!" a drunken Forsythe called after him. "You've chosen well."

"Honestly," Victor muttered as the crowd parted before him. "After that display, I don't know if I should marry you at all."

"Absolutely you will marry me." Miss Abbot shook the blow from her hand. "Now you know that I shall defend the truth to the utmost."

As they passed from the drawing room, another formidable spectacle faced them.

"Victor Anthony Wyndell! Are you spurning young ladies?"

A ripple of terror, so familiar from his childhood,

ran up his spine. There stood his mother, fists on her hips, rage in her face. When she used his full name, he was in serious trouble. Behind her stood Miss Parnell, her eyes very red from crying. Supporting her daughter was Lady Parnell, also looking rather upset.

His hands froze on Miss Abbot's arms, bringing her up short. He looked from mother to mother to daughter.

"No. For I would never be involved with anyone who would spread untrue rumors about our kind hosts."

A sharp, mocking laugh rang out from Miss Bitner. "Untrue?" She laughed again. "I know all about The Agreement."

Both Lady Parnell and her daughter gasped.

"You weren't supposed to say anything." Miss Parnell moaned.

Lady Parnell gripped her daughter's arm. "Cornelia…" she warned.

Mrs. Wyndell, listening to this exchange, slowly inched away from the Parnells. Victor reached out a reassuring hand, hoping to pull her closer. At least they knew who had leaked the knowledge of The Agreement. Even if they had found and destroyed it, it was too late.

Then his gaze lit on yet another figure behind this crowd, one whose face was frozen in unpleasant surprise. *Oh no.*

"Felicity Anne Abbot! What are *you* doing here?"

Everyone turned to the voice of Mrs. Abbot.

Immediately, Victor released Miss Abbot. She was not alone. Lady Chester stood behind her, avoiding everyone's gaze. If the heat of his mother's wrath was bad, it was nothing compared to Mrs. Abbot's cold disapproval falling upon them all.

Miss Abbot swallowed. "Hello, Mother."

****

Felicity wanted to curl up inside herself. Why oh why didn't she depart when Lady Chester had shoved her out of the party? And how did her mother return so quickly?

Mrs. Abbot looked about the circle. "Lady Parnell, Mrs. Wyndell, and the rest of you. You all are coming with me. *Now*."

No one dared brook Mrs. Abbot, especially a cowed Felicity.

She followed her mother out the front door, not bothering to check if the others obeyed as well. "Really, I only popped by when—"

But her mother waved away her pathetic excuse. "Don't bother. I know you've been here the whole night."

"How—"

"People talk. Lady Middlestone had a few things to say about you."

Lady Middlestone! But how had she run into Mother, unless she'd left to attend whatever party her parents had ended up.

Felicity followed her down the pavement and up the steps to Grandmama's townhouse. If only she could have disappeared into the fog. Oh, her mother's wrath would fall heavy on her tonight!

Lady Chester abandoned her party. There was nothing more she could do now. The whole thing had dissolved into a terrible mess that would surely make the papers tomorrow. Lady Parnell came along, her daughter a frightened little thing, and the Wyndells.

Somehow, Miss Bitner and her bloodied nose had disappeared. Felicity tucked her hand behind her skirts. Miss Smith would have been proud.

Once inside the house Mrs. Abbot led them into the small parlor by the front door. No fire burned, and only a single lamp, brought in from the hallway, illuminated the chilly little room. Felicity shuddered at its resemblance to the Chesters' cloak room. The little clock ticked on the cold mantel.

"I kindly bid you all to wait here." Mrs. Abbot's voice laid the steel of command under those words.

If everyone were smart, they would remain where they were. Felicity certainly would not dare budge an inch. Mrs. Abbot left them there to ponder on their sins.

Mr. Wyndell leaned toward Felicity. "What's happening?"

"We are all in serious trouble."

She knew her mother's style. Mrs. Abbot did not berate one in public, but withdrew to a more private location—like this parlor—before laying the terror of her disapproval upon the miscreant.

"What are we waiting for?"

"Judgment Day."

Felicity's throat had gone dry. No amount of swallowing alleviated the tightness. She wanted to clutch Mr. Wyndell's hand and not let go. But what would her mother say? Technically, she and Mr. Wyndell had not been properly introduced.

And she'd *kissed* him!

Her mother most certainly did not need to know that.

Lady Chester sat on the settee, her arms wrapped tightly about her stomach.

Lady Parnell and her daughter clutched together, Miss Parnell's face pressed into her mother's bosom, her shoulders heaving.

Mrs. Abbot returned promptly, an unfolded piece of paper in her hands. "I'm sure most of you will recognize this."

The Agreement. It was smaller than Felicity imagined. She'd envisioned a large piece of parchment, like a royal decree. This was a simple letter-sized piece of stationery, with the Chester crest on top, a simple statement of a few lines, and four signatures.

Mr. Wyndell's jaw dropped. "The Agreement was here the whole time?"

Lady Parnell jumped. "How do you know about The Agreement?" Her voice trailed off at the end, heavy with guilt.

Mrs. Abbot fixed her with a very strong glare. "How does anyone know about The Agreement?" She held up the paper. "Someone told."

So strong was Mrs. Abbot's glare, Lady Parnell shrank back, turning as if to protect her daughter from that fearful gaze.

Mrs. Abbot held up the smallish piece of paper. "This is what we had written: 'We the undersigned hereby agree that we shall never speak of the events of tonight. In exchange for our silence, and for the preservation of her dignity, Lady Chester agrees never to play cards again in public, either at a party or other gathering, or with guests whilst at home.' And here are our four signatures, none of them signed under duress."

At this, Lady Chester blanched. Felicity was willing to lay a year's worth of pin money that Lady Chester had very much signed The Agreement under duress. Her mother had a knack of getting her own way.

Mrs. Abbot rolled up The Agreement. "Lady Parnell, you have brought dishonor upon us all."

"That is not true!" Tears formed in Lady Parnell's eyes. "I was not the one who cheated at cards!"

Felicity gasped. Everyone in the room looked to her.

She clapped both hands over her mouth. So *that's* what The Agreement was about? Lady Chester cheated at cards, got caught, and everyone at the table—her mother, Lady Parnell, Lady Chester, Mrs. Wyndell—all agreed to keep such a dishonorable matter to themselves, in exchange for Lady Chester never playing cards again?

Truly, she did not expect that to remain unquestioned for long. The Chesters were famous for their card parties, and Lady Chester was a renowned player. So why cheat?

All this over a card game?

Lady Abbot was unmoved. "Who said anything about cards? There are other ways of being dishonorable."

Mrs. Wyndell shook her finger in Lady Parnell's face. "You told your daughter about The Agreement."

"Don't you shake your finger at me!" Lady Parnell drew herself up in indignation. "*You* told your son."

Mr. Wyndell cleared his throat. "She only told me a piece of paper existed. I never knew the contents or the nature until now." He scowled at her. "My mother never betrayed The Agreement."

Lady Parnell folded her arms. "So how did you know about it, then? Hmm?"

Mr. Wyndell answered that one. "Rumor from

Miss Bitner. You heard her yourself. You told your daughter, who told Miss Bitner, who chose to use it as revenge against Miss Chester."

A small whimper escaped Lady Chester's lips. "Is that what happened? Oh, poor Clarice. Ever since we announced her betrothal, she's been subjected to such vicious rumors."

Mr. Wyndell pointed a finger to Miss Parnell. "There's your origin."

Miss Parnell cried out, "I never said anything about Miss Chester."

"No, Miss Bitner did. She had quite a lot to say."

"This is what happens when you cannot keep your mouths shut. From now on, none of us in this room will ever speak of The Agreement. No one will mention it exists, much less the contents." Mrs. Abbot turned to Victor and Felicity. "This specifically includes you."

Felicity swallowed. "But what about Miss Bitner? She knows about it as well. And she's not here."

Her mother folded her arms in her firm, do-not-trifle-with-me stance. "She has proven herself untrustworthy." To Lady Parnell, she said, "I'm sorry, Leticia. We'll have to get rid of your niece, socially."

Lady Chester drew herself up. "I agree," she added with quite a bit of fire. "She actively tried to destroy my daughter's betrothal and ruin my family in the process." Her fist slammed into the cushions of the settee.

A sob exploded from Lady Parnell's lips. "And my daughter? She didn't mean any harm." Tears coursed down her face. Fear of her own social ostracizing smothered the heat of her indignation.

Mrs. Abbot shook her head. "That's a very dangerous trait—not understanding just how powerful rumor can be. Why did you tell her in the first place? You know we agreed to keep silent."

Lady Parnell fumbled at her reticule for a handkerchief. "I simply wanted someone to talk to. She's all I've got."

Mrs. Abbot's face softened somewhat. "I understand loneliness. Still, you had us. We could have talked to each other. That's what this was about—supporting each other. Lady Parnell, you will make her keep her silence, or we will get rid of her socially as well."

Miss Parnell cried out and hid her face once more in her mother's shoulder.

Another sob escaped Lady Parnell's lips. "You can't do that."

"You broke The Agreement. These are the consequences."

"But my crimes aren't nearly as bad as Lady Chester's." She stuck a finger at her. "She actually cheated."

Lady Chester swallowed. "That may be. But I have adhered to The Agreement. Since that day, I have never played cards." Her voice shuddered as she spoke. "And I will never play cards again. At least I may regain some honor in that."

Mrs. Abbot stepped closer to Lady Parnell, practically looming over her smaller form. Miss Parnell hastened away from her mother, possibly fearful of Mrs. Abbot's wrath spilling on her.

"Your dishonor is just as bad. You betrayed a confidence. Through that, your actions nearly destroyed the hopes of an innocent young lady. Adhere to The Agreement, or your own daughter's chances will lay in tatters."

Lady Parnell collapsed to the settee, making Lady Chester abandon it. She did not faint, as Felicity supposed she might. Lady Parnell's grief overcame her. Her shoulders heaved with sobs, and she wailed loudly. Her daughter rushed over, not so much to comfort her, but to commiserate. Mrs. Abbot and Lady Chester stood and watched as the Parnell ladies clung to each other in their grief.

Mrs. Wyndell squirmed over by the fireplace. When the lack of conversation became too awkward for her, she blurted, "I never broke The Agreement."

Lady Abbot's gaze never left Lady Parnell. "Technically true. But revealing the existence of The Agreement came pretty close to the line. From that one little detail, your son and my daughter worked out The Whole Situation all by themselves. If they could have done it, so could others. That's why, from now on, we will disavow all knowledge of The Agreement as well as its contents, under peril of ruination."

Mrs. Wyndell shut up. She nodded her head.

One of Felicity's heartstrings pinged in sympathy. Mrs. Wyndell was only doing what she thought was best, if a bit misguided. Her actions did lead to Felicity's meeting Mr. Wyndell.

To think she'd kissed him *three* times tonight!

From a writing desk under the window, Mrs. Abbot brought forth a pen and ink. "Mr. Wyndell, Felicity, Miss Parnell, you shall also sign this agreement and be bound by it."

At the bottom, Mrs. Abbot scratched a few amendments, namely, that the undersigned would never reveal the existence of The Agreement nor its contents.

She handed the pen to Mr. Wyndell. He held it poised for a few moments. Eventually, he signed.

Felicity would never be able to get out of not signing, not with her mother standing over her. She, too, added her name. Miss Parnell shrank back when The Agreement was thrust under her nose, but she signed it meekly.

Mrs. Abbot sanded the new signatures. She folded The Agreement and tucked it into her bosom. "I'll have to find a new home for this. I thought it anonymously safe at my house. Now that's no longer true."

Lady Parnell raised her head. "I don't think that's fair that you keep The Agreement."

Mrs. Abbot raised an elegant eyebrow. "I am the only one who has not acted questionably. Of us all"— and her gaze included Mr. Wyndell and Felicity—"I am the most trustworthy."

Mrs. Abbot personally escorted everyone out of her house as dawn lightened the fog in the streets. Mr. Wyndell offered his arm to his dejected mother. As they departed, he gave Felicity one last look over his shoulder. He left without a word.

She watched him from the front parlor window. He and his mother, like the other ladies of The Agreement, disappeared into the mist.

She did not fight the tears that fell down her face. *Well, there would be no marrying him now.*

"You will go immediately to bed. We shall speak of this on the morrow." Mrs. Abbot's voice was tight.

From the sounds of it, not only would she not be marrying Mr. Wyndell, she would be marrying nobody else. As far as her mother was concerned, Felicity might not get her Season after all. How could anyone sleep after a life sentence like that?

As Felicity slipped out, she hesitated a moment before closing the door. As she peeked through the crack, she saw her mother remove The Agreement and place it into the chimney of the lantern until it caught alight.

****

After enduring the most severe scolding of her life, Felicity took to her bed for three days. She picked at the breakfast tray a footman brought her. She stared sightlessly at the canopy of her bed, listening to the carriage wheels outside. She opened her wardrobe and stared at the lovely clothes that would never see a Season party.

What a disaster her one and only crush had been. Tedious, overcrowded, poorly catered, and rife with rumor and scandal. Granted, she had met Miss Smith, someone who expected nothing. If it hadn't been for the curse, Felicity could almost have envied Miss Smith and her carefree attitude.

At least she got to watch Miss Smith punch out her Mrs. Manton. Alas, that particular scandal had not made it into the papers, nor had her punching out of Miss Bitner. *Shame.*

The more she thought about it, the more she was sure Miss Bitner was behind the binding of Mr. Wyndell. If she hadn't been there to free him, who knew what disaster could have happened?

And then there was Mr. Wyndell, the only bright point of the whole party. If she had not sneaked over there that night, she would never have met him.

Oh, after her debut—which looked like never— they might have been introduced. But would he have remembered her? *Possibly not.*

Now, she would never see him again.

"Felicity Anne Wyndell." She tried the name on one more time before putting it away for good.

What a shame. It fitted so nicely.

She flopped back onto the bed. *So this is what being the victim of scandal felt like.* Only now, in the end, did she understand everyone else's concern. Once scandal had spilled out, there was no putting it back in its bottle.

One of the servants knocked on the door.

"Go away," Felicity muttered.

"Your mother bids you come down."

"My mother can go to hell," Felicity replied, somewhat shocked at her own language. If one was to be the victim of scandal, failing to keep up appearances couldn't possibly do her more harm.

"You have a visitor."

Felicity sat up. "Who?"

****

Five minutes. That had to be a record in dressing for guests. Felicity tossed on the first morning gown her hand touched in the wardrobe, and she swatted in annoyance at the maid's attempt to dress her hair.

"Whoever it is will already know about our disgrace. They will not care about the condition of my hair."

Nevertheless, Felicity twisted up her locks and secured them with a couple of pins. She dashed down the staircase, heedless of grace and decorum. Someone came to call? They asked for her?

Miss Smith was the only person who came to mind. Felicity had posted a letter to her the other day.

Felicity skidded to a halt before the parlor. She took a breath, smoothed her skirts, and opened the door.

The figure who rose from a chair was not Miss Smith.

"Hello, Miss Abbot." Mr. Wyndell clutched his hat to his chest. "I hope you are well."

He was here! Felicity moved forward, her hand outstretched.

Her gaze caught her mother's tight expression.

Mrs. Abbot sat stiffly on the couch, her hands clutched in her lap.

Felicity's feet slowed. "What is it?"

Had The Whole Situation, despite their best efforts, gotten out? Had Mr. Wyndell come to inform them that everyone involved was socially ruined forever?

Mrs. Abbot said nothing. She looked away. And was that a sigh of resignation? If rumors of the scandal had gotten out, of course she would not be pleased.

Mr. Wyndell fumbled with his hat, nearly dropping it. He abandoned it to the table, where it promptly fell off. Both he and Felicity stooped down to fetch it, and almost knocked each other over. Mr. Wyndell caught Felicity, and together they rose.

"This is awkward," he said.

"But not the most awkward moment we've had."

He shook his head. "I meant, my being here. See, my mother does not know. And your mother does not approve."

Felicity brushed at her skirts. She looked to her mother. "Approve of what?"

Her mother did not answer.

"There is too much scandal in my family," Mr. Wyndell said. "My mother's behavior the other night."

Felicity gasped. "Surely that is not enough for censure." Certainly not compared to Lady Parnell's.

He had not released her hands but held them gently, lovingly. "Then there is my brother's behavior."

She gave him a quizzical look. If his brother had been involved in a scandal, she could not bring the specifics to mind.

"Oh, that one is largely forgotten, except during moments of great inconvenience. And then there's my uncle and his unfortunate wife."

That one Felicity remembered. "So what does this mean?"

He drew her hands close to his chest, so close she could feel his beating heart.

"It means that your mother thinks it entirely inappropriate for me to pay court to you."

Court? Felicity's own heart beat a rapid tattoo.

"Yet you came. And my mother did not turn you away."

He took a deep breath. "That is because on my own merits, I am nearly impeccable." He leaned over and whispered in her ear, "If you don't mind a younger son with no career prospects."

At this, Mrs. Abbott perked up. "What are you saying?"

Felicity ignored her. "What about your clocks?"

That smile she always hoped for spread across his face. "I wanted to talk to you about that. I do not receive much, as a younger son, but I receive enough for a comfortable, if unfashionable, living. I want to design clocks. I don't know if you could call it trade, as I do not manufacture or sell them. I merely design them for a watchmaker of my acquaintance. The designs fetch a handsome price, as they keep excellent time."

An accurate clock? That would be worth something indeed. "I have never seen one of your clocks."

He gestured to the mantel. There, where the old clock used to be, sat a new one, simpler in design, with clean, elegant lines.

"A gift for you."

A gift! No wonder her mother hadn't thrown him out on his ear.

"Your mother disapproves of me, Miss Abbot. My mother disapproves of me. She would surely have an apoplectic fit if she knew I was here. But do you disapprove of me? I never meant to get anyone involved in a scandal, least of all some—"

Felicity put a finger to his lips. "Hush. I got myself involved. I have a propensity for that, you see. One cannot have truly experienced the Season without rubbing elbows with scandal." She pressed herself closer to him. "The question I would ask is, can you bear to court a young lady who gets herself involved in scandal?"

So close was she, he took an involuntary step backward.

"I do not recall any other scandal."

"I recall you are entirely unsuited for a career in the Church."

Perplexity crossed his face. "I am?" Then the memory came to him. "Oh."

Felicity rose up on her toes, took his blushing face in her hands, and thoroughly kissed him. *Scandal indeed.*

Mrs. Abbot gasped audibly. "Felicity Anne Abbot!"

Felicity ignored her.

After all, once the banns had been read, she would only answer to the name of Felicity Anne Wyndell.

A word about the author...

Heidi Wessman Kneale is an Australian author of moderate repute. When she's had too much of reality, she opens a book. She specializes in science fiction, fantasy, and romance in hopes of helping her fellow humans escape.

Visit her at:

http://romancespinners.blogspot.com

http://tinyurl.com/heidikneale

~*~

Titles by Heidi Wessman Kneale at The Wild Rose Press include:

As Good as Gold

For Richer, For Poorer

Marry Me

The White Feather

~*~

If you enjoyed *Currently Unchaperoned*, or any of Heidi's stories, leaving a review at your favorite book retailer or reader website would be much appreciated.

Thank you!